A Better Man

Cheryl Barton

Published by: CRBarton Productions, LLC

CRBarton Productions, LLC
P.O. Box 962
Reisterstown, Maryland 21136
www.crbarton.com

Ordering Information:
Quantity sales. Special discounts are available on quantity purchases by corporations, associations, and others. For details, contact the publisher at the address above.

Orders by U.S. trade bookstores and wholesalers. Please contact prez@crbarton.com

Cover Photo: www.pixabay.com

ISBN: 0997877901
ISBN-13: 978-0997877908

Prologue

Phoenix squirmed to the left and then to the right trying to take in more of the amorous feeling flowing through every part of her body, starting at the top of her head to the tip of her toes. She kept her eyes closed tight knowing if she opened them, she would look into the face of the faceless man. This was a man without a face who gave and gave to her, only taking after he knew that she was completely satiated beyond anything she had ever experienced before.

She loved that his touch knew her body and that he knew exactly where she needed him to focus, giving her the most intoxicating pleasure. His hands were masterful as they covered every pliant part and his tongue, which glided ever so wonderfully across her skin, should be labeled as a lethal weapon since it slayed her into submission time and time again. Who was her mystery man, she thought. Why couldn't she *see his face?*

She wanted to see his face and when she tried to open her eyes to get a glance, her eyelids felt as if they were being held closed by weights. The heaviness was becoming a distraction from her ability to concentrate on the wonderful feelings flowing through her body, so she stopped trying and concentrated on what delightful thing he would do next to elicit yet another moan of aroused delight from her. Who are you? She wanted to shout out, but couldn't. Who could make her feel this good every time he touched her?

It had to be Carson, she thought. It had to be the man she loved, whom she believed returned her love as fervently as she gave hers to him. Each time she parted her lips to call his name to let him know that she enjoyed his ministrations, nothing came out.

Phoenix wasn't the vocal type in bed with a man like she wanted to be, but what she was feeling warranted her cries of pleasure and her words of encouragement. She wanted and needed to call his name with every breath she expelled from her lips. There isn't a woman anywhere who experienced this kind of lovemaking and didn't yearn to call out her lover's name with exhilaration. Why wouldn't his name slip from her tongue? Clearly he had no problem getting his tongue to work because he was giving her the work-over of a lifetime with it. One minute his tongue was soft and smooth and the next, without warning, it was hard and demanding, letting her know that he wanted it all.

Her mystery man was calling her name, letting her know how much he enjoyed the feel of her under his strong, exploratory hands and the taste of her on his lips and she fought to return the sentiment. What was wrong with her? Why couldn't she see his face? Why did his voice sound unfamiliar as he said her name over and over again? Surely it was Carson; it had to be. Who else could it be?

Phoenix let her confused thoughts invade her mind while he lover continued invading her body. She shivered when she realized it was possible the faceless man wasn't Carson. The erotic shiver was followed by a minute of shame at the thought that she enjoyed the faceless man's attention even though she knew it may not be Carson. That minute of guilt turned to exuberance thinking that somewhere there was a man who knew her body and played it like a drum.

Carson never pleasured her to the point of exhaustion from oral caresses like this before. She loved making love with him, but he was more of a taker than a giver. Being with him was always an enjoyable experience, but she wished she knew how to be the kind of woman to ask for more. With her faceless lover she was getting more and then some more and still yet even more and she hadn't even shared with him what more for her would be like. It was obvious he didn't need any instructions because he was hitting every spot over and over and she couldn't seem to get enough.

On instinct, she reached down as his head swirled

around and around matching the movement of his tongue on her sensitive nub and gripped his shoulders to hold on as her body surged higher and higher. She noticed how much more muscular he was than Carson. Thinking back to the feel of him inside of her body, she knew her faceless lover was more muscular in other ways too; ways that took her over the edge time and time again, sometimes one night right after another.

Phoenix felt her body reaching for the stars as her release came within reach. She wanted it more than she wanted her next breath, but she wanted to know who it was that knew her body better than she did. Who else could know what it craved? How could he know what enthralled her the most?

'Who are you?' she asked in her head because she still couldn't get her lips to work. 'How do you know what I want and need? Why would you always put my needs ahead of yours? Why am I enjoying making love with you when I have a fiancé that I love and adore?'

Carson was good at pleasuring her orally, but not this good. This faceless god wasn't just a master, he was the instructor. She got the feeling he wrote the book on all this pleasure-filled.

'Who are you?' Phoenix screamed in her head yet again. For a split second her lover lifted his head, still faceless and whispered in a husky raspy voice, "I'm a better man."

His deep, seductive voice laced with passion and desire for her was more than her senses could take.

She didn't have a chance to react or respond before he again lowered his head back down and with the next stroke of his tongue, her body sizzled and then shattered into a million pieces as she exploded and soared higher on a plateau of hallucinogenic heat. His mouth possessed her, claimed her and she gave herself over to him, not caring who he was. Her only thought was that she never wanted him to stop. The powerful feeling stirred even more embers causing them to burn through her like a hot, hot fire when she suddenly woke up and sat straight up in bed.

Startled and wide away, Phoenix found herself taking in big gulps of air to catch her breath. She looked around at her decorative bedroom in shades of purple and white and knew she was in her own darkened room and gone was her faceless lover.

Still breathing as if she'd just run a marathon, she looked to her left and saw Carson sound asleep in bed next to her. Clearly what she experienced wasn't reality, but another dream like so many she'd been having lately. She'd never wanted so much and had been given just that.

Feeling her heart rate slow down, she slid down under the soft, white down comforter that covered them and was about to turn to Carson to snuggle up close when she remembered him telling her he had problems sleeping with someone being that close to him. She wanted to reach out and pull him to her to feel the closeness she'd just felt in her dream, but knew that wasn't to be.

Phoenix nibbled on her lips as she struggled with the after-effects of her sensual dream. She wanted Carson, she loved Carson, but until he gave her what she needed, her ultimate desires were still encased in her dreamland.

Carson had shown up hours before, drunk and already too tired to make love and she relented allowing him to give her yet another excuse.

Phoenix turned toward her side of the bed and tried to fall back to sleep. Part of her wanted to fight falling back into any more dreams of the faceless man, knowing her thoughts of love and lovemaking should be about Carson, the man whom she would soon walk down the aisle to say 'I do' to. Secretly, she hoped that the faceless man would invade her dreams once again and perhaps reveal the face of the man who loved to satisfy her. It appeared to be his greatest pleasure. Her last thought before falling to sleep was, she wanted the man who considered himself the *better man*.

Chapter 1

Phoenix knew it was morning, but like most days when daylight flowed through her big bay windows, she struggled to get out of bed. There was one thing she learned as a young child and that was her hatred for early mornings. At twenty-eight, she would prefer that her day started around noon, giving her a few more hours to adjust to the new day. If she were in the profession she really wanted to be in, she could probably set her own schedule. As a human resources manager for one of the largest hotel chains in the world, she knew she had a responsibility to get up and out because people depended on her and they did so early in the morning.

Finally opening her eyes and rolling over to snuggle close to the love of her life even if he didn't want it, she was shocked to see that she was in bed alone again.

Carson Stone, the love of her life had slipped out either sometime right before the sun came up or within the past hour. She didn't hear him moving around or showering, so he must have been moving around quietly to not wake her. She preferred being woken up by him, especially if she knew he needed to get going. She assumed he had a lot to do, even though she wasn't quite sure what that was.

Carson spent more time figuring out what he wanted to do with his life than actually doing anything about it. That's what you can do when your father owns the largest chain of hotels in the country. It's easy to get up each day without a care in the world when you were born rich. She, on the other hand, like her brother and sister had to actually work for a living. Even if she didn't she knew she still would because of the sense of satisfaction that came with getting and having your own. She loved Carson, but hoped the rest of their lives wouldn't consist of him still trying to discover a career, years into their marriage.

So far, Carson had gone through several jobs working for his father's hotel chain and nothing lasted for more than a year or so. They'd been together two years, engaged for six months and she was still waiting to see what his plan was for an actual career. All she'd ever seen him do was party, something else he told her he'd slow down doing. She knew that nightclubs profited greatly just by having him make an appearance and they paid him handsomely just to show up, wave and flirt. She hoped that wasn't what he considered enough once they were husband and wife.

Meeting Carson, heir to the Stone Towers hotel chain a month after she started working at one of his father's hotels was the beginning of a whirlwind romance. She was fresh out of graduate school with her degree in human resources management and ready to tackle the world. Love came fast for her and she knew she was exactly what he needed to tamper down his playboy image, something his father told him he needed to work on.

When they'd met, Carson was the talk of the magazines and social media sites due to his love for all things female. His father wanted a different image for his son who would one day run the Stone Towers empire. Carson knew that running the company was in his future and he hoped his father would make the decision to turn things over to him much sooner than later. His father was hesitant and was waiting until the day came that Carson showed him that his wild ways were behind him. He expected a more wholesome, business and family man image and Carson would either submit to the request or spend his life going from one party to the next.

The once playboy, now fiancé had some time in the early morning hours slipped out of her bed. He had been doing that a lot lately and she hoped it was for a business opportunity and not because he'd found a better bed to be in. She pushed that thought from her mind. She'd seen many stories about his wild ways and hoped that they were all made up, especially since the moment he'd put a ring on her finger, asking her to marry him. They were planning to build a life together and were getting married in less than a year. Telling him over and over that it was time to find his lane in the business world wasn't something she wanted to worry him about since his father was doing a good job of that on a regular basis. When they were together, she tried to make their time about them and not about what was next for him. Still, she wondered where he could have gone so early in the morning, not making a sound that would wake her up.

No doubt she was wide awake now, though disappointed. She loved waking up in the morning to enjoy some time together before they both headed out. Grabbing her cell phone, Phoenix checked to see if he'd left her a text, but saw nothing. She loved sending him little messages throughout the day to let him know she was thinking about him. Carson once mentioned that just because he didn't send her a text throughout the day, didn't mean he wasn't thinking about her. She liked knowing that, but the thought of him taking the time out of his busy day to say hello or to send a few words wouldn't hurt anything, but that was her Carson.

Looking around the loft apartment she lived in compliments of her brother who owned it and was currently in Paris on a photo shoot, she saw no signs of a note saying good morning or telling her why he had to leave without as much as a few words telling her to have a good day at work. Knowing it wouldn't be like him to leave any kind of note, she didn't know why she even looked around for one. Instead of worrying about it, she fixed a quick breakfast and prepared to leave for work.

Grabbing the makings for a quick omelet, her favorite breakfast food, she turned on some music to get motivated to start her day. Over the sound of the music, she heard a noise that sounded as if it were coming from the hallway outside of her loft, thinking perhaps it was her new neighbor. There had been a note in her door from the building owner that the loft across the hall had been sold and soon she would see or hear someone, so she shouldn't be alarmed. There were only two lofts on the top level while the other eight floors had four lofts on each level. The bottom level housed a gym and a private entrance to the underground parking reserved for tenants and their guests only.

She was renting the loft from her brother who'd be gone for over a year. He didn't want to sell it and when he told her he was going to take the job, she offered to live in it so that it wouldn't stay empty.

The loft was huge with two bedrooms, a large open floor plan in the main room that her brother had used as his photography studio. She loved the rustic look of the brick wall interior and there were big windows that went from floor to ceiling on three walls including the large master bedroom. She loved the loft and enjoyed the quietness of being the only one on the top floor. She sometimes heard sounds, but none as pronounced as what she'd just heard as she walked over to the door and listened, but heard nothing. Shrugging it off, she went back to making breakfast so that she would have enough time to shower and get to work without being late. She was sure if the source of the noise was a new neighbor, she would meet whoever it was soon.

**

Gavin Black was excited about his move to Chicago. He was in need of some downtime and after spending a few weeks in Hawaii to regroup, he was ready to move ahead beyond the turmoil of the last few months of his life.

A failed relationship and his move to temporarily step away from the multi-million dollar company he'd started were his attempts of a new outlook on life.

At age thirty-two, Gavin was one of the youngest multi-millionaires in the country and well on his way to being in the billionaire's club. Though he loved the life it provided him, he hated the spotlight and preferred to live as far off of people's radar as he could. His attempt to do that now had him sporting a neatly trimmed mustache and beard in hopes of getting by with a little anonymity until he decided it was time to go back to the life he'd walked away from. He knew there would be no chance of no one recognizing him, but his plans to live incognito for a while would be aided if he could change his appearance while he lived amongst the great people of the city of Chicago.

He entered the building that housed his new loft apartment ready to get settled into what would now be his new surroundings. He entered the elevator and after it reached the top floor, he exited just as he heard a sound in the hallway and his eyes landed on a sight of beauty exiting the loft across from his. He'd heard there was one tenant in the loft across the hall and was happy to hear that and hoping it meant less traffic back and forth. She looked up at him as he walked toward her and the first word that came to mind was stunning.

Phoenix turned to lock the door after leaving out to head to work and she heard a sound and turned to see a very tall, extremely handsome and definitely in shape man coming down the hallway carrying a box. She locked the door and walked down the hall toward who she assumed was her new neighbor. As she got closer to him, he smiled at her and she smiled in return.

"Good morning," she said, being all neighbor-like.

"Good morning to you. I'm Gavin. I'm moving into the loft across from you today."

"Great. I'm Phoenix and welcome to the building. I heard I would be getting a new neighbor soon and thought I'd heard a noise this morning."

"Sorry if I disturbed you. I brought a few things up, but asked the moving company to wait and start after nine hoping we wouldn't wake up many neighbors."

"It's quite alright. I was already up heading to work. It was nice to meet you Gavin," she said shaking the hand he extended to her.

"It was a pleasure meeting you too, Phoenix. I like your name."

If she had a mirror, Phoenix knew she would see herself blushing.

"Thank you. I was named after the city where my parents met," she said smiling.

"It's a lovely name and thanks for the welcome to the building. I guess I'll be seeing you coming and going and if I'm ever making too much noise, just tell me to be quiet and I will," he said smiling pleasantly.

"I'm sure it will be fine. I'm a bit of a music lover myself and I'll have to remember to keep my music down now that I'm not the only one on this floor."

"Well, it was nice meeting you Phoenix and I'm sure I'll see you again soon."

"Good luck moving in," she said pushing the button for the elevator. It opened immediately and she looked at him one last time before getting in.

"Thank you," Gavin said reaching his door to enter.

Phoenix watched him place the box on the floor while he searched, most likely for his key. She couldn't help stealing a glance. He was strikingly handsome and irresistible to look at. She wondered if he was married and who the lucky woman was if he were.

Smiling one last time and hoping he didn't catch her ogling him, she walked into the elevator and waited for the doors to close. Gavin was an exquisite specimen. Carson was handsome, but Gavin was gorgeous. She snapped to reality realizing she'd, for the first time, compared Carson to another man.

Taking the elevator down, she couldn't help visually going over her neighbor's amazingly good looks. He was tall, over six-feet, with broad, muscular shoulders and powerful thighs that showed clearly through jeans that were made to fit his body perfectly. His hair was cut close and she loved the rugged look of the mustache and growing beard. There was no doubt he was serious about a workout regimen because he was toned with no sign of body fat.

When the elevator rang letting her know she'd reached the garage level, she realized she was too focused on her handsome neighbor and she'd only talked to him for a few minutes. She walked to her car and got in and immediately dialed Carson to say good morning and to let him know she missed him. Other men aren't supposed to be a distraction to an engaged woman as she removed all thoughts of her neighbor.

"Hey you," she said when he answered sounding as if he were out of breath.

"Hey back. Are you at work?" Carson asked.

"No, I'm just leaving out. You didn't wake me when you left this morning. I was hoping a little loving would be in order to start my day since I called it an early night last night and you were clearly drunk when you finally showed up. What got you up and out so early?" she asked.

"I wanted to get to the gym before the crowd showed up and I'm going to a meeting with a club owner who wants me to make an appearance."

"An appearance? That's it? You're still doing those?"

She heard him exhale on the other end.

"Phoenix, you know people like to pay me to show up hoping it will bring in a crowd. I get them in and they pay me handsomely. I'm meeting the owner this morning who flew in from Vegas to meet with me about a big event he's hosting. After that, I'm meeting with my father to talk about money. He thinks I'm spending too much of his and not deciding on what I want to do to make and spend my own."

She was surprised to hear that his father was in town considering he hadn't told her before now.

"Your father's in town? How long has he been here?"

"Just a few days. I had dinner with him the other night. I thought I told you that," he expressed.

Phoenix held the phone out and looked at it as if it were a snake about to bite her. Carson knew he hadn't told her about his father's visit and once again, he tried to play her as if she wouldn't figure out that he deliberately kept that information from her. It wasn't the first time, but she wished it would be the last, putting the phone back up to her ear.

"No you didn't tell me that. I would have loved to join the two of you for dinner. How much longer will he be here? Maybe we can have dinner together before he leaves."

"Babe, I don't think he's going to be here beyond today. My mom isn't with him, so he's flying back to California later today. If we weren't going to talk business, I'd invite you to join us, but you'll be bored and I'm sure he'll spend most of the time talking down to me anyway and you don't want a front seat to that."

"He doesn't talk down to you. He's looking out for you and wants you to be the best."

"Trust me, he doesn't do it in front of you, but he

does it and as for wanting the best for me, yeah, well he has a strange way of showing it. I may not be like my sister the doctor or my brother, the owner of his own string of restaurants, but I'm the debonair one who will one day take over the hotel empire if he would let me at the table."

Phoenix could hear that Carson needed words of encouragement and that he wasn't looking forward to the chat with his father.

"I think he knows you're trying. He never expected you to settle down and propose marriage to me, but you did. You're showing him that you're ready to be what he needs you to be."

On more than one occasion she knew that his father had told him he was tired of reading about his playboy antics on every news station. He needed to make a change and she was more than happy to be a part of that change.

"Hopefully he notices a change in me," Carson said somberly.

"He only wants what's best for you. He wants you to find your niche and focus on that. His frustration comes out of worry for your future. Maybe the discussion won't be so bad."

Carson exhaled loudly on the other end.

"Yeah, maybe. Listen, I need to finish this workout and then get going. I'll call you later."

"Will you come see me tonight or we can meet at your place?"

"I'll call you later to let you know. I don't think it will

be a late evening for me and if it is, I don't want you out that late and I know you need to get up early. After all, my father counts on you to keep his hotel running like a well-oiled machine."

Carson laughed and that made her feel better. She knew he didn't like when his father made trips to Chicago under the premise of having a business meeting when he was actually checking up on Carson.

"Okay, well, I'm on my way to work and I should be home around eight. I'm meeting my sister after work to talk wedding stuff."

"Tell Reese I said hello and I'll talk to you later."

"I love you," she said to the empty phone line. Carson had already hung up and she was sure he hadn't heard her expression of love or her reference to the wedding. If he had he certainly would have returned the affection. Not giving it too much thought, she pulled out of the garage, driving by one of her new neighbor's two parking spots where one was occupied by a big, black, sleek SUV. Just when she thought she'd gotten her mind off of her neighbor, he invaded her thoughts once again.

Chapter 2

Gavin spent the morning unpacking or at least some semblance of it. He'd been in his new loft for three weeks and he was still living out of boxes. There was no need to rush and unpack since he wasn't planning on going anywhere anytime soon. He needed to get some order to the catastrophe that was his loft, especially since one of the assistant's he'd hired to help with unpacking wasn't scheduled to start for a few days. Tonight he was planning to entertain a woman he'd met at a restaurant his first night in Chicago and he needed to at least make a path to the bedroom, where he hoped they'd spend a little of their time together.

Meeting women has always been an easy task for him and not just because he was extremely rich. Before he had the idea to start GNAB Technologies, the company that made him rich, women were drawn to him and he indulged in his share. He was looking forward indulging again later when his date showed up. Luckily, she was looking for a noncommittal, friends with benefits relationship which is all he had to offer at the moment. He'd given a few years of his life to a relationship that turned out to bite him in the behind and he was planning on staying clear of anything that wasn't casual. He preferred women who knew the game going in so that in the end, there were no hard feelings.

Tonight should be a night with one of those women looking to get her toes curled without the drama of anything serious. He'd hate for her to get a look at his place in a state of disarray, but he wouldn't get everything in its place before the evening. It wasn't as if he didn't have the time and he hadn't encountered any distractions.

As he moved around, his thoughts drifted to Phoenix, his neighbor across the hall. She was a beautiful woman and over the past few weeks, he'd run into her and a man she'd mentioned to him was her fiancé. It was clear they didn't live together because except for a few sightings, the mystery fiancé didn't spend a lot of time coming and going. They'd had several conversations in passing and he knew that her fiancé was the infamous Carson Stone, of the Stone Towers hotel chain and empire and also playboy extraordinaire. He couldn't imagine the Carson he knew from the media coverage of his every move was engaged to marry someone who wasn't a part of his wild and crazy lifestyle. He didn't remember seeing her beautiful face plastered all over magazines alongside

Carson's.

Phoenix, he'd learned, was more reserved than the women Carson was known to entertain. Theirs seemed like an odd relationship since it was clear Phoenix had no desire to be a part of the entertainment lifestyle filled with stars, paparazzi and one party after another.

Gavin knew he had no place to judge since his last relationship ended up in the toilet which had completely blindsided him. He thought he'd found the perfect match only to discover his ex was far from that.

From the few chats he'd had with Phoenix, there was something special about her that made him feel the need to be protective of her and from what he knew of Carson, someone needed to protect her. She was too good for Carson, but it wasn't his place to get involved.

He picked up and moved a few boxes when he turned at the sound of his cell phone ringing on the table across the room. Reaching it and seeing the caller, he answered it.

"Are you getting settled in yet?"

Gavin knew the answer without looking around.

"Not even close. I'm still living my life out of boxes," he admitted to his best friend Ellis Mays who was calling from Silicon Valley, headquarters for the company.

"Well, tell me you are at least catching up on chapters for your book. One of the reasons for this big change in your life was to focus on your writing."

Gavin wished he could say that was true, but for the past few weeks, he was suffering from a writing drought. He sat down at his computer, yet nothing new was added to the few chapters he'd already written.

"No such luck, but let's keep hope alive. Once I get everything unpacked and have this place looking more like a home, I'll be ready to dive back in. All I have are the few chapters I wrote while in Hawaii."

"Is Isabella there to help you get unpacked yet? I thought her first day was earlier this week."

Gavin decided to give his other personal assistant, Isabella, a few days off. She'd come with him from California to help keep him on track with his book and other personal assistant tasks.

"I gave her a couple of weeks off to get her own family settled in and the other assistant she hired to help me unpack and get things set up around here hasn't started yet. It's just me left to fend for myself and you know how that goes. I haven't lifted a finger to do much, but I need to. I have a date later tonight and since she's coming here, I should have had this place together by now. Have you had Isabella's office wired and set up yet with all of the equipment she's going to need?"

Even though he didn't plan on needing Isabella as much as he did when he ran his company, Gavin still wanted her to have office space to work out of. He didn't want her cooped up with him in his loft working each day.

"I'm doing that this week. I don't see why she's going to need all of that equipment if all you're going to be doing is focusing on finishing your book. Hey, it's not like you're still running a multi-million dollar high technology corporation anymore when you needed assistants working around the clock who had the best equipment within arms-reach."

"You're right. That's your job now along with the board, but you know it would be hard to get used to not having someone take care of everything that I don't want to have to deal with. Besides, I'm still working with a few start-ups, lending them my expertise and I do need an assistant to keep that work organized. I emailed you the schematics of the loft and how I want the office set up here. How soon can you get that done? I know this is asking a lot, but I want my team from there to set it all up."

"Hey, anything for our chief executive officer," Ellis added.

"Haha, but I'm not the CEO anymore, you are."

"Right. I'm your best friend, Gavin, and if no one else knows, I know that moving that title from you to me is for paper documentation only. True, I'm doing the work now, but one day when you decide to come back and take control again, you'll be back where you belong and not hiding out someplace writing novels. I still don't know how you go from CEO to author without blinking."

Gavin didn't know how he did it either, but he needed a change in his life. His company, GNAB Technologies had been one of the fastest growing technology companies in the world. Not only were they big in computer technology, but they were also the biggest gaming company in the world. He had taken his love for video games into a new realm of gaming that allowed a user to play war games virtually as if they were actually in foreign countries. The virtual technology his company had created was the first of its kind and within two years of settling in Silicon Valley five years ago, he had released his first video console and games and he was propelled to the top of the game when his system and games surpassed the biggest gaming companies that had lived at the top for years. He had become richer than he ever dreamed he would be and fame and fortune thrust him into the spotlight, something he immediately shied away from. The media scrambled to get pictures of him and dive into his life and were surprised there wasn't much to find out about him.

He'd been born in England and moved to the United States when he was in middle school. Making friends was hard for him because kids made fun of his accent, so he spent his free time alone or with his sister Layne and his brother Luke. They adjusted to life in the U.S. much better than he did, especially after he found entertainment in video games. His love for them had him thinking of ways to improve on the gaming experience from his younger years until his college years where he'd met his best friend Ellis Mays.

Ellis was a wiz at programming and along with his own expertise in programming and design, he'd built GNAB technologies in the basement of his parents' Encino Valley home.

One day after graduating college, he pitched the idea of his company to his father to get him to back it since he had no real money of his own. His father, CEO of his own financial conglomerate, having great faith in his vision, gave him five hundred thousand dollars to start his dream and the rest, as they say was history. Now, seven years after he first hatched the plan before even starting his company five years ago, he was burned out and needed a break from the fast-paced gaming and technology world. He knew he would never be able to walk away from that world for good, but for now, he took advantage of the much needed break.

"Hey, did I lose you? Did you drift off to sleep or something?"

Gavin rejoined the conversation when he realized he had been reminiscing about the past. Some parts of the past he wanted to leave there and never think of again, but any trip down memory lane was also a visit to the parts he'd like to forget all about.

"No, I'm here. Sorry about that. My mind wandered for a minute. I'm good and like you, I don't have a clue how I leaped from one to the other, but this time away is definitely something I needed and you know that. This book thing came out of nowhere, but I'm really interested in it. I've been that anonymous CEO for a long time and though the news loves my company, not many people know a lot about me and writing this book is not about the money, but it's about how I got where I was so fast and hoping to inspire young minds to follow their dreams to success. I agree with the publisher that the story needs to be told and there is no better time to do it than right now when I have the time to do it myself. It will keep people from assuming what my life is like and writing unauthorized stories about it. I'd rather tell my own story."

"So no ghostwriter like I know a lot of celebrities do?"

Gavin knew he wouldn't think of doing that. If he was going to tell his story, he was going to tell it and write it himself.

"No, none. No one knows my story like me and being such a mystery all these years, I'm tired of people making up stories about who they think I am."

A pause in Ellis responding told him what was coming next.

"How into you and your life are you going to get?" Ellis asked hesitantly.

"Not that deep and I know what you're thinking and no, I'm not getting that personal. I'm going to keep the book focused on my life and the company and what drove me there, leaving out anything about my personal life, especially that relationship. That's a part of my life I never want to see coming off of the pages of a novel right at me. I've moved on and clearly she has, so there is no reason to rehash any of it."

"Yeah, I hear you and I understand. Last year was a rough year and thankfully you and Natasha preferred that your private life stay private and your ups and downs weren't fodder for the national rag magazines."

Hearing her name made Gavin sick. No woman had

ever done to him what she'd done and even though he tried to justify what she did by blaming himself, it didn't hurt any less. That part of his life is over now and he was in a new phase of life where there was no need to look back.

"Yeah, that's a good thing. I'm glad I was able to stay off of the public radar because I lived like a hermit for so long and she didn't mind living there with me until, well, you know and that's water under the bridge. I'm keeping anything about her out of the book. There is no need to tarnish her or try to tear her down for the sake of a few dollars compared to what I make each year. I'm donating any money I make from the sale of the book to charity. That's one of the first tasks I'm going to give to Isabella. I need her to research some charities that I don't already contribute to yearly and make sure all of the money from book sales and appearances are donated."

"That's a good idea. I believe the book is going to be a huge seller once people get a look into who Gavin Black is. I need to know what you want me to do about your house. You said you didn't want it anymore. Are you sure you're not going to come back to it one day when you're ready to come back to the company?"

"If I do come back to the company one day, and that's a big if, I'll build a new house. Go ahead and get a realtor lined up to sell it."

He heard Ellis whistle on the other end.

"That's going to be a huge payday. You spent forty million building it and it's worth twice that much now.

I hear there's already been interest in it."

"There was a lot of interest in it when I lived in it. There was some sheik from some country who, at one time, offered me three times its value. He had a daughter who loved it and he wanted to buy it for her."

"I think I know who that is and I believe he is still interested. I've seen some correspondence about contact from him. I'll get a realtor on it this week. What about your other properties?"

Gavin hadn't thought a lot about the other properties he owned. There was the house in England, the house he'd recently built in Hawaii, his house and condo in Los Angeles, his New York City apartment and his house in Miami.

"The only house I need to sell is the one we talked about and I'll think about the others. I don't see a need to unload the others since I still plan to spend time in them and Luke and Layne like having a private place to stay when they travel."

He didn't openly admit that the only reason he focused on that one house is because he had lived in it with Natasha for two years. Their relationship crumbled and the last encounter that brought about the end of their relationship had taken place in that house. He knew he never wanted to be in it again.

"I hear you," Ellis said.

"I do want my boat brought down to Miami where I want it to stay. I'll get Isabella on that when she's finally settled in. See, there's already a list of things for her to do," he quipped which made Ellis laughed too.

"I'm not going to keep you long from your unpacking, though I'm sure you're not going to get right back to it. I was calling to check on you to see if you'd changed your mind and if not, I wanted to be sure all is good."

"It's all good on this end," Gavin quickly admitted.

He started to ask Ellis about work, but knew that once he started asking questions and getting answers, he wouldn't be able to tear himself away from the day to day of the company and besides the board members, that was now Ellis' job.

"Good. I'll get the team to Chicago next week to get your office set up. Is the loft big enough for the setup you want?"

"Yeah, this place is humungous. It's the only loft with three bedrooms and one of those rooms I'm turning into an office. I understand even the loft across the hall from me only has two bedrooms and mine is significantly larger. I'll need some electrical upgrades made to accommodate all the outlets and power I'll need. Then I'll need the equipment set up. I plan to stay connected to my smaller team of programmers from the office and I want to be hardwired to connect with them."

"Cool. I'm glad you're not completely disassociating yourself with the company and you're staying connected."

"I know that I'll never be able to completely walk away from the company that I built, but this time away will be good for me. I needed to step away and I also know that I don't have a care in the world because you're at the top looking out for everything."

"I got it covered and you know I've got your back. Get back to your unpacking and I'll let you know what day next week the team will be in Chicago."

Gavin hung up and looked around the large open space of his loft. Even though the loft was large, it didn't compare to the size of the house he'd walked away from. He had completely picked up his life and moved to Chicago, a place where he was hoping to blend in with the crowd. Luckily, he was smart enough to create a shell company to buy the building which included his loft so that he could stay off of people's radar. He knew that it was more of people's personal life than there business acumen that kept them in the media day after day and because he never gave interviews or talked about his personal life, no one cared what he did or where he went and he was grateful for that. What he needed most of all was privacy.

Chapter 3

"Hey Phoenix."

She turned to see Gavin walking into the building. He looked like he was coming from running. His powerful arms and legs were glistening with sweat and she almost missed recognizing him with his hat sitting low over his handsome face. Even covered in sweat he was intoxicating.

"Hi Gavin."

"You look nice. Hot date with Carson?"

She smiled.

"Not really a hot date. We're supposed to have dinner with some friends of mine. We've been scheduling and rescheduling this dinner for months. What are you up to this evening besides getting in a late evening run? Are you staying in to get some writing done or are you planning a night out on the town in Chicago?"

"No, I have some friends in town for today only and I'm meeting them for dinner. I just need to shower and change and get back out the door. Are you going to be okay standing out here waiting? The sun is about to go down" he said looking around, not seeing Carson anywhere.

"Oh, I'll be fine. We're already running late and I don't want Carson to have to park, so I told him I'd be out front. Now that we have a doorman and security at the entrance, thanks to the owner of the building, I feel safe standing here. You know, I've lived here over a year since my brother moved out of the country and leased it to me and we never had security or a doorman until you moved in. You must have brought some good vibes with you. I understand from one of the owners on the first floor that they've been asking about it for years, but the owner of the building didn't want to foot the cost. He said that the individual owners of each loft would have to split the cost equally and either everyone agreed or it wouldn't happen. I don't know about anyone else, but I never got anything else about it until one day last month, I came home to a note that said they were building a guard's desk on the first floor that would monitor elevator usage and the front door. Apparently security wasn't as tight on all of the floors as it is on the top floor. It's nice to know that there will be a doorman at the door around the clock. Any idea how any of this came about?"

Gavin knew exactly how it came about. He had a problem with the lack of security and though he lived a low-key life, his privacy meant everything to him. He wouldn't tell her that when he purchased his loft, he had also purchased the building and the land it sat on. It was now owned by one of his many companies and someone would have to dig extremely deep to find out he was linked to it. He was responsible for the around the clock security and doorman services and was also planning on making upgrades to the lighting around the building and in the below ground garage to be sure everyone felt safe. He noticed there were a lot of women living in the building and now that he owned it, he felt responsible for their safety.

"I have no clue, but it's good to see. I hear other upgrades are coming soon. Did you see the notice in your mailbox about that?"

Phoenix remembered seeing it and wondered if she would get a bill for the upgrades. She was affording the lease from her brother only because he was supplementing it."

"I did and I'm waiting for the bill to drop in my mailbox for all the upgrades. Besides the extra lighting, each loft is getting a high-tech security system along with cameras pointed to the hallway outside of their door and the front door to the building. I like that a lot. Sometimes I get random buzzes and I have no idea who it is since the call button chooses when it wants to work."

Gavin had no plans to bill any of the tenants for the upgrades. They should have been done long before he bought the place.

"I hear these upgrades are going to be top of the line. I checked into this and found out that none of us are being billed for any of it. They were plans the building owner had been planning all along, but never did and then the new owner jumped right on it. The cost of these lofts alone should more than cover the upgrades, so I don't think you have anything to worry about. I'm going to get going since I'm already late. Are you sure you don't want me to wait down here with you until Carson shows up?"

Phoenix waved him off, already pissed off that Carson was over a half-hour late. They had agreed she'd be downstairs waiting when he pulled up at seven for dinner and it was already going on seven-thirty.

"No, I'll be fine. I'm sure he'll be here any minute now. Go ahead so that you're not late for your own night out. Have fun," she said when he walked toward the door.

Gavin turned around.

"You too."

When he disappeared into the building, Phoenix grabbed her cell phone and called Carson again. She hated that he was never on time for anything. He should have been, considering he knew she was standing outside waiting for him as they had agreed. She became even more annoyed when he didn't answer her call.

**

Dressed and ready to head back out, Gavin had to go back into his room to grab his keys. Coming back out

34

into the main loft area, he turned again to head back into his room to grab his cell phone. He couldn't seem to think straight wondering why his mind was focused on Phoenix standing outside of their building waiting on her fiancé. While he showered, images of her standing outside alone invaded his thoughts. It wasn't his place to say anything, but he would never ask or expect a woman to wait for him outside of a building and he didn't care how much time it would save them. Nothing mattered more than a woman's safety. There was something about Carson that he didn't like and though he found Phoenix extremely attractive, he didn't want to chalk his dislike for him up to the fact that he had an interest in her, which he was finding he did.

He'd been living in the building for three months and enjoyed talking to her and learning about her, though he felt bad that he wasn't as open about sharing all parts of his life with her as she was with him. He hadn't lied to her about anything as much as he was purposely leaving things out. He had gone through great lengths to protect his identity and he wanted to keep it that way. He knew soon enough he would be found out, but for now, he was enjoying the peace of his neighbors not knowing.

Phoenix was nice and had been since the moment he moved in. She always greeted him with a smile even on days when he knew she didn't want to smile. He never said anything, but he could hear her and Carson arguing about one thing or another and yet when she encountered him right after, she would be smiling and friendly.

They would talk about all kinds of things whenever they saw each other, especially if they happened to be in the gym at the same time. She was genuinely kindhearted and though he would never say it out loud, he had a feeling she cared a lot more for Carson than he did for her. They argued constantly about his lateness to everything and about his lack of steady employment. He'd seen Carson's face plastered all over social media with one unflattering headline after another. He also knew if Carson wasn't so self-centered, he would probably recognize Gavin even with the change in his appearance, but Carson was all about Carson.

For the life of him, he could not picture him and Phoenix as a couple. She didn't appear to be the partying or groupie type. She wasn't flashy though every time he'd seen her, she was impeccably dressed. Tonight, seeing her standing outside, she was a vision of beauty.

She had been wearing a fiery red dress that hugged her body, enhancing every single one of her curves. Her daily workout was proof that time spent in the gym was well worth the effort. He had never seen more beautiful legs on any woman before. He could tell she loved pampering herself with polished nails, every hair in place and even with the small hint of makeup, her skin was flawless. She had a natural beauty that he loved, especially her naturally coiled hair. The hints of blond throughout added an eccentric look that he loved.

Carson didn't seem like her type. He knew from pictures of him with other women that he liked women with large body enhancements, especially breasts and he loved long, permed hair and weaves on women. Before Phoenix, he'd never seen him with a woman whose body and hair were natural. He didn't want to diminish the woman that Phoenix was because he knew that he would be lucky to have a woman like her who was full of life and didn't live to be eye candy for a rich and famous boyfriend. She instead opted for the backseat to his life, being seen out on the town with him when she had to be and not because she looked for an opportunity to be. He liked that about her.

When they talked, he got the feeling she and Carson got together because she was the opposite of the type of women he was linked to because of his fame and fortune. He liked her because she was the kind of woman a man wouldn't mind taking home to his mother and father and she was the type his parents would like to see him settle down with. Gavin should know because from what he could tell, she would be the type he would take home to his own parents, if he was ever planning to do that. He'd tried that once and it didn't turn out too well for him.

The kind of woman Phoenix was is the kind of woman he thought he'd found in Natasha, the woman he thought he would one day marry. At one time, he thought she was everything he'd wanted and until the very last day that he'd seen her, he never thought differently. Perhaps Phoenix walked around with the same clouded glasses on that he'd worn when it came to taking a good look at his own relationship.

He looked around his loft one last time, grabbing his IPad and left to meet his guests. He shook off any idea that it was his business what Phoenix did in her personal life since he was just her neighbor. Just his luck, he would move into a building with a neighbor who he had an inkling was the full package. He never found that within a few months of meeting anyone. He knew he needed to shake his interest in her. She was engaged to marry another man and clearly she was in love with him.

**

"What do you mean you're not coming?" Phoenix yelled into her phone. She didn't care who may be walking by and could hear her yelling. She was livid.

"Baby, listen, I have this meeting that is running over and this could mean big things for me, so I need to stay here."

"But..." she tried to get out.

"Go have dinner with your friends and tell them I'm sorry I couldn't make it. We'll reschedule the couple's night another time. I love you and I'll call you tomorrow."

Before she could get another word out, the phone line went dead because Carson had hung up on her. She stood out on the sidewalk in front of her building looking like an idiot, waiting an hour for a man who didn't have the decency to tell her an hour ago that he wasn't going to make it. This was another in a long line of dates he cancelled out on and his excuses were getting more and more planned. If she didn't love him as much as she did, she wouldn't put up with it anymore. She was trying to be the supportive fiancé by not making waves when he pulled stunts like the one he'd just pulled on her.

Now what? she thought. She could still make dinner with her friends and once again make an excuse for Carson's absence. She hated being the third wheel to another couple and then she'd feel like she needed to spend the entire night making apologies for Carson, which she found herself doing a lot. Her friends would understand, but she wasn't in the mood; not anymore. She turned and headed back into the building. She had to get up early the next morning for work anyway, so perhaps the night turned out the way it needed to.

As soon as she got to the elevator and pushed the button, the door opened. Getting in, she thought of what she'd say when she talked to Carson after his antics from tonight. They needed to have a talk so that he would know that she expected him to be as considerate of her as she was of him. This is not how she wanted their life as husband and wife to be and they needed to put things like inconsideration of each other's time to bed before the wedding.

The elevator door opened on her floor and standing on the other side was Gavin looking all charming and handsome dressed in all black and his usual staple of a hat on his head. She was hoping she could get to her loft before running into him since he'd seen her standing outside waiting.

Gavin looked Phoenix square in the eyes when the elevator door opened.

Looking in her face, it was the first time he'd seen her upset and not smiling. When she saw him, she tried to plaster a fake smile on her face, but it didn't work.

"Are you alright?" he asked when she stepped off.

Phoenix tried to keep her head down so that he wouldn't notice how upset she was. She wasn't usually rude to him as she ignored him and walked toward her door.

Gavin let the elevator door close as he watched Phoenix walk away. Something was obviously wrong.

"Phoenix?" he said hoping this time she would answer him.

She stopped walking and turned back around as he took a few steps toward her.

"I'm sorry. I'm not usually rude."

"I know that, but I can tell something is wrong. Last I saw you about an hour ago, you were standing outside waiting for Carson. What's wrong?"

With her head held down and her eyes on the carpeted floor, she spoke.

"He didn't show up."

"What?" he said with anger behind his words that he couldn't explain.

"Carson didn't show up."

"Wait, do you mean he left you standing outside for an hour and never came to pick you up?"

"That's exactly what he did. After calling him for the

twentieth time, he finally answered and said he had to cancel. He was caught up in some meeting and couldn't get away. Before I could get more than a few words out, he told me to go ahead to dinner with my friends and apologize to them for his absence. He hung up before I could say anything else."

"Did he know you were already outside for an hour waiting?"

Phoenix tried to put on a brave front as if his actions didn't bother her.

"I'm sure he assumed I was still inside waiting on him. He probably forgot that we were meeting outside of the building. It's not a big deal. I'm sure he was in an important meeting that could make or break his career. I told you he was making some big moves these days to try and prove to his father that he will be ready to take over the company one day soon."

Gavin was enraged. Not only did Carson leave her standing outside for an hour, but she was making an excuse for his behavior.

"I don't care what he had going on, there is no excuse for leaving a woman standing around waiting for an hour and only after you call him does he make up an excuse. Don't make excuses for him, Phoenix."

He tried to sound calm when he spoke, but he was furious. No woman deserved to be treated that way.

"I've been here before. That's the downside to being engaged to someone like Carson."

Gavin noticed she didn't say 'being in love with' someone like Carson. That said more than a little bit.

"Are you going to be alright? I've never seen you look down and that doesn't mesh well with how beautiful you look tonight. A woman as beautiful as you should never have a sad look on her face."

She did smile then and it wasn't a fake one. She liked Gavin and she knew whatever woman garnered his attention was a lucky one.

She'd seen a few women come and go since he'd moved in a few months ago and some she knew had spent the night with him. In the morning, if she ran into one, there was always a glow about her, smiling like she'd had the night of her life. She had no doubt he knew how to treat a woman. Gavin didn't know her well, but he still cared about her and any woman could appreciate that. Everything about him says he leads from his heart and never for selfish reasons, a trait that Carson was missing.

"I'm going to be fine. If this wasn't a repeat state of existence for me, I may second guess that, but I'm all too familiar with being the fiancé of Carson Stone. I'll be fine. Aren't you going to be late for your dinner?"

He didn't respond and she knew he was torn between going out and caring about her feelings which were now hurt and she knew it showed. He didn't want to leave her alone feeling sorry for herself.

"I should get going, but I want to be sure you're okay."

She reached out and touched his arm to reassure him. The moment she did, an electric shock caught them both by surprise. It wasn't the kind you got from being on carpet, but it was a shock that made her aware of him like never before. The shock made her center on him and as she looked into his eyes, she saw something deep and intense that made her feel instantly connected to him. Where did that come from, she thought. She pulled her hand back and wiped it on her dress as if that would remove the feeling of closeness she felt with him.

"I'm fine Gavin, really I am. I'm going to go inside to relax. I have no business going out tonight anyway. I have a lot of work to catch up on and I have to get up early in the morning."

"Okay, well I won't be out too late and if you need to talk or anything, knock on my door any time."

"Thanks for being a great guy," she said before turning around.

"Have a good night and try not to let anything get you down. Life is too short to be consumed by anything that doesn't make you smile."

"Thank you and I won't," she said plastering on a smile even though she was furious at Carson. She opened her door and went inside just as Gavin walked into the elevator. She leaned back against her door and exhaled as if she had been holding on to her breath for a long time.

"What a man! Where do they manufacture men like you and where can I get one to train Carson," she said out loud.

Chapter 4

"He stood me up again, Reese."

"What!!"

Her sister was shouting so loud, she had to move the phone away from her ear.

"You heard me," Phoenix added.

"You know I don't like that bastard and the way he treats you. Why do you put up with it? Is it for the money and the lifestyle you'll live as the wife of the man who will one day run the Stone Tower empire? I don't understand the draw? He is a real jackass and he's been that way since the beginning. I know you love him and somewhere in that selfish body of his, I think he loves you too, but something genuine is missing and I hate to see him treat you this way."

"Over dramatic much?" Phoenix asked her sister after she spilled all of her true feelings about Carson.

"Not dramatic enough?" Reese shot back, shocking her.

"I don't want to argue with you about Carson yet again. He is who he is and I knew it the day I got involved with him. I'm not looking to change who he was when I met him; that would be wrong. I love him even with all of his faults."

"Are you sure? Wait, don't answer that. I know you do on some level and I'm not questioning your love for him or his for you. I'm saying you're my sister, I love you and I don't like how he treats you as an afterthought. That's all I'm saying and we don't have to argue about your personal life, but when you share it with me and I want you to, you should know that I'm going to be honest."

Phoenix smiled. She hated hearing criticism, but she loved that her sister told her like it was. That's why they were not only sisters, but best friends.

"I know and that's why I tell you everything. You give me exactly what I need. Carson and I need to work on our relationship and we will."

"Good, now tell me about this handsome neighbor of yours."

Phoenix laid across her chaise lounge and turned the volume down on the music, which she had been blaring and singing to. Music was her first love and it always made her feel good hearing and especially singing it.

"I don't know a whole lot about him other than his name is Gavin Knolls and he's fine."

"Gavin what? Spell it."

She did.

"Knolls."

"Why do you need it?"

"I'm going to look him up."

"Not now Reese."

"Okay, okay."

"He's some sort of writer, working on a novel. When I tell you he's fine, that's an understatement and considering he's also extremely thoughtful, he's like a woman's dream man. He lives a pretty quiet existence, though I've seen some very beautiful women come and go. He must have a very active sex life because I swear these women have a look of satisfaction that screams about a night of pure pleasure they experienced. He has an assistant, Isabella, who comes over several times during the week and another assistant who does a lot of shopping for him."

"You think they're rolling around in the sheets too?" Phoenix chuckled.

"Only you would think like that. I don't know and I don't care, but I doubt it. Isabella is quite a bit older and seems like a mother figure. Either way, it's none of my business and it's none of yours."

"Whatever! What kind of book is he writing?"

"I don't know. He doesn't talk much about it and I don't see him too often, just in passing or sometimes in the gym. He's full of mystery. He has a loft that's the largest in the building and you should see the cars he drives. When he first moved in, all I saw was this beautiful black truck, but now he also has a black

Jaguar and when I tell you this car is in a class by itself, I mean it. It's definitely top of the line and from what I can tell, I don't think he has a job, so perhaps he's a self-made man or something. I don't know because I'm not that kind of nosey neighbor. I don't like digging around into people's lives and I don't want you doing it either."

She heard her sister groan on the other end, but knew that she would do as she asked and not dig.

"Alright I hear you. Have you heard from our brother lately?"

"No. I pay my portion every month and all is good. I talked to mom last night and she said she talked to him last week and that he was doing fine. Andre is knee deep in his latest job and doesn't have a lot of time for communication. I'm going to send him a hello email later this evening and you should do the same."

"I know I will," Reese said.

"Good, now can we talk about my wedding since I have your undivided attention? I want to schedule the cake tasting and the final fitting for my dress."

"Is Carson going to make it to the tasting? I know you said he wanted to be a part of the cake selection process?"

Phoenix heard the sound of doubt in her sister's voice and let it go without acknowledging it. She didn't want to get back into talking about him and all of the many things he does wrong.

"Yes and as soon as I have the date and time on the books, I'll let him know so that he can make a plan to be there with us. It should be exciting tasting all those flavors."

"I'm excited too and I can't wait. Getting you married is my top priority and since Carson's family is footing the bill, I say we go all out!"

Laughing along with her silly sister, she almost fell out of the chair.

"Funny Reese. I know it looks like we have a blank check, but I still want to be conservative where I can. The price of my dress alone could buy someone a nice home. Remember his mother is going to be with us. I need to get it scheduled since she'll be flying in for the tasting. All I have to do is pick when, since the where has already been determined. She's contracted with one of the best pastry chefs in the world, so I know every sample is going to be delicious."

"What's going on with the venue?" Reese asked.

"We're still going to do the wedding at their house in Weston, Massachusetts. You know that's one of the most elite parts of Massachusetts. I hear it's valued at almost two million dollars. I know that's small potatoes for them, but that's huge for me. The planner his mother contracted for me is coming into town when we do the tasting since his mother will be here."

"Girl, this is going to be some wedding. Is Andre coming in for the wedding?"

"I told him about it and he said he wouldn't miss it. He told me not to get a photographer or videographer because of course that's his line of work and he has that covered. That's one expense I don't have to give Carson a bill for. It's overwhelming the amount of money being spent on this wedding."

"Oh, please. They are happy to be marrying their playboy son off to help clean up his image. I bet they would spend anything to make that happen."

She'd like to doubt everything her sister said, but she knew the words were true. Carson needed to put that image of himself to bed once and for all and having him engaged to someone not prone to living in the limelight was exactly what he needed. Even knowing that, they still loved each other which was important to note. Carson had his faults, but so did she and together, they were going to have a fairytale kind of love and marriage and she couldn't wait to be his wife."

"Have you and Carson decided where you're going to live after the wedding?"

"He wants to take over the west coast hotels, so probably in California where he wants to build a house in Hidden Hills, in Calabasas. He says his parents are going to buy us property there for our wedding gift and will have the house of our dreams built. I'm going along with whatever plans he has. I told him I still wanted to work for the hotel and he didn't think it would be a problem taking over human resources there. That would mean I'd be responsible for the largest hotels in the chain and that's exciting!" she exclaimed.

"I can't believe my baby sister is about to marry into one of the richest families in the country. That's exciting."

"Reese, it's not all about the money. I love him."

Reese didn't say it, but she was thinking that it wasn't her sister's love for Carson that she questioned; it was his love for Phoenix that she had an issue with, but she would never say her true feelings out loud about that.

"I know you do and I'm excited about your love. Just promise me you'll have the talk with him about the two of you being on the same page."

"I promise I will. I need to run out to the store. Carson wants to make that night up to me by coming over and spending a quiet evening watching television and cuddling. I'm going to cook us a nice meal, one of his favorites and I need to pick up a few extra things. I'll call you next week about the cake tasting."

"Phoenix, it's ten o'clock in the morning on a Saturday. You have all day to do that unless you're doing dinner at noon."

"You always got jokes. I was already up and dressed after working out in the gym and I have to do some things and I only told you about that one."

"Okay, I'm going to stop picking. I love you sis."

"Love you too, Reese."

Already dressed in a sweat suit for running errands, Phoenix grabbed her phone, keys and left. She and Carson had some alone time to make up for tonight. He had called several times over the past few days since the dinner debacle and apologized for skipping out on their date and like always, she forgave him after he promised to make it up to her. She hoped he meant it this time. He was running out of chances.

**

"That should be it Isabella. I'm sorry I have to put you to work on a Saturday. I try to let you have your weekends to yourself and your family and hopefully these two small tasks won't take you too long."

"Thank you Mr. Black and I promise you it's not a problem at all. Oops, I keep forgetting to call you Mr. Knolls so that I can get used to the pseudonym."

"It's okay to use my real name when we're alone or talking on the phone."

He'd instructed those around him to go by his made-up last name so that he could keep his privacy as long as possible. He didn't mind if they slipped up every now and then, especially when there was no one around to hear it.

"Okay, that's good to know and I don't mind working on Saturday. I dropped my kids off at the mall to hang out with their friends and my husband is finally painting my kitchen, so my day is pretty much free. I hope you are taking some time to relax today and not focused on working on your novel. You've been in a slump with your writing lately, but you promised me only fun things on weekends."

Gavin laughed. Isabella was a mother figure who worried about him constantly. She was definitely the best assistant he ever had and that's saying something considering he'd had quite a few when he was at GNAB Technologies. If he ever went back, he wondered how much he would have to offer Isabella to pick up her family again and move back to California to continue working for him. He hesitated asking her to move to Chicago from California where she worked for him at the company, but she quickly accepted after conferring with her husband. They looked forward to a change of pace and someplace new. Her husband worked in real estate and Gavin helped him get a job in Chicago by making a few calls. It also helped that he paid Isabella triple what a typical assistant at any other company made.

He liked her the minute he'd hired her four years ago. Luckily, she was well versed when it came to knowing how to use all of the latest technology. A lot of what they needed to confer about could be done virtually especially after Ellis had sent a team to install some new communication equipment in her home and in the small office he'd purchased that he had yet to visit. Isabella worked out of it every day even though he told her she didn't have to. She preferred it, giving her the opportunity to get out and about every day. He even threw in new computers for her husband and kids and a new gaming system that she said her kids practically lived in front of during their down time. He got great pleasure out of doing things for others.

"I promise that I have no plans to do any writing today. I'm still drawing a blank anyway and hope that the motivation to pick my writing back up again will come soon. That deadline is coming up fast."

"Pace yourself and don't worry about it too much. The words will come when they're supposed to. I'll get you this information in a few hours and send it right over to you."

"Thank you, Isabella. I don't know what I would do without you," he said pulling into his parking space in the garage under his building.

"You will never have to find out. Have a good day Mr. Black," Isabella said cheerfully before hanging up.

Gavin hung up and as he exited his car, he saw Phoenix pulling into one of her two assigned parking spaces. He hadn't seen her since the night Carson had left her standing outside of the building backing out on their date.

"Hey neighbor," he said when she exited her car.

"Hey to you too. How have you been?"

"I've been great. I haven't seen you in a few days. How are things?" he asked as she went around to the trunk of her car.

When he saw that she had several bags, he walked over to help her.

"Things are great."

"Let me help you with those," he said, pulling the bags from her car.

"Oh, thank you. I appreciate it."

Gavin grabbed all of the bags and followed her to the elevator. He watched her as she walked and couldn't help but admire the gentle sway of her hips. Having an hour glass figure, her hips flared adding a little extra movement to her walk. There was no way he could deny how sexy she was and he didn't care who she was engaged to. Phoenix was a beautiful woman and it never hurt to look.

They got in the elevator and silence welcomed them on the ride up as they tried to avoid acknowledging they were staring at each other. He would look at her and she would look away and then she would look over at him and then she'd look away. He refused to turn away. He believed in direct eye contact.

"So, how is the book coming along?" Phoenix asked, breaking the silence.

"Slowly, but I'm okay with that. I haven't had much inspiration. I need the down time, so it's all good."

Gavin didn't want to talk too much about him so he deflected the conversation to her.

"How is work for you? They still have you working hard?"

"Extremely hard. I've been setting up new customer service training for all of the staff in all of the hotels, starting with those here in Illinois. That's kept me extremely busy, but I love it."

Gavin looked down into the bags he was carrying.

"It looks like you're preparing for a feast," he said.

Phoenix perked up.

"Yes, I'm cooking a feast for Carson and me for tonight. He's finally carved out some down time and we're hoping to reconnect tonight. I haven't seen him since the night he skipped out on dinner."

"Good food and even better company will definitely do the trick. He's a lucky man to have a woman who loves and cares for him the way you do."

Phoenix blushed.

"Thank you. I think he is pretty lucky too!" she

quipped.

The elevator door opened and they walked down the hall in silence. Phoenix opened the door and looked to take the bags from his hands.

"Go ahead in. I'll bring these in. They are pretty heavy," he said, following her in.

"Thank you," she said. She knew they were heavy and was happy she didn't have to carry them.

Gavin looked around.

"This place is nice. Where do you want me to put the bags down?"

"Thank you. You can put them on the counter over there," she said pointing to the island in the kitchen area.

Walking over, he moved around a big box that sat in the middle of the floor. He remembered the day the box was delivered weeks ago. He looked down at it and saw that it was a large bookshelf.

"Hey, I remember seeing them bring this big box up. You haven't gotten anyone to put this together yet?"

"I've been waiting for Carson to do it," she stumble out.

Say no more, Gavin thought.

"I see," was all he replied.

"He said he would do it, but hasn't found the time to get around to it yet. I didn't think he would anyway since he's not the handy type and I've never seen him with a tool in his hands. I'm planning to call a friend of my sister's to ask if he could put it together. Be careful moving around it."

Gavin laid the bags down.

"I have some time and can put it together. I'm quite handy with a screwdriver. I even have a tool box, if you can imagine that. I'm quite good with my hands," he added.

Phoenix turned away from his stare hoping he wouldn't see the heat that rose in them when he mentioned his hands. The minute the words were out of his mouth, images flooded her mind of all the things she knew he could probably do with those hands. Somewhere she knew there were some lucky women walking around who already knew.

"Oh, you don't have to do that. I can call someone to do it."

"Phoenix, it's okay. I could have this together in a couple of hours. If you don't mind the intrusion and the noise, I can go grab my tools and be out of your hair before your evening begins."

She lightened up knowing that Gavin was being neighborly.

"If you're sure you don't mind."

"I don't mind at all. I didn't have anything planned until later this evening. I'll run over to my place and grab my tools and be right back over to hook you up."

She watched as he walked off and once again, she felt a sudden rush of heat travel through her body. He had an innocent way of saying things that made her think of him naked and pleasuring her in ways unimaginable, at least to her.

First he mentioned this hands and when he

mentioned returning with tools to hook her up, the visual of him using his tools had her breaking out in a sweat. She needed to pull it back. She was attracted to Gavin, which was clear and she couldn't think of a woman who wouldn't be. Still, she needed to stop letting her thoughts run away because she had Carson and she didn't need the distraction even from a man who, without knowing it, showed her where her own man had shortcomings. Handyman or not, Carson could have tried putting the bookshelf together or offered help in finding someone to put it together. Every time he entered the loft, he walked around it like it wasn't sitting in the middle of the floor.

Shrugging it off, she went to empty the food from the bags as Gavin knocked and then entered. She saw his excitement over helping her out and secretly wished she could see the same in Carson. She knew it wasn't fair to compare the two of them, but she couldn't help herself. The differences were more than obvious.

**

"Gavin, I just landed. I'm only here for a few hours unexpectedly for an extended layover. I've got about five hours to kill," Ellis said as soon as Gavin answered.

"You're here in Chicago?" Gavin asked.

"I am," Ellis replied.

After putting the bookshelf together for Phoenix, he had settled in for a relaxed evening at home. He was going to spend the evening looking through the latest financial records for the company as well as for his other smaller companies. He still hadn't received much inspiration when it came to adding more to his book, so other work would take his mind off of the fact that he was falling for his neighbor who was probably getting herself together for a night of dinner and lovemaking with her fiancé. He was jealous because he knew incredible women like Phoenix were hard to find and Carson had her.

He enjoyed talking to her while he fixed her bookcase. He was done sooner than he thought and would have loved more time to talk to her especially about her love for music. Her voice was miraculous and for a minute, the few times he'd heard her, he thought that he was listening to a professional artist. Phoenix had a voice that would match any of the current artists who sat at the top of the charts. He couldn't believe she wasn't singing professionally.

She mentioned that at one time in her life, a career in music was her dream, but she didn't want to be one of those starving artists and went with what she thought would be a more sensible career. Hearing her casually sing left him with no doubt that getting her in the recording studio was a great idea. She had a voice that was undeniably ready for the world.

Phoenix amazed him more and more each time they talked. She could have been the type of woman to use Carson to get ahead and he definitely had the money to help her get a music career going. Knowing that, he could see that she was a jewel and didn't want to use Carson for her own gain.

Gavin was intrigued and not just a little. He could

have any woman he wanted and he was fixated on one that was engaged to another man.

He looked at the time and it was only nine in the evening and he could get to the airport in no time at all to connect with his best friend. He needed something, anything to take his mind off of Phoenix. He'd heard Carson when he arrived about an hour ago, no doubt late again since he rushed to put the bookcase together when Phoenix told him she as expecting him around six. He smiled at himself and the level of jealousy he felt knowing how lucky a man Carson was. He knew he needed some distance.

"I'll be on my way to the airport in a few minutes. I didn't know you were flying this way. Business or pleasure?

"Business. I would have told you about it, but the original plan for the layover was for me to stay on the plane as they added additional passengers and we would only be here while they gassed up the plane. Now we're told there are problems with the plane, so we had to disembark and the flight won't get out for a few hours. You feel like a few drinks and maybe a few steaks while I'm here?"

"Of course. When have you known me not to want a steak? I'm on my way."

Gavin hung up and went in his room to change. Remembering to grab his wallet and keys and the hat he liked to wear that helped hide his face, he opened the door and was locking it when Phoenix's door opened at the same time. He looked over and saw

Carson leaving out. He wondered if he was leaving because he forgot something or if he was leaving for good. His second thought would certainly fit who he knew Carson was, arriving an hour ago and already leaving. He'd only met him a few times coming out of her place and each time, Carson never did more than nod his head, never speaking.

"Gavin, right?"

He turned when Carson said his name.

"Yes, that's right."

Gavin didn't hide the fact that he didn't care for him, but he was important to Phoenix, so he played it off as much as possible. He didn't want to stop and talk to him, so he walked the distance toward the elevator with Carson in tow.

"You know you look familiar to me. Is it possible we've met before?"

"I doubt it," Gavin replied, standoffishly. The last thing he wanted to do was engage in a conversation with him.

"Right, so I hear you put the bookshelf together for Phoenix earlier today."

"Yeah, well she mentioned it had been sitting in the floor in the box for a few weeks and I offered to put it together for her. It wasn't a big deal."

He could hear the tension in Carson's voice that said he wasn't happy about the idea that he helped her out.

"Right, right. So the two of you are quite chummy now huh?" Carson asked nonchalantly.

Gavin heard annoyance in his voice and didn't like

where the conversation was going. He also didn't like beating around the bush. It wasn't in his character and he turned to face Carson full on.

"You have something to say, then say it. Obviously you do because you've never said a word to me before when you've seen me. What's the deal?"

Carson avoided eye contact, but spoke to him without looking directly at him. He was a few inches taller than Carson and noticed he avoided looking up at him, probably feeling intimidated. Carson was only a big man when it came to the amount of money he had, definitely not in stature or personality.

"Okay, here it is. I would appreciate it if you wouldn't lend anymore helping hands to my fiancé. I had that bookshelf covered and was planning to put it together tonight when I got here. To my surprise, it was already put together and she had even started stocking it with little trinkets. I'm not trying to ruffle any feathers here and I don't want to assume you have an ulterior motive for being helpful to my lady. She seems to know an awful lot about you considering you're only neighbors."

All Gavin could think was there was nothing worse than an insecure man. If he was taking care of his woman the way he should be, he wouldn't have to worry about being jealous of any man Phoenix may encounter. His patience had officially worn off.

"Are you done?" he asked with a little more power behind his voice than he wanted.

Carson signaled that the floor was his.

"Well, to begin with, I don't have an ulterior motive and you're right Phoenix and I are neighbors and I consider her a friend and that is it. I helped her bring in some bags earlier, I saw the bookshelf that I remembered being delivered a couple of weeks ago and I offered to put it together. I did that and as soon as I was done, I went back to my place. We didn't even have a lot of conversation because she was cooking for her evening with you. If for any reason you feel like I overstepped a boundary, then I apologize and I will certainly apologize to Phoenix. I have no problem not lending a hand if that's what she wants considering helping a woman who needs help is what my parents raised me to do and not leave a woman to walk around a box in her floor for weeks before I take action to put it together. Now, just so we don't get this conversation twisted, you don't intimidate me and I don't take instructions from you. If you don't want a man offering your fiancé help, then perhaps you should make sure you're around to do the things that a fiancé should be doing to help make her life easier. You would think her safety, well-being and comfort in life would be a priority for you. If it's not, don't beat your chest like you're the king of the jungle in my face because I'm not impressed. Are we done?"

He didn't back down, making sure Carson knew he wasn't a chump and wasn't to be challenged. He didn't care how much money his family had. It made him an arrogant prick and his least favorite person. He waited to see how Carson would react and he lessened his stance when he watched Carson step back and look around, playing it cool.

"Yeah, well, I'll take care of my fiancé."

"You do that," Gavin said.

When the elevator came, he got in and expected Carson to follow him in. When he didn't, he pushed the button to close the door and rode down to his car. His initial assumption was that Carson may have heard him leaving out and decided to act as if he was leaving out at the same time in order to confront him. When he didn't get in the elevator, he assumed he had then gone back inside to Phoenix.

Gavin walked to his car and had been sitting in it for a few minutes putting the address to the airport in his GPS when he was about to start his car, heard a noise and looked up to see the elevator door open and out walked Carson. He shook his head. Apparently he didn't go back inside with Phoenix, but decided to not take the elevator down with him. He didn't care as long as the playboy got the message. He wasn't one of those flunkies who followed Carson around like a puppy because of who his daddy was. Maybe now, he'll do a better job of treating his woman the way she should be treated.

He pulled off and headed in the direction of the airport, never looking in Carson's direction.

Chapter 5

Phoenix tried not to seem moved by her best friend Adrienne and her sister Reese's comments about her relationship with Carson. They had stopped over so that she could get more planning done for the wedding before the wedding planner showed up and dismissed all of her ideas for her own wedding.

Her sister and Adrienne were sharing the maid of honor duties and their opinions meant everything to her. They also wanted to talk about her bachelorette party, the one that older members of her and Carson's family would not be invited to. Somehow the conversation had turned to Carson.

"Girl, as much as I want you to marry into this rich family, I want you to be happy first and are you sure you're finding that happiness with Carson? I mean, seriously, I can't believe another man had to put that bookshelf together for you. I was here the week it was delivered and you said the men laid it out in the floor because Carson promised he would do it later that night. Now you're telling me weeks later and he never found the time to do it? That's just pathetic," Reese said, not holding back on her opinion.

"I know, I know," she replied.

"What did he say when you told him your neighbor put it together?" Adrienne asked.

"He didn't say anything. He thought I had called a company to do it and he got quiet when I said Gavin had done it. He asked me what was Gavin doing in here and I told him he helped me with the bags from the garage. I would have had to make two trips if he hadn't helped me," Phoenix explained.

"Well, I'm sure that didn't go over too well. You know that ego of his didn't want to hear that. How did the rest of the night go?"

"It went fine," she lied.

"Hmm," Reese replied, then smiled.

Phoenix rolled her eyes playfully and continued.

"We had dinner and when we were about to relax and watch a movie, he remembered some clients he was supposed to meet for dinner. He's brokering a contract for cable advertisement for the hotel. There were some representatives in town that he wanted to schmooze with and forgot it was the same night."

She didn't want to tell them that she knew when he arrived, he had no plans to stay beyond dinner. He was dressed for a night out on the town and not for one to lounge around and chill with her. She let it go and enjoyed dinner anyway. She waited to see when he would announce he was leaving and around nine, his phone rang and she knew that was the moment he would come up with his exit strategy and he did. There was no need to tell that part to Reese and Adrienne. They would find more reasons to slam Carson and she wasn't in the mood for it.

Reese looked at Adrienne and they turned and looked at her with suspicious looks.

"You fell for that?"

"Not tonight Reese, please," she pleaded.

"Okay, well it's getting late anyway. Did we have anything else we needed to talk about while you have us here? Adrienne filled out all of the other dates in your planner and we still need to find mom a dress. I'll pick her up for our fitting and we can help her find something. She's going to the cake tasting too, so that's the perfect time to do it. Has Carson's mother found her dress for wedding?"

Phoenix looked at her facetiously.

"Girl, she has a personal stylist who is making her dress for the wedding. I asked her what it looked like and she wasn't sure yet. She told me it would be the color I asked her to be in, but that's all she knew about it so far."

"Girl, that woman is going to show up at this wedding trying to out dress you and you know it. You know she has to have all the attention when she walks in a room."

Phoenix knew that, considering Mrs. Stone was the

beginning and the ending to everything, but not her wedding day. She didn't plan to have anyone outshine her.

"Well, she can try it, but it's my wedding day and no one will steal the spotlight away from me. Wait until you see this body in that dress," she joked, framing her curves with her hands and spinning around.

Reese laughed out loud.

"Just say the word baby sister and I'll throw a bowl of punch on her."

They all laughed.

"I have to get out of here. Rodney and I have a standing date night tonight and I don't want to keep my man waiting," Adrienne said, standing to leave.

"Well, since I came with you, that's my cue to leave too. Are we done?" she looked to Phoenix.

"Yeah, we're done."

Phoenix was feeling a little jealous of Adrienne and her relationship. She and Rodney had a standing night of the week for date night and according to her, there were times when she forgot and he would remind her. She missed the days of Carson having more time for them to have date nights. She remembered when someone asked her parents what was the secret to their long lasting marriage, her father replied, 'never stop dating'.

Phoenix got up and walked them to the door while keeping her melancholy thoughts to herself. She was in the hallway giving them hugs when the elevator signaled it was landing on her floor. They all gawked as

Gavin exited looking like a star in every woman's dreams. He had a sexy confidence about his walk that had them all holding their breath as he approached.

"Damn," Reese said and Phoenix nudged her in the ribs.

"Stop it," she whispered before he got close enough to hear them.

"Good evening ladies," Gavin acknowledged when he reached them, tipping his hat to them.

"Oh, this evening just got better," Reese said giving him a good once over.

"Stop it Reese," Phoenix said, embarrassed by her sister's lack of tact.

"Hey Gavin. This is my sister Reese and my best friend Adrienne. They were just leaving," she said nudging them on.

"I was thinking of sticking around for a bit," Reese said before Adrienne pulled her along.

"You have a man, remember?" Adrienne said as they reached the elevator.

"It was nice to meet you Gavin. Phoenix has told us what a great neighbor you are."

"It's nice to finally meet you ladies. Phoenix talks about you all the time. I hope to see you again soon."

"It will be our pleasure," Reese said just before she was pushed into the elevator by Adrienne.

Phoenix shook her head at her sister who wasn't known for holding her tongue.

"I'm so sorry about my sister. She can be quite curt when she speaks and it's often done without thinking first."

"That's okay. I've got a sister too and I understand."

"Yeah, well, no one has a sister like mine, but I love her anyway," she laughed.

When the hallway got quiet, but neither of them moved, Gavin spoke first.

"I haven't seen you since the day I put the bookcase together for you. How did dinner turn out that night?"

Phoenix really wanted to lie, but she couldn't summon the words to do so. Something about Gavin made her want to tell him the truth and she looked forward to his male perspective on things.

"It was a quick dinner and he had to leave earlier than I thought he would. Something about a business meeting."

"Sorry to hear that. I know you cooked all afternoon as a surprise for him."

"Yeah," was all she could think to say.

"Did he enjoy it?"

Phoenix was mad that she didn't know. Carson ate and never acknowledged anything about it or the fact that she'd spent the entire day cooking some of his favorite things.

"Yeah, sure," she replied.

She had nothing good to say and she stayed away from saying anything too bad because that would reflect on her as well as her choice of the man to be with. Carson had his good and bad like anyone else, but even she knew it shouldn't be an excuse considering she wasn't engaged to any of them; she was engaged to him.

"I ran into Carson as I was heading out and it was kind of early. I was hoping it wasn't the food?" he jested, hoping to lighten the mood. When she laughed, he laughed with her. God, she was so beautiful, he thought.

"It definitely wasn't the food. My mother taught me early how to burn in the kitchen and that's not literally burning anything. He's handling a big advertising deal for the hotel chain and it's the first big deal his father is trusting him with. There were some representatives in town that he wanted to show a good evening to."

So, Carson preferred showing a good evening to strangers and not the love of his life, he thought to himself. Classic move of a prick.

"So, in other words, he ruined your plans for a quiet evening together?"

"Yeah, you would think I would be accustomed to it by now. It was fine, because after cooking all day, I was exhausted. At least he ate every bit of it, including dessert, so it turned out okay. I had a lot of wedding stuff to think through, so that gave me a chance to do that."

Gavin didn't comment on her attempt to make yet another excuse for Carson. He saw how the man was dressed and he was definitely dressed for a party with a younger crowd, not for meeting marketing executives to discuss business. It wasn't his place to question it and he wouldn't.

"I'm glad dinner turned out great. How is that

bookshelf holding up?"

Phoenix lit up thinking about how nicely it fit into her décor and anyone would think it was professionally constructed if they saw it.

"It's wonderful and thank you again for doing that. You're a man of many talents I see."

"That's me, a man of many talents."

To anyone else, Gavin saying those words would have just been words, but to her, they sounded erotic especially when his voice appeared to drop an octave and his piercing stare went right through her. Was she picking up on hints of him flirting with her or was she imagining it? Was she flirting with him and not realizing it? She didn't know, but she felt the temperature in the hallway suddenly rise and she needed some cool air.

"Well, I'm thankful for your talent of putting bookshelves together because mine looks magnificent."

Gavin's response got lost in his throat. He wanted to respond with something neighbor-like, but his mind was thinking of blurting out words that said how magnificent she looked and he knew that was going over the line. It was time for a quick exit.

"I'm glad I could help. I have some paperwork to get to so I'll say goodnight. I'll see you soon," he said.

"See you soon," Phoenix said right before she closed and locked her door.

She went inside and plopped down on her sofa. There's trouble in paradise, she thought. Every woman wanted a man as attentive and thoughtful as Gavin and without trying too hard, he was showing her what was missing in her own relationship.

**

"Man, what the hell am I thinking? I can't fall for this woman. She's engaged to another man and it's obvious she's in love with him. I'm telling you he treats her like crap, though I know it's not my place to judge or do anything about it."

Gavin vented to Ellis on the other end of the phone. He'd called him to talk about the design for a new game he had been thinking about when the conversation turned to his sexy neighbor across the hall.

"Gavin, there is nothing wrong with liking this woman as long as you know where the line that you shouldn't cross is drawn. Who she loves or doesn't love is none of your business and it doesn't matter how bad he treats her unless he's putting a hand on her and in that case I would say call me before you knock his ass out so that I can have bail money ready for you. Otherwise, stay out of her personal business."

Gavin tried to gather his thoughts, but for the past hour, all he'd been able to think about was Phoenix and her beautiful smile. He tried not to focus on her and so far it was a losing battle.

"I hear you, Ellis. Can you believe this guy tried to raise up on me over a bookshelf? I could have laid him out then, but I held back. He thinks he moves everybody the way he does those who follow his every footstep. He backed down when he realized I wasn't swayed by his fame, which is all in his mind and in the money he throws around."

"Do you think he knows who you are?" Ellis asked.

Gavin wasn't as well-known as some celebrities, but someone like Carson would know, but again, Carson's world involved Carson.

"I don't know. He may recognize me, but the name on my mailbox and everything else about me says Gavin Knolls, not Gavin Black. There was some brief recognition, but he couldn't figure out where he knew me from. At that point, the conversation got a little heated, so the focus went to what I was saying and not who I was. Besides, he has a problem looking people straight in the eye. He never really looked at me hard unless he did so at a time when I didn't see him. He would have to really dig deep and want to know who I am for it to show up. I think he's too self-centered to even care. He doesn't care about anyone, but himself and the next event he can get to where he's the life of the party and all attention is focused on him."

"You're just getting your life back together after all of that Natasha business and the last thing you need to do is get wrapped up in more drama with a woman. Let it go and get back to working on your book and this new game you called me about."

Ellis was right. He hadn't done much writing since he moved into the loft and he was losing focus. His manager and publicist were sending him messages daily asking about his progress and he had nothing new to share.

"I know you're right and Manny and Lester at the

publishing company have been on me to get more chapters written. She's just a beautiful woman, inside and out. I can't help that I'm attracted to her. She's one of the good ones and he's treating her like she's one of his groupies."

"I'm not saying you need to help being attracted to her. From what you tell me and from the pictures of her I was able to scrounge up on the net of her out with playboy Carson, she is gorgeous. Still, she is engaged and unless the feeling is mutual, back off and remember there is a line, brother."

Gavin exhaled knowing every word Ellis spoke was true. He was developing feelings for Phoenix and he knew that was unavoidable. He tried, but every time he saw and talked to her, he liked her even more. What was avoidable was putting her in an uncompromising position by acting on how he was beginning to feel about her knowing she was in love with Carson, bad guy or not.

"I know man. I just can't figure out what she sees in him. It must be all that money, though I don't peg her for that type. Then again, I'm not good with pegging types am I? I sure got Natasha wrong."

"You didn't get her wrong. She got blinded by the money and that made her a target for those who thought they could get some of your money out of her by getting close to her. There is no way you could have known how close someone would have gotten to her. The fact that she was hooked on prescription drugs clouded her judgment and she easily hooked up with someone without thinking clearly. "

"Not just one someone," Gavin corrected. After the relationship ended, Gavin found that Natasha had hooked up with a couple of guys and they didn't really want her as much as they wanted to find out more about him.

"Don't do this to yourself. Natasha is done and there's no better time than the present to remember that. Whatever the reasons are that Phoenix is with Carson, they are her reasons. She's not asking to be rescued from him, so don't start devising a plan. You have women who love dropping panties whenever you are around before you even ask them too. Why this woman when there is a plethora of them to get with?"

"That's just it. I'm not trying to get with Phoenix. I really like her and I shouldn't, not her, but that doesn't mean it's going away. I'll deal with it just as I have been doing."

"What's up with that woman you told me about that you've been seeing?"

"That's just something casual and it works for what it is. We don't really have a vibe outside of the bedroom and eventually that gets old; at least for me it does."

"It's time you got back out there for something more than just bed hopping. That's never really been you and a hot body to cuddle up with is a good thing, but you've always been the type of guy who's looking for more than that and now that you've met Phoenix, you see what you're missing out on. Just watch yourself because you liking this woman could lead to disaster.

She's not just involved with someone, she's engaged. Let it go. Now, does a brother need to start singing the let it go song?" Ellis wisecracked.

"Don't even try it," Gavin chortled.

"I'm just saying."

Yeah, I know and I will. I'm trying to be low-key here in Chicago and the reason for coming here was so that I could blend in and have as much anonymity as I can until someone recognizes me and makes the connection. The less I'm out the better chances I'll have for that. I'm not searching for a relationship and I'm not even sure I need to get that involved with anyone right now. That wouldn't help with my trying to be low-key here."

"Dude, you can forget that. I give it a few more weeks and someone will make the connection. You are one of the richest brothers in the country and people know that face, especially the women. You can't hide it for too long and I don't care how much extra facial hair you grow or how many hats you wear or even the change in how you dress, you'll be recognized soon. Replacing the five thousand dollar suits for jeans and sweats won't hide the fact that you're Gavin Black. For now, have some fun even if you have to sneak it in and have it sign a non-disclosure agreement. You need something to occupy your mind besides your neighbor and her relationship."

Gavin chuckled.

"I hear you man. I'm staying out of it and I'm going to try to get in front of this computer and knock out some words. Before I do, let's talk about this new game and I want to hear what happened at the last board meeting."

He settled in to let Ellis run down to him everything he'd missed at the board meeting. Though he was no longer CEO, he was still a member of the board and he'd given his vote to Ellis for any decision making that needed to be made. He wanted to know what he voted for during the meeting. For a little while, he'd get to refocus his thoughts on something other than Phoenix Graham. He would follow Ellis' advice and mind his own business.

Chapter 6

"Not many men can pull off all that facial hair like you can Mr. Black," Isabella said as she cleared his work table of stacks of papers.

Since moving to Chicago, he may not have gotten much work done on his book, but he'd come up with an idea for a new game and he was looking forward to working with a select few at the company that he trusted to keep the secret about it. He'd laid it out for Ellis and he could hear his excitement over the phone. He personally wanted to assemble his own team to pull it together. He liked being able to still do business when he wanted to and not because he had to.

"Thank you Isabella. It's taking some getting used to. I've never liked facial hair other than a mustache and very trimmed goatee, but this is working for me especially as long as I keep it shaped up. I need you to order two design tables for me and I'm going to be converting some of the space on the lower level of the building into a small office space for when my team comes into town. I'll need lots of office equipment for it. I'll have Helena from the Silicon Valley office give you a call with what I'll need. We'll need all of the hookups and tight security codes and fire walls for those who will have access."

Isabella took notes as he rattled off a to-do list for her.

"I think I have everything. I'll get on this when I get home."

Gavin looked at the time.

"You'll do no such thing. Look at the hour, it's getting late. You can take care of this tomorrow or later in the week. The upgrades on the space won't be completed for another two weeks. Let's get everything in there after the work is done."

"Tomorrow it is. Only if you make me a promise," she said.

Gavin leaned back in his chair knowing she was probably going to give him a speech about too much work.

"What promise is that?" he said.

"Get out of here tonight and go have some fun. I know you're trying to spend most of your time indoors to protect your identity, but stop doing that. You are who you are and you shouldn't run from that. You can put protections in place to keep people away from you. Do you want me to get Wallace from your old security detail here? You may need him and I don't want you vulnerable to media or random people walking up to you. You're too important for that."

"No, I'm good. I've been trying to go without a security detail to keep attention away, but when I need it, I'll call him to get it in place. I also promise to get out of here and have more fun," he said.

"Do that instead of keeping yourself locked up in here all the time."

She was right. He was spending most of his time at home avoiding people.

"I promise you I will get out tonight. I was thinking of taking in a new movie. There's a new Sci-Fi movie out I've been dying to see and I think I'm going to take a break from anything work or book related tonight and go see it. Thanks for the suggestion Isabella. I hope you and the family have something fun planned for tonight."

"We are going out for pizza and ice cream to celebrate my son making the track team."

"Congratulations to him. Well, have fun," he said as she prepared to leave, after making sure she'd straightened up everything.

"I'll talk to you tomorrow and see in you a few days," she said before walking to the door where he followed her out. Now that his building had security and a doorman, he called down on his newly installed security system to let them know she was on her way down and would need an escort to her car in the garage.

Gavin waited until she was in the elevator before

walking back to his door. As soon as he reached it, he heard loud voices coming from Phoenix's apartment. She and Carson were arguing again and since she was shouting loudly, he knew that they were arguing because he had once again stood her up and she was angry. The way she was hollering, she had to be extremely upset.

He hated the misery Carson brought to her life. She couldn't enjoy it enough because she spent most of her time, when not working, arguing with Carson or making excuses for his tired behavior. Ellis was right. It was none of his business. He went back into his own place and shut the door. Thirty minutes later after he grabbed a quick shower and dressed, he heard Phoenix's door open and slam shut. The door slammed so hard, he felt the floor beneath his feet vibrate. Even though what happened between Phoenix and Carson wasn't his business, he still wanted to be sure she was okay. He grabbed his cell phone to call her remembering that they had recently exchanged cell phone numbers in case of an emergency.

He was dialing her number when he heard a soft knock at his door. He rushed over to it and looking at the video screen on the wall that had a camera that pointed to the hall and he saw Phoenix on the other side of his door. He opened it quickly hoping she was okay.

"Gavin, hi. I hope I'm not interrupting anything."

"No, not at all. Are you okay?" he asked, joining her in the hallway. Though he had dressed for the movie, he didn't have anything on his feet. He pulled his door closed and watched as Phoenix slid down to the floor as if she were totally exhausted. He followed suit and sat down across from her with his back against the wall of his loft.

"Yeah, I'm fine. I got into another fight with Carson. I know you don't want to hear about my drama with him, but I needed some fresh air. I wasn't sure if you were home or not."

"You want to talk about it? Tell me what happened? I may not be able to help, but I can be a sounding board if that's what you need."

She smiled up at him, though he knew she wasn't in a smiling mood.

"You are a great guy. Why aren't you married with two point three kids yet?" she asked humorously.

Gavin relaxed, crossing his legs at the ankles.

"Believe me, it's not because it isn't what I want. That just hasn't happened for me yet."

Phoenix shook her head to clear it.

"Well, walking the path and getting to that point is no walk in the park, I kid you not," she admitted. She wanted that and thought she was on her way until she began questioning her own choices.

"I'm all ears."

When she looked over at him with a serious look on her face, he settled back to let her vent.

"To begin with, why didn't you tell me he said something to you about staying away from me and not helping me with anything anymore? He shouldn't have done that. You told me you ran into him, but you didn't tell me the two of you had words."

Gavin couldn't believe that coward Carson had actually told her about their discussion.

"It wasn't my place and he was just acting jealous. If he treated you better, he wouldn't have anything to be jealous about."

The words slipped out before he could pull them back. He was supposed to be staying out of her business and not giving his opinion. He should be listening.

"I'm sorry about that," he said. "You need a sounding board, not my unsolicited opinion."

"Don't be sorry and it's okay. Carson doesn't own me as if I'm a piece of property and he doesn't make decisions of who can and cannot be around me, something I made very clear to him tonight. I told him we were neighbors and friends and that there was no harm done in you putting that bookshelf together for me. I have no idea why he wanted to act all he-man like. It's not a look or persona that works for him. I don't get all jealous when we're out and woman after woman comes up to him whispering and hanging all on him as if I'm not even there."

"That's a lot to deal with I'm sure," Gavin interjected.

"You have no idea. I see articles and social media posts about him being at this event or that event and yet I don't remember getting an invite to those same functions. I questioned whether he wanted to be married to me and he made it sound as if I was exaggerating. I told him we never go anywhere or do anything that couples do. Every time we go anyplace, it's with a large group of people. I'm not sure he understands the basics of having a date with just me unless it's behind closed doors. We had one hell of a fight tonight and he stormed off as he usually does. I know how this will play out. In a few hours, I'll get a text apologizing and promising he'll do better. He'll make a plan for us to go out on a date for some one-on-one time and then after he thinks things are better between us, he'll come up with an excuse to cancel as he usually does and I'll forgive him as I usually do. It's all so frustrating. I don't want to get too into your personal business, but do you have a girlfriend or anything? I don't want you to think I'm spying on you or anything, but I've seen a beautiful woman or two coming and going. Do you have these same problems?"

He didn't want to lie and what she needed was honesty.

"No, I'm not in a relationship with anyone at the moment. I occasionally date," he said, avoiding eye contact. He wanted to be honest, but he didn't want her to look too deeply into what he called, 'occasional dates". In other words, he dates for the intimacy of it without any commitment. He wasn't sure he was ready to leap into anything serious yet, but he enjoyed the company of a beautiful, sexy woman. As long as the women didn't have any issues with his desire to keep things casual, they both walked away with what they were seeking, sexual pleasure. When Phoenix looked over at him with a questionable look on her face, he knew his attempt at being honest and elusive at the same time didn't work.

"So, does occasional dating have the same meaning as friends with benefits?" she asked sheepishly.

"That's exactly what it means," he acknowledged.

"Oh," was all Phoenix could think to say. Looking at him, she had no doubt any woman lucky enough to share in a friends with benefits situation with him was doing so happily. The man oozed sex. She looked at how he was sitting across from her on the floor and even in that position, he looked like he should be gracing the cover of a male model magazine.

"I hope that doesn't make me seem bad in your eyes. I'm honest with women and it's all mutual. I know that sometimes people have a hard time seeing that kind of friendship as meaningful, but it's actually a matter of putting your wants and desires on the table and going with it with no shame in wanting just the intimacy and friendship."

Phoenix smiled at his honesty. It wasn't for her to judge and she could appreciate a man who was upfront about his wants instead of leaving a trail of broken hearts behind him. She could imagine the attention he would pay to a woman and the stamina he possessed. She'd seen him working out in the gym on the lower level of their building and even when he was completely covered in sweat, he still continued on where any other man would have stopped to gather himself. Images of him pleasuring a woman and plying her with affection temporarily distracted her until she coughed and realized where her mind was taking her. She needed to refocus when she knew thoughts of her fiancé should be what her mind was focused on, even when she was angry at him like now. What was she thinking having steamy thoughts about her neighbor?

"Not at all. You're adults and you don't get what you need if you don't speak what you want. Is that how you see relationships in general?"

Phoenix should know since she falls into the category of never expressing her needs, but going with what's given. She wished she could express to a man exactly what she wanted from him, especially when it came to intimacy. With Carson, he always took the lead and their lovemaking was always what he thought it should be. Though always enjoyable, she still felt like something was missing.

"Not at all. I love the thought of being in a one-on-one relationship with a woman. I have every intention of doing so when the time is right and I meet the right woman. I recently ended a relationship with a bad breakup and I haven't had time to think about getting back into the dating game yet with the thought in mind that it could lead to a relationship. With my last relationship, we didn't have the same issues you and Carson have. My problems in that relationship was I trusted too much and too easily even though something was telling me to be more careful. I gave her the attention a man should give a woman and we did all of the things I know you wish Carson would do with you and yet it wasn't enough. She also had some issues I didn't know about and maybe it was enough and some people just aren't meant to be together forever. I also think our relationship goals were different. I don't have any hard feelings, though. It was what it was and I've moved on."

"That's a great way to look at things. I know what my relationship goals are, but I'm not sure I know what his are or if he even has any. Things are not where I'd like them to be and I'm hoping what's going on with us is temporary."

Gavin could hear the disappointment in her words and could sense how badly she wanted things to work out, but relationships have to be worked out together with two people on the same page.

"You have to know what his goals are and how they line up with yours. I know you love him and I'm sure he loves you. He asked you to marry him and that means something. Carson has been a party guy for so long that now that he's found someone he loves, he hasn't learned how to put that part of him to rest yet, but I think he will because he loves you and you love him."

Phoenix already felt better, hearing him giving her good advice and just being an ear for her to vent to.

"You're right. Stresses about work and the wedding could be getting to him. I'm trying to be patient, but I have a concern that this same behavior will carry over into our marriage and I don't want that."

"Then you work to fix those things before the

wedding. If you really love him, it will be worth the effort in the end. Now, enough of this talking that's only bringing you down. I was about to head out to check out a Sci-Fi movie. Would you like to come along, strictly as friends of course? I haven't done much since I moved in here and my assistant told me to get out of here and have some fun or else. I don't think there's a rule that says two neighbors who are friends can't go check out a movie especially if both could use a breath of fresh air. What do you say?"

Gavin was making another mistake, but couldn't rescue himself from the big foot he'd just put in his mouth. There was no way he should be inviting her out anywhere knowing he was falling for her. He needed to keep his distance. Maybe she would decline and save him from himself.

"That sounds like a great idea," Phoenix said getting up. "I haven't been to a movie in a long time and I could use a distraction right now. Are you sure you don't mind me tagging along?"

"Not at all," he admitted and meant it.

Damn, he thought. He was really in trouble now and stood when she did.

"Okay, well the movie starts in about an hour. How fast can you be ready?" he asked.

"Let me grab some shoes and my bag and I'm ready."

He smiled happy that she didn't need an hour to get ready for a movie. He knew a lot of women would disappear behind closed doors and come back out over an hour later. He liked her get up and go attitude. She was like a breath of fresh air and he liked it; he liked her.

"Okay, I just need to grab some shoes and I'll meet you back out here in the hall in a few minutes."

Phoenix moved with an excitement she hadn't felt in a long time. The last time she'd gone to check out a movie seemed like it had been ages ago since Carson hated darkened theaters. She chalked that up to his love for the spotlight being on him and in a dark theater, he was just another person in the crowd. She quickly grabbed shoes and searched for her phone and checked it to be sure it was powered up. She was smiling like a little kid going out on her first date.

"Wait, this isn't a date," she said to herself. "This is just two neighbors going out for a movie. She was even planning to pay for her own ticket and popcorn. That would help it seem like less of a date and more like two friends hanging out. As she turned off the lights and headed for the door, deep down, she wished it was a date. She knew that Gavin would be the perfect man for a perfect date and wished it was Carson who had invited her out for a movie. She needed that kind of night and she and Carson could use a date night.

Chapter 7

Phoenix relaxed as Gavin drove them from the movie theater. The movie was fun and the time spent enjoying an evening out was great. Gavin had been the best friend to go to the movies with. There was no pressure and after much push back from her, he let her pay for her own movie ticket, popcorn and drink. She smiled when he told her if they ever decided to have another outing like this again, he was never agreeing to letting her pay her own way again. He felt awkward and she laughed at how uncomfortable he seemed when she walked to the window to pay for her own ticket. He was truly a man's man and he was definitely a man used to taking care of a woman.

She liked and appreciated that he wanted to do that, but she didn't want to tell him that her reasons weren't about her being every woman, but more about making sure she saw the evening as two friends just hanging out and not a date. She was getting comfortable with him and could see herself forgetting she was engaged to another man.

They had talked some before the movie while they waited for it to start. He told her more about his twin brother and sister, Luke and Layne, both were juniors at the same college in Florida. Hearing him talk about them made her think of how much she loved her own brother and sister and how close they had always been. She learned even more about him and the more she learned, the more she liked. How could a man like him still be single? She knew that he'd had a bad relationship that apparently impacted him enough that he still hadn't jumped back into the dating game. She wondered what could have been so bad.

"Thanks for letting me share in your movie night. This is something I needed more than I could have imagined. I can't remember the last time I've been to an actual movie theater and the movie was good. I can remember my brother being in love with all those super heroes when he was young. I never enjoyed them until I was grown."

"I've loved them since I was a young boy and with all of the technology available today, I love seeing the special effects."

Phoenix listened quietly as Gavin talked about the behind the scenes special effects as if he were a pro and she got excited watching how he lit up talking about it.

"You are such a mystery. If I didn't know any better, I would say you were all things technology."

Gavin smiled at how perceptive she was. She picked up on a lot of things about him, though he hadn't shared that part of him.

"I'm not really a mystery," he said, looking over at her while they were stopped at a light. Something sparked when he looked at her and the intensity he thought he'd felt earlier in the night was back again. He was feeling drawn to her and his radar was telling him that she was becoming just as drawn to him. For a split second, his mind drifted to a place where she was no longer engaged and he would be able to express his want and desire for her without any guilt of coming between her and another man. The man she had brought her unhappiness and misery and like all women, she deserved to be loved and cherished like a precious gem. She was deserving of every bit of the love and affection she wanted and needed and he knew if he were given the chance, she would never have another day of sadness. Playboy Carson wasn't the man for her, but it wasn't up to him to make that decision for her. He needed to draw back his attraction and remember she needed a friend.

"Do you feel like stopping while I grab something to eat to take back home?" he asked.

"No, not at all. I'll get something also."

"Well, since we're both hungry, why don't we stop off and eat some pizza. I've fallen in love with the Chicago deep dish pizza."

Phoenix had to remind herself this was not a date, though it felt like one and it felt like the best date she'd ever had in her life. It was a simple outing, but a great one and she wasn't ready to go back to her empty loft yet.

"That sounds like a good plan."

Gavin made a quick turn and within seconds, they were pulling up to his favorite place to eat.

**

"So tell me what would make a man like you who is obviously kind, considerate, far from self-absorbed decide to stay in the single lane and out of the dating game? You mentioned something about a bad breakup? I don't want to pry if you don't want to talk about it."

Gavin actually did want to talk about it. The only person he'd shared the details with was Ellis. He hadn't even shared what happened in his relationship with anyone in his family preferring to tell them that the relationship ended amicably. His brother and sister knew a little more than that, but he kept the deep and dirty parts to himself.

"I don't plan to stay in the single lane forever. I recently made a lot of changes in my life and that included ending a relationship that I thought would have me out of the single lane permanently one day, but that didn't happen. Instead it woke me up to the reality that I was racing through life doing bigger and better things in my professional life, but my life in general was passing me by."

Gavin looked at Phoenix contemplating how much to tell her and decided he had nothing to lose by being honest. There was something about her that made him want to tell her anything she wanted to know about him. He knew there was more to their interaction for him than it was for her and he needed to be careful of the line Ellis reminded him was there.

"I feel like that sometimes and I don't know what to do about it. There are days that fly by so fast that I can't remember what I did the day before that took up twenty-four hours," Phoenix admitted.

"It can be an overwhelming feeling and cause you to check your own reality. It worked for me and that's how I ended up here in Chicago."

"Is that why you're writing this book? Is it about the reality check and what it has meant to your life now?"

"Not exactly. It is a book about my life, but I'm writing it because I know that people want to know how I got where I am, but it has nothing to do with the reality check."

"I'm thinking I need a reality check. I'm doubting my relationship with Carson and this isn't the first time I've done that. I know people see us together and wonder what is that playboy doing with that woman who barely likes to put on a pair of heels unless she's going to work. I know I'm different than the women he's been seen with over the years, but I thought that maybe that's what makes us work. I think it's our differences that are pulling us apart. He started out being attentive and fun, but right after we got engaged, he changed. He had calmed down a lot and was trying to get more focused on planning a life together. I get the feeling that I'm keeping him from being the person he really wants to be. I think he's being pressured by his parents to tone his life down and he figured it would look good if he proposed to me."

"Are you saying that Carson is with you because it improves his image? You are a beautiful woman and any man would be glad to have you with him, so I hope that's not what you're insinuating."

Two points for you, she thought, appreciating his observation.

"No, not at all. I know I'm a great catch," she said smiling. "I believe that his intentions in the beginning were genuine. We were attracted to each other, but I also know that he wishes I was more of the party animal like him. That's the one thing we don't have in common. I attend lots of things with him because I should as his girlfriend, but that spotlight isn't for me. I want Carson, not Carson's lifestyle, money or fame. No one in my circle understands why I am still with him and there are days I ask myself the same thing."

As much as he liked her and would like to see her away from Carson, he would not be that guy who talked down on another guy to pull his woman away. Phoenix was a smart woman and she would need to figure out what she really wanted. He was enjoying being her friend and he would stay in the friend lane and give her friendly advice.

"You may be different, but there is something that holds you together enough for you to say yes to marrying him, so whatever is wrong, you should work on it together. Life is too short to not be happy and if

Carson is who makes you happy, then be happy. You have to be in it together or it won't work. Believe me, I've tried and even though I knew there were issues in my relationship, I ignored them thinking they would work themselves out and they didn't, so here I am in the singles lane and putting my life back together again in a way that makes me happy. Believe me when I tell you Carson loves the spotlight, but it isn't all it's cracked up to be. It's one reason I stay out of the spotlight, not letting people into my life to scrutinize who I am and what my life is about."

Phoenix put the slice of pizza she was about to bite into down on her plate and put her full attention on Gavin. He was a mystery.

"Okay, now you really have me curious. What is it about Gavin Knolls that people want to know? You said you were writing your book about your life. Who is Gavin Knolls?" she asked curiously.

Here goes nothing, Gavin thought.

"Well, my name isn't Gavin Knolls, it's Gavin Black."

Phoenix sat straight up. She knew he looked familiar though his appearance had changed slightly.

"I know who Gavin Black is and I knew you looked familiar, but I couldn't put my finger on it. You are that Gavin Black? You're the tech guru who made millions from a start-up that has become one of the biggest and fastest growing technology corporations in the world? That's you?" she asked again, surprised.

Gavin had already braced himself for her questions. He noticed the change in her demeanor the minute she knew who he was.

"Yes, that's me."

"I don't do a lot of social media and the news I get, I pretty much watch on television or hear from my gossiping sister and not the papers, so I'm not familiar with a lot about you other than you weren't one to be in the media and you shied away from interviews especially about your life."

"That's true. A lot of what I did to build my company was done behind doors and that's where I spent all of my time, indoors and focused on work. I was lucky that the personal life of a nerd wasn't much fodder for the entertainment world. That was why I was able to end my relationship and it didn't make the headlines."

"How bad was the ending?" she asked.

"I was planning to propose to my girlfriend and so I cut a business trip to Japan short and flew back to our home to surprise her. Though I didn't care for the limelight, she was someone who thrived on it. She liked the party scene and when we met, she was on her way to becoming a model, something she decided not to do and instead opted to focus on being my girlfriend. We traveled around the world and indulged in the best of everything. What I didn't know was her indulgences when I wasn't around. Without going into too much detail, let's just say, she wasn't in our bed alone. The guy had the nerve to actually pitch me on a video game idea he wanted to sell me when I caught them in my house together. Though he bedded my girlfriend, it was me he wanted to connect with and sleeping with her was an added bonus. Apparently it wasn't the first time she'd done that. I guess being in a relationship with me wasn't enough for her or I was too busy not giving her the attention she needed. Either way, I'm not making excuses for her behavior and I'm not taking the blame because she knew what she was doing, but hey, it was a relationship and either you're in it one hundred percent or you're not. If not, then it's time to move on and find what's worth fighting for."

Phoenix looked at Gavin as if he were an anomaly.

"You mean that don't you? A woman would never have to question herself or doubt you if she were involved with you? There are some really good men out here, but there are some who look for an opportunity to conquer every woman they meet."

"Well, I'm not a conqueror unless it's in the business world. I have a sister and a mother along with other female relatives and friends and I treat women the way I would want them to be treated. I believe women deserve only the best from any man she's involved with. One of the reasons why I've been able to really move on from my relationship with Natasha and not hate is because she showed me I wasn't what she was looking for. She aimed high, but it wasn't where she really wanted to live. She wasn't ready for a man who was committed to her, faithful to her, who loved and cherished her and would give her the world if she asked for it."

"Have you had any contact with her since the breakup?"

"I have and the conversation was civil. I told her there were no hard feelings other than she brought men to my home and anything could have happened to her or me. My feelings about her infidelity weren't harsh at all and I even surprised myself with that. Relationships aren't marriage and you can walk away whenever you want, but don't hurt someone by sneaking around and being unfaithful. That could leave someone scarred when it comes to another relationship."

Phoenix was intrigued. She'd never had this kind of open dialogue with a man, other than her brother, about relationships. Too often, men will tell a woman what he felt she needed to hear and not what she should hear and Gavin's outlook on relationships was giving her insight into how she sees relationships. Since he was being all honest, she decided to plug away a little more into his opinion.

"What would you say to a woman who was in a relationship and found herself attracted to you while you were attracted to her as well? Would you consider it unfaithful for her to not divulge that information to the man she's involved with?"

Gavin looked Phoenix in the eyes and felt a heat rising between them. How ironic that she would ask him a question like that? Was he reading more into her words than their actual meaning? He knew he was attracted to her, but could she really be talking about herself? He didn't want to assume, but it was a tell-tale kind of question.

"I don't consider it unfaithful if neither have physically acted on it. Sometimes you can't help if you are attracted to someone even if you're in a relationship. It's unfaithful the moment you cross a physical line. That's just my thought on it. That doesn't make it a global response. I do know that as long as that woman is still involved with that man, I wouldn't cross a line and put her in an uncomfortable position, but if she finds herself single for any reason, then I hope that we would have a chance to explore beyond just friendship."

Gavin heard his words and they were too true. The look in her eyes told him that his words were playing havoc with her psyche. He had a feeling she was in fact talking about herself and she was just as torn over developing feelings for him as he was over what he was starting to feel for her.

"It sounds like that woman would be in quite a quandary."

"What would you do?" he asked.

"I think my actions would vary depending on the state of the relationship. I would stick it out in my relationship as long as there was something to hold on to. If the day came when that was no longer the case and I felt that the other person would be worth taking a chance on, I would do it. Everyone deserves to be happy and who knows, happiness may be on the grass that appears to be greener on the other side, though I've heard the old saying that grass isn't always greener on the other side. I think I'd be willing to find out."

Phoenix held her breath when she saw the heat in Gavin's gaze. They were playing a dangerous game as the scenario they'd just talked about ran through each of their minds. In another time, place and circumstance, this could be very interesting. If Carson hadn't been messing up so bad, would she allow her mind to drift to a place where she and Gavin would leave the restaurant and head back to a bed in one of their lofts?

Gavin saw that Phoenix was obviously torn and he didn't want to see her in that position. It wasn't his intention to have her questioning her own relationship and he wasn't in the woman stealing business.

"You do know this is just talk? I would never insinuate that you should do anything that wasn't honorable, but I believe in happiness at all costs. You only live once and it shouldn't be wasted, especially on a bad relationship," Gavin added.

"Ain't that the truth," she replied.

Though they couldn't seem to take their eyes off of each other, Gavin knew it was time to go. Any more talk could be too revealing and they needed to stop before things went too far. He would pull back on his growing feelings because they were becoming obvious to her and he didn't want to put any pressure on her knowing she was already struggling with her relationship with Carson. If she wanted to come to him, it would be because she wanted to after she was clear of Carson. He wouldn't wait, but he wouldn't put on any weight. After holding her gaze for far too long, he broke eye contact and looked away.

"Well, now that I'm sure we've both had enough pizza to have us working out around the clock for days to work it off, it's getting late. Are you ready to go?"

Phoenix reached for her wallet to help with the cost of their meal.

Gavin stopped her when he saw what she was about to do.

"Don't even think about it. Now, I let you get away with it at the movies which was a first for me and that felt weird, but if you're reaching for money, don't."

"Friends remember? Doesn't that mean we split the cost?"

"Maybe in your world, but friends or not, I never want to see a woman coming out of her pocket with money to pay for anything when she's with me. I wouldn't do it with any other female I know and I won't with you either, no man should."

"You are some guy Gavin Black," Phoenix said. She'd been out several times with Carson where he had no problem letting her foot the bill even though he had enough money to throw away. He'd told her he believed in equal rights since women were always screaming they wanted it, so he had no problem letting a woman pick up the check every now and then. It wasn't even a matter of picking up the check when they had dinner for his birthday or some other event to celebrate them, but Carson expected it and a time or two, it did bother her that he wouldn't bat an eye when she pulled out her wallet when he failed to reach for his.

"I'm a man who was taught by my father to always take care of the women in my life because since the beginning of time, that's what men did."

"Does that mean one day you will marry a woman whose only job will be to take care of the home while you take care of everything else? What if your woman had her own wants and desires as far as a career? What if she wanted to be just as successful as you are?"

"I believe a woman can do whatever she wants to do and if she has worked to get there, she deserves to walk her own path to success. I would help her in any way she needed and I would celebrate every achievement she made. A woman's place is wherever she wants it to be, whether it's at home or in the workplace. It's my job to support and love her and her choices."

Phoenix didn't know what to say. She and Carson had talked a few times about life after they got married and even though he told her he didn't care if she worked or not, she got the feeling he didn't want that. He wanted her to stay at home and push out babies while he took care of them. She loved working and she got satisfaction from seeing her college degrees being put to great use. She couldn't wait to have a family of her own, but she wanted more than just that and felt that she could give equal time to both.

"Are you going to continue working after you and Carson get married?"

"I'm planning on it. I'm not sure he's thinking that way. We've talked about it, but I don't think he told me what he really felt about it. That's my plan though."

Gavin stood and came around to help her up.

"Carson is a lucky man," he whispered.

Phoenix smiled. Carson was lucky, but was she?

Chapter 8

"So, what happened to the playboy for the cake tasting today? I thought he was going to join us and bring his mother along?" Reese asked as she, Adrienne, her mother, Phoenix and the other bridesmaids walked into the hotel where the cake tasting was taking place.

Phoenix wished she had an answer, but she didn't. As usual, Carson called and cancelled at the last minute citing some important meeting he couldn't miss, saying she didn't need him to taste cake anyway. He would be happy with whatever she chose. His mother was still coming as far as she knew.

"He had a conflict he forgot about and told me to go ahead and select what I wanted. His mother is still coming and her driver should be bringing her by in a few minutes. We are a little early."

Reese gave her a non-patient look.

"Seriously, I need to get a copy of this excuse book

Carson pulls all of his excuses from. I need a few to have on hand when I want to get out of attending something I never had any intention of going to. Are you sure he's going to show up for the wedding? I could pay someone to sit on him and drag him down the aisle. I don't think he's going to do it willingly," she sneered.

"Stop it Reese before mom hears you," Phoenix whispered when their mother had walked a few steps ahead of them while talking to Adrienne.

"I'm just saying, this guy is the pits. You know I want to see you happy, but I feel like I wouldn't be honest if I didn't tell you to check your relationship. I think there is a link in the chain that's not closed as tight as it should be. Is he going with you to select the items for your wedding registry or should I block off the time to go with you?" Reese asked, snidely.

Phoenix knew she was being flippant, but she knew Reese would have her back and always speak the truth.

"Let it go Reese," she said.

Reese looked at her impatiently. They needed a moment to talk in private.

"Will you all excuse me and my sister for a few minutes?" Reese asked, pulling her away from the group toward a secluded area.

"What are you doing?" Phoenix asked.

"What the hell are you doing? I want to know right now, with it being just you and me, do you really want to marry this guy? I know my timing is crazy, but you are my sister and I love you, but Carson is not the guy for you. Is it the money because it really can't be love? This guy doesn't love anyone, but himself. Did you see the social media photos of him I saw posted last night? I saw the date and time and they were taken on a night that the two of you were supposed to have dinner with us and he lied and gave you an excuse about a business dinner. He didn't look like he was having dinner to me. He looked like he was freaking some trashy girl in a club. I was ready to throw a condom at the photo he was so all up in that."

Phoenix turned her head so sharp she felt a pain.

"I don't trust any of those photos. They can be pulled from years ago and you know photographs can be manipulated."

Reese looked at her questionably, not sure this is the same person she grew up with.

"Who are you? Is this my sister I'm talking to? Even you can't believe the words coming out of your own mouth. This guy is playing you or using you, but he's not loving you. If what you want is to walk down that aisle and marry this guy then there is nothing I will do other than stand up there and support you, but make sure it's what you want. I've seen some pretty steamy stories about him in the media lately and those photos are not manipulated. Every time I talk to you he's pulled a new trick with a new excuse and you suck it up and forgive him."

Ever since her night out with Gavin at the movies a few weeks ago, Phoenix has found herself questioning her relationship. Without knowing it, he'd said words that made her question her desire for a man who didn't make her a priority. He didn't appear to show as much interest in their wedding as she did and though she believed he cared for her, she didn't feel loved. She felt tolerated and that wouldn't make for a great, loving marriage.

Phoenix was working hard to keep their relationship together and he appeared to still be living the single life. She guessed since they weren't married yet, he was actually single and free to do as he wanted. Perhaps being in a relationship didn't mean as much to him as it meant to her. He hadn't done anything to hurt her or disrespect her, so she felt like she owed him the benefit of sowing a few wild oats before they got married. He wasn't being unfaithful, he was just being Carson. He was still the man she fell in love with and agreed to marry and she would go through with it. No one was perfect, she thought.

"I'm three months from my wedding Reese. There are so many people, especially women, who would like to see that day never happen, but I'm not one of them. Can you be happy that I'm happy?"

"Are you? Are you happy? Can I be honest with you?"

Phoenix tried to muster up a smile.

"Sure, why stop now!" she exclaimed.

"What about Gavin?"

Phoenix looked at her sister perplexed. She didn't know why she would bring up Gavin.

"It's me, your sister. You tell me everything even

when you don't tell me everything. I know that you've grown attracted to him and I can't blame you. From what you tell me about this guy, he sounds magnificent and if I'm correct, there's an attraction between the two of you that you've both been fighting. I know you have been especially after all the time you've spent avoiding him lately after that night at the movies and conversation over pizza. You do remember you told me all about that and how that night left you feeling."

"I haven't been avoiding Gavin," she lied.

"Like I said, it's me, your sister, and I know you. I know whatever you talked about had you thinking and re-thinking your relationship with Carson. There is nothing wrong with that. You should be re-thinking it as far as I'm concerned. Remember you told me you felt a vibe with him that you have never felt with Carson and it scared you. You were scared because though you are completely devoted to Carson, there is something in you that is drawing you to Gavin and I have no doubt he feels the same way about you. You almost admitted to me that since that night, you've been avoiding him and trying hard to work things out with Carson. You're trying hard because you know that Gavin is the kind of man who, without knowing it or doing anything, he makes you realize your best isn't better for you. Carson may be a good guy, though I don't see it and you know that and I don't think he's the guy for you. I want more for my baby sister when it comes to love and happiness. I've seen more frowns than smiles on your face over the past few months and I don't like it. The only time I've seen you smile were the times you've told me a thing or two about Gavin."

Phoenix tried to let her face deny everything her sister was saying. She didn't care how true her words were. She had been purposely avoiding Gavin. The fact that she hadn't run into him lately could be that he was avoiding her too. Something happened between them that night across the table over pizza. There was no doubt that by the time they left, they each knew that they were mutually fighting an attraction. She was thankful for the gentleman that he was because if he had asked, she would have put her commitment to Carson in the back of her mind and gone home, literally, with Gavin. She would never admit that much to her sister or anyone else.

"Gavin and I are friends and that's it and I haven't been avoiding him as much as I have just been busy. Between working overtime and preparing for this wedding, I've been keeping late hours."

She was about to continue when she saw an awkward look on her sister's face.

"What's that look for?"

With a candor, nonchalant attitude Reese smiled like a cat who had been let into the hen house.

"Oh, I was waiting for you to say you were keeping late hours because you and Carson had spent a lot of late hours making up for all of the times he stood you up, but I guess that didn't happen."

Phoenix smirked.

"If I didn't love you like a sister, we would be

scrapping right now," Phoenix said jokingly.

"Oh, that's the south-side girl I know and love. I'd like to see her come out and get Carson in line. For now I'll keep hope alive and give you the support you want and need. Just know that if you decide that you want to drop him and knock on Gavin's door, I'm all for it. That's a man I know would never leave my sister and gallivant off every chance he got. Just promise me that if you feel like you don't want to go through with this marriage, you will tell me so that I can help you plan the getaway."

Phoenix laughed so loud, she had to cover her mouth to keep others from coming over to see what was going on.

"Only my sister would come up with something like a scheme for me to play the runaway bride."

"Well, not actually. I was thinking more of doing it before we actually got to the day of your wedding. It would be less dramatic, though more fun. I wouldn't want an embarrassing moment for you either. I'm just saying, let a sister know if I need to stand up for my baby sister and tell Carson, his stuck up mother and all of their money to take a hike. Money isn't everything especially when it comes to you."

Phoenix turned when she heard a noise and saw Carson's mother show up with an entourage of five or six people. That woman never travels without a host of people at her beck and call, she thought.

"Speaking of his mother, she's here."

"Last chance, sis. I bet there's a back door we can

slip out of."

Phoenix laughed and playfully pushed her sister.

"I'm good sis and thanks for looking out. I'll be fine, you'll see. Let's go join the party," she said, walking ahead.

Phoenix walked toward the group with a plastered, phony smile on her face as her thoughts turned to Gavin. She had been avoiding him because she feared the feelings that were growing for him. She felt like a cheat and it seemed dishonest to have any kind of feelings other than friendship for another man.

**

"Gavin, why are you in Chicago," Luke asked. His brother had called after returning from a European trip studying abroad in a partnership between his school and a college there.

"I told you and Layne I would be staying here for a while."

"I know, but why Chicago?" Luke pushed.

"There's no reason in particular I chose Chicago other than I have always loved this city."

"Let me see if I have this right. You're living in Chicago now to write a book? Are you going through some kind of mid-life crisis?"

Gavin laughed.

"First of all, I'm not middle-aged, so I'm not going through any kind of crisis. Second, I don't always have to live big and flamboyant. You know that's never been your brother. I can live anywhere and thanks to my success, I get to choose anywhere I'd like."

"Are you sure? I might know a doctor I can send you to if you need some counseling. Hey, you know I'm always looking out for your well-being."

"You make sure you're looking out for your own well-being. How was Europe?" he asked.

"Europe was great. I can't wait to go back and I'm hoping my big brother wouldn't mind footing the bill for me to go back for the summer."

"If that's what you want I've got it covered. Just make sure you're being safe. You could find yourself in trouble if you're not careful and there won't be a guide from your school to keep you in line like this semester."

"I know, I know. I already have the place picked out where I want to stay."

"I have a house there already and you can stay at the house?"

"Ah, Gav, that house is too big. I'll email you the information for where I want to stay. Have you talked to Layne?"

"I talked to her yesterday. She wants to come visit me to talk about something. She wouldn't tell me what. Do you know what it is? It sounded kind of serious, though she tried not to let me hear the seriousness in her voice. It must be big if she's coming to me and not going to mom about whatever is going on. Should I be worried?"

"I know what it is and no you shouldn't be worried. I won't tell you because she wants to tell you herself. Just be open-minded when she comes to talk to you. We have always been able to come to you with things that we can't take to mom and dad and this is one of those times for Layne. When is she visiting you?"

"She should be here this weekend for a few days now that school is out for the semester."

"Just hear her out okay?"

Gavin wanted to be worried and almost demanded that Layne tell him over the phone what was going on, but he'd always had a great open and honest relationship with the twins especially with the age difference and they knew they could trust him with anything. He would give Layne what she needed and right now what she needed was his confidence and support."

"I will."

"Good. I was calling to check in and to also see how the ladies are in Chicago. Are they keeping your bed warm? I know how you can be. The ladies love them some Gavin Black."

Having ladies like him was never a problem and it wouldn't be now if he could keep his mind off of one beautiful lady in particular.

"The ladies in Chicago are just as lovely as the ladies anywhere else."

"Are you seeing a different one every night or have you fallen back in love?"

"Love? You're reaching now," he chided.

"Wait, there is a woman and not just any woman. Who is she? You can tell me."

Gavin knew he could, but he wasn't going to.

"It's nothing I can't handle."

"Just don't bring home another Natasha. That one was crazy, bro."

"I know, I know. Listen, I have some things to get back to. I'll talk to you in a few days and send me the information on your trip. I'll make sure you have access to whatever you need while you're gone."

"Hey, when do Layne and I get the trust fund you set up for us? You could give me access to that and you wouldn't have to foot the bill for everything."

"Right. Not happening little brother. Neither of you are ready for that kind of responsibility over that kind of money. You'll get it at age thirty and that's only with a college degree under your belt and until then, whatever you need, let me know."

"I love you Gav. I'll call you later this week. I need to call Layne now before she has a heart attack. I haven't talked to her since I got home and she's been blowing up my phone for three days. "

"Alright. Take it easy and watch the women."

"I should be telling you the same thing."

Gavin hung up his phone and secretly wished someone would have told him to watch the women because one in particular had been invading his mind, day and night.

He hadn't seen Phoenix other than in passing in the elevator or the garage and other people always seemed to be around. They seemed to avoid eye contact and rushed to get away from each other. He didn't like the distance, but it was best. Slipping up and telling her how he felt about her could cause problems in her relationship. Good or bad, it was her relationship and he needed to stay clear.

Chapter 9

Phoenix was about to exit her car in the underground garage when she looked up to see Gavin pulling into his parking space. They were about ten spots apart, but she could clearly see into his car to know that he wasn't alone. She let go of the door handle and sat still. She hadn't seen him for more than a few glances as they passed by each other for several weeks.

She continued to watch as he got out of his car and went around to open the door for a woman. She watched as the woman got out of the car and Phoenix thought she must be some type of model because she was exquisitely beautiful. She was tall and slim in an all-white outfit from top to bottom. She was definitely younger than Gavin, but she seemed thrilled with him as they laughed and talked like they were a loving couple. She was jealous as she watched him take a suitcase out of the car as they then walked arm in arm to the elevator. Whoever she was, Gavin was happy to be in her presence and the excitement of having her with him was evident.

As the elevator came and they got in, she could see the joy on Gavin's face. That was the look of a happy man.

Rather than go up into her lonely loft apartment, she turned her car back on and decided to go for a drive. What was it really about Gavin that had her so intrigued?

Gavin had been living in the building for months and whenever she saw him with a woman, each was more flawlessly beautiful than the last. The one she saw him getting in the elevator with was no different. Her jealousy of the woman ramped up when she remembered Gavin had been carrying a suitcase with them, signaling the woman would most likely be staying the night or even the weekend.

She missed Carson and seeing how happy Gavin was with his lady friend made her miss the connection they shared at the beginning of their relationship. She hadn't seen him for a few days and when they talked, the conversation seemed to turn towards arguing. She asked him if he still wanted her and he assured her it had nothing to do with that. He was busy trying to get a life started so that he would be able to take care of them and not live off of his father's money taking handouts as he was currently doing. She respected that, but wished he'd find time for them to get back the love and passion, especially the passion that had been missing for a while.

She missed spending all night with him and waking up in the morning to continue the lovemaking that would start the night before. Lately, he would make excuses that always ended with him being too tired. She'd never heard of men who didn't want to make love every chance he got, especially when she would spend the time buying sexy lingerie just for him knowing how much he loved seeing her in it. That hadn't worked lately either and it made her question where he was getting his loving from. She knew if he wasn't getting it from her for more than a few days a week, he was getting it from somewhere, she feared. They were drifting apart and she didn't know how to fix it.

As she pulled out of the garage and into traffic, her phone rang and she used the hands-free system in her car to answer her mother's call.

"Hey mom!" she said with a lot of excitement.

"Hi baby. How are you? I was expecting to hear from you last night about what you thought of my dress for the wedding."

After the cake tasting almost a week ago, they shopped for a dress for her mother which she loved.

"Mom, I told you that night that I loved it."

"I know, but I wanted to be sure you really, really loved it. I want to look incredible for my daughter's wedding to the rich and handsome Carson Stone."

"You're going to be beautiful mom. I was thinking about calling you and you happen to call me."

"Oh? Is everything okay?"

Phoenix wanted to open up to her mother, but didn't know how she would sound questioning marrying Carson only a few short months before the wedding. Maybe she was getting cold feet that she heard could happen. She wanted to be sure she was making the right choice.

"Everything is fine mom. Can I ask you a question about you and dad?"

"You can ask me anything about everything. What's going on?"

She hesitated knowing the conversation may alarm her mother, but she needed to open up to someone and though she and Reese could always talk about everything, she didn't need her sister's type of opinion. She needed to hear from someone who may have gone through doubts about marriage. Her sister, though she loved her dearly, went through a man as often as she changed the gas in her car. She knew that her sister had literally met the last guy she was seeing while pumping gas in her car.

"Carson is what's going on."

"Is he okay? Has something happened?"

"He's fine and nothing has happened. When you and dad met, did you know he was the one for you? Did you ever have any doubts about marrying him?"

Her mom fell silent and that worried her.

"Phoenix, are you having doubts?"

It was honesty now or never, she thought.

"Yes mom, I am and I don't know what to do about it. Can you tell me about your experience? Perhaps I'm just having pre-wedding jitters."

"Well, when I met your father, I didn't like him very much. He was cocky and made a play for me to impress his friends. Let's just say that first encounter didn't work to his benefit. A few weeks later, we ran across each other again when he was alone and he was a totally different person. I knew that he had been acting a fool for his friends, but alone with me, he was the kindest, nicest guy I'd ever met. Our love wasn't swift, but it was deep and I never doubted it. I knew I wanted to marry him and the minute he asked me, he couldn't get the words out fast enough before I screamed yes. There has never been a moment that I have ever had any regrets, not before we got married or after. You shouldn't have any reservations if marrying Carson is what you really want to do. What are you feeling?"

"I'm feeling like he doesn't really want to get married or be in this relationship, but that he has to."

"What do you mean that he has to? I didn't raise you to be with a man for anything other than deep, devoted love. You know to never settle for anything less than that."

Phoenix could hear the worry in her mother's voice and didn't mean to upset or startle her by her doubts.

"I know mom. You know the kind of guy Carson was when I met him. He was the playboy of all playboys and he wanted me. I was excited about that and we had a lot of fun in the beginning. Now it seems like we have to work extra hard just to tolerate each other. We never do anything, we barely talk and I have to avoid all media if I want to stay in a secure place about our relationship. There are pictures of him with women all over the place."

"Are those compromising pictures?"

"Not really mom. Just pictures of him partying and hanging out, getting drunk with women hanging all over him. You would think being engaged would have him staying away from wild activities, but it hasn't. I find myself questioning what I'm accepting from him and I feel like I've been walking around with blinders on in order to stay in the relationship instead of telling him that his wild lifestyle makes me uncomfortable. I barely see him and if I do, he's in between one thing or another and he's gone quicker than he arrived. He has no interest in all the wedding planning and when I asked him about the guest list and his groomsmen, he tells me the event planner will handle all of that for him. In all honesty, I don't feel loved mom."

When her mom emitted a loud breath on the other end, Phoenix felt like crying.

"Oh baby. I'm sorry. What is Carson thinking? Are you sure you want to marry him? You know you don't have to and I don't care if it's the day of the wedding. If you're not sure, don't do it. I don't want to see you setting yourself up for a life of unhappiness. Who Carson is, is exactly who he will probably continue to be. How much can you live with? What's driving you to continue with the wedding if he doesn't make you happy while you're engaged? I know that some people may say you should stick with it and make it work, but that's not who your mother is. I want you to commit to him if that's what you want, but if you have any doubt, then you need to re-think your decision to marry him. A loveless marriage is no marriage at all. Do you love him?"

"I love him, but I don't love who he has been lately. I feel like I'm an afterthought. I feel like he is out living his life and then he remembers I'm here, so he takes some time out of his busy schedule to pay me a visit to show me he's still around. I don't know if he's still in the game one hundred percent."

She had more she wanted to share with her mother, but she felt ashamed over the admission.

"I believe in one hundred percent or nothing."

"Maybe it's not just him mom."

"What do you mean? What aren't you telling me?"

Phoenix hesitated.

"It's mom and you know you can tell me anything and it stays between us. What is it Phoenix?"

"I met someone that I can't seem to stop thinking about."

Another long pause from her mother and she wished she hadn't blurted it out. She couldn't take the words back now.

"I'm sorry, what did you say?" her mother asked.

"There is this guy and no, nothing has happened. I am and always have been committed to Carson, but I met a guy who lives in my building that's really, really nice. I've gotten to know him since we're neighbors and the more I know about him, the more I feel like I'm missing something in my relationship with Carson. I don't want to compare the two of them because I'm not involved with this guy. Have you ever talked to your friends and wonder why they are with some of the men they are with? I have and I've become that woman that I would talk about. I've become that woman who settles for being treated in a way that's less than I deserve. I see the signs and I've been seeing them a long time, but I've been ignoring them. Am I so desperate for a man that I would do that to myself? This guy I met hasn't made a play for me, but just talking to him I can see where I'm settling for less and there are days when it really hurts."

"Phoenix, I'm going to tell you this from my heart because I'm your mother, I love you and I always want to be honest with you. Don't you marry Carson if that's not what's in your heart. I don't care how much time and money has gone into this. If he doesn't treat you right, the way you've watched your father treat me all these years, then you walk away. Do you hear me? You were raised to demand respect and love because you deserve it. I would never tell you to run into the arms of another man and you shouldn't, not on the rebound. This guy may be a really nice guy, but all men are nice when they want you and you know that. You thought so with Carson and it seems to me that something is missing in your relationship that needs to be addressed and fixed before you get married. As far as this other guy is concerned, you can't help being attracted to someone. It's human nature, but don't run to him because you're lonely or you feel neglected by Carson. If Carson is not the one for you, then you make sure you end things for that reason, not because you find yourself attracted to and thinking of someone else. If you find someone else better for you than Carson, then so be it, but you don't do it without doing the right thing, which would be telling Carson what you are thinking and see if you can have an honest conversation with him. I hate to say this, but perhaps, he doesn't really want to be married either. You'll never know if you don't talk about it. Get your mind off of this other guy and deal with what's going on between you and Carson and if this other guy is the direction you eventually go in when you're free and clear, then you do that. You're too young to not have choices for yourself."

Phoenix felt better hearing the words she needed to hear from her mother. She had been avoiding talking openly and honestly with Carson and it was time she did so.

"Thank you mom. I knew I needed to talk to you."

"Yes you did and you can anytime you want and need to. You have your talk with Carson and then you call me so that I will know if I need to take this dress back before I get it altered."

Phoenix laughed when her mother did. She felt better as she drove around the streets of Chicago. She turned back towards home after their call ended. Gavin or no Gavin, she and Carson had issues they needed to work out and she needed to stop avoiding her neighbor. Her mother was right, she was either in it with Carson or out and Gavin would have no place in her decision making. She still wanted to be his friend and he had done nothing to deserve her avoiding him and treating him like he'd done something wrong. She was the one with torn feelings and she needed to get herself in check and deal with the issues concerning what looked like a failed relationship.

** **

"So this is the new place huh?" Layne said settling in on the chair in front of his entertainment system.

"Yes, you like it?" Gavin asked while taking her bag into his guest bedroom.

"I love it. It's the kind of place I need."

"Layne, you don't need a place this big. Your apartment near campus is fine and your room at home with mom and dad will suffice for now until you graduate and get a job to afford your own place."

"You're really going to make me get a job and pay for my own place aren't you?"

Gavin looked at his sister and her play to win him over with her sad face, fake and all.

"Don't even try that fake look with me because you know the puppy dog look in the eyes only works on mom and dad, not your big brother who knows better."

Layne grabbed the remote and turned the television on.

"Whatever. What do you have to eat around here?"

"There's food in the fridge and snacks in the cabinets. Before you ask, yes there are makings for a salad since I know you live off of them. There's also lots of fruit, enough that should last even after you go back Monday. Now, are we going to talk about whatever it is you want to talk about that had to be done in person?"

"Not now. We will though. For now I just want to enjoy visiting my big brother. I've missed you," she said laying back to relax.

"I've missed you too Laynie."

"Enough to make me a sandwich and salad? I am a guest, after all."

"I guess so since you're visiting. Tomorrow you're cooking for us both."

"I was hoping tomorrow you'd take me out to eat and show me around Chicago."

"We'll see," he said.

Gavin walked toward the kitchen to fix her what she requested. He was happy to see her and didn't mind waiting on her, for now. Soon, she needed to tell him what brought on her sudden visit. He would always be concerned about her and Luke and if they needed him, he would be there.

Chapter 10

Gavin stood in the hall outside the loft door waiting for
Layne to come out so that they could go out to grab
something to eat and he promised her Chicago pizza.
They still hadn't talked and she'd be leaving in two days
to return home. Whatever it was didn't seem to bother
her. He would wait until she was ready, but would push
her if Monday came and she still hadn't talked to him
about the reason for her visit. He was expecting Ellis on
Sunday after he agreed to go with him to some party to
meet a music producer who was interested in doing the
music score for Gavin's next video game, which was
slated to be a monster on the gaming circuit.

"Let's go Layne," he said, opening the door and
hollering in for her. When he'd first walked out, she
was with him, but then decided to change her shoes.
That was over ten minutes ago and he was still waiting

in the hall. He was hoping to get her to open up over pizza.

"I'm coming," Layne screamed back. "One more minute."

Gavin shut the door again and waited. He probably should have gone back inside and plopped down in front of the television. He had a feeling Layne would be more than a minute.

As he stood waiting, he pulled out his cell phone to check his emails from Isabella. They were stacking up and he owed her several responses before Monday. He started reading through them when the elevator door opened and out walked Phoenix in all of her glory. The woman took his breath away every time he saw her. She smiled when she saw him and he smiled back. Seeing her was like a breath of fresh air and he missed that since they hadn't had time to say more than a few hellos over the past few weeks.

"Hi Phoenix."

"Hi Gavin," she said.

"You look beautiful as usual," he said.

"Thank you. You are looking quite dashing yourself. Headed out for the evening?" she asked. She knew he had a weekend guest and assumed they were heading out for a date, possibly to dinner.

After talking to her mother, she called Carson to ask if he wanted to do dinner and as usual, she waited for him to show up and he never did. He called after midnight the night before saying he had to take a flight to meet his father for an important meeting and he was running late for his flight and forgot to call her to cancel. For the first time in a long time, his lack of attentiveness didn't faze her.

Gavin's phone rang and she was about to go inside her place when he asked her to wait. As she did, she thought back to her conversation with Carson the night before.

"Hello?"

"Hi baby," Carson said. Normally she would smile, but she wasn't in a smiling mood with him.

"Hi. I thought you were coming by tonight? You promised we could go out somewhere and have some fun. We needed this night, Carson," she explained.

"I know, but I had to catch a flight on my dad's private plane to join him for a meeting I forgot about. My assistant didn't put it on my calendar like I asked her to. I know I promised, but I needed to meet a potential client and this time my father was at the meeting. He's getting a firsthand look at how I conduct business and it was an opportunity I couldn't pass up."

Phoenix stopped folding clothes when she realized what he'd said.

"Wait, you're out of town? I didn't even know you were gone. You couldn't tell me that before you left? No excuse about you running late. There is this invention called a cell phone and you could have called me quickly to say you were leaving town," she said in an angry tone.

"There wasn't any time. When my father called and asked if I had already landed for the meeting since he sent the plane for me, I couldn't tell him I forgot. I would never hear the end of that, so I rushed to get ready and hopped on the plane. Then it was one meeting on the phone after the next. I've called you a few times, so you have to admit I tried."

"You could have left a message saying that considering we had a date night tonight, something we haven't had in a very long time. After nine or so, I didn't even expect you anymore and my phone is in my purse."

"Phoenix, you've been busy at work and I've been giving you space with all of the wedding stuff so that I'm not in the way and you know what I'm trying to do on this work tip. Why are you getting upset?"

"I'm upset because I miss you and we need time together. I'm concerned that you don't feel the same way. We have barely seen each other over the past month or so. Don't you miss me?"

"Baby, of course I miss you. I love you and I promise things are going to be better once we're married. This is just a busy time for us both."

"Don't add me to that equation. I'm never too busy for you, but you can't say the same thing. I know what you're trying to do and I respect that, but don't you think our relationship deserves just as much time?"

"We're about to be married Phoenix. You'll have me all to yourself all the time. How much more time with me do you need?"

"Okay, you know what, you're right. If you don't see a need for alone time with me, I guess I'm over exaggerating. My bad. I guess a being in a relationship doesn't mean you actually spend any time together."

She heard Carson sigh on the other end.

"Don't be like that. I love spending time with you. Just let me get through this and when I come back Monday, I'll give you all my time the entire week. Can you take some time off from work? Maybe we can take a quick trip to an island for a few days. I bet that's something you can use. You sound a little stressed and I'm guessing it's all of this wedding stuff."

Surprise, surprise she thought. Carson had never come up with a plan for any kind of vacation for them. That was always left up to her.

"That would be great and I can get a few days off. Do you want me to make the arrangements? Where do you want to go?" she asked forgetting she was supposed to be angry at him.

"Yes, make the arrangements for wherever you want to go and put it on my black card. You have the account information. Just tell me when, where and for how many days and we're off to paradise together to reconnect. How does that sound?"

Phoenix smiled with delight. This is what she's been wanting all along from Carson. She wanted time for the two of them to have fun and be all about each other as if others in the world didn't exist. It looks like she was about to get her wish. Now, perhaps she could get the old Carson back and she could wipe away any doubt about marrying him. She loved him and he loved her so there was no reason they couldn't make it work. She was willing if he was.

"That sounds wonderful and I can't wait. I'm glad you thought about this."

"Baby, I've been thinking about doing this for a while. I was going to surprise you with it, but it looks like we were going in different directions at the beginning of this call. I'm glad we're back on track and I can't wait to see that sexy body of yours in a string bikini. I'm thinking something in white. I only hope I don't get arrested for indecently devouring you in a public place."

"I'm ready to be devoured. We need to connect like that in a major way."

"I know and I'm sorry about that. I'll make it up to you, I promise. I'm thinking of keeping you naked the whole time. Maybe a bathing suit won't be necessary."

"Hey, I don't need one or any other clothes if that's what you'd like."

"Yeah baby, that's exactly what I'd like. I have to go. I love you."

"I love you too," Phoenix said hanging up the phone and dancing around her kitchen. Perhaps all was not lost, she thought

Gavin ended his call just as his door opened and out walked the woman she'd seen him with the day before in the garage. She'd spent the night before wondering what kind of evening they were having, like some jealous teenager.

"Hello," the woman said to her. Up close, Phoenix could tell she really was much younger than Gavin as she'd suspected when she saw them in the garage. She looked to be in her early twenties.

"Hello."

Phoenix looked shyly from the woman to Gavin.

"We're on our way out for pizza. Would you like to join us?" he asked.

"Oh, no. I wouldn't want to intrude on your date."

Layne broke out laughing and pointed toward Gavin.

"Him? My date? I don't think so. I think there are laws and religious passages against that type of thing," Layne said.

Gavin looked at her with a stern face.

"Not funny Layne," he said embarrassed.

Phoenix caught on the minute he said her name.

"Wait, you're Layne, Gavin's sister."

"Yes, I am the infamous Layne, the better looking one of my siblings. You are?" she said reaching her hand out.

"Oh, I'm sorry, that's rude. I'm Phoenix. I live across the hall here from your brother. He didn't tell me you were so beautiful and yes I can see how you're the better looking of the two of you," she kidded.

"Both of you have jokes. Yes, this is my sister, the comedian. She's here for the weekend hanging out and getting in my hair. I promised her a night out around Chicago tonight since I have plans for tomorrow. Now that you know that this isn't a date, you can join us if you like?"

Phoenix thought about it and thought it best she

stayed home to catch up on some work that she hadn't gotten to during the week. Wedding details had taken control of her whole week.

"Thanks for the offer, but I think I'm going to call it a night, relax and get some work done. It was nice meeting you Layne. Gavin, I hope to see you again soon," she said.

"You will," he replied and added a look that said he meant it. The chill she felt running through her body didn't leave her cold, but hot and wanting.

Where the hell did that come from, she thought.

After they walked to the elevator, she went inside and locked the door, smiling brighter than the morning sunshine. She would never tell anyone that her smile was because the woman she saw him with wasn't a date, but his sister. She was elated and ashamed at the same time. It gave her pleasure knowing the woman wasn't a love interest.

She walked away from the door shaking the thought off. She had a man, not a great one, but a man and her thoughts needed to be on him and hoping he would get himself together.

**

"You like her don't you?" Layne asked as they pulled out of the garage.

"What?"

"You heard me Gav. You like her and not just like her a little bit. I could see it in your eyes and all over your face."

Gavin ignored her as he pulled into traffic and

hoped she'd change the conversation.

"We're going for pizza, but did you want to do anything else tonight? Remember I told you tomorrow night I'm going to meet a producer with Ellis, so I'll be gone until really late."

"Ellis is here with his fine self?" she asked.

"Stop it Layne. Ellis is a married man."

"He's married, but I'm not dead. I know a fine man when I see one and I'm not the only one. I see that Ms. Phoenix likes her some Gavin too, huh?"

He loved his sister who never learned the art of being subtle.

"Phoenix is engaged to be married and is not checking for your brother."

"Are you really going to try to convince me of that? I'm a woman and I know when a woman is into a man and Phoenix is definitely into you. Didn't you see how her demeanor changed when she realized I was your sister and not your woman? She was all set to be jealous of me, thinking I was your date. Yuck!"

"Funny, Layne," he laughed.

"I saw the look of disappointment on her face when I walked out and grabbed your arm. I did that on purpose. I love the look on women's faces when they have ideas of getting you naked in their heads and then they see me and think we're a couple. I don't know why people can't see the resemblance. We look so much alike, except for the hairy beard thing you have going on that I hate."

"First of all, never open your mouth and say the

word naked to me ever again and you're too young to know anything about what Phoenix was thinking."

"Keep telling yourself that. There are a lot of things you think I'm too young for that I'm not. I could tell you some stories."

Before she could continue, he stopped her.

"Whoa, there are some things I don't mind you talking to me about, but others, leave that for mom or your friends. In my mind, you still play with Barbie dolls!" he shouted.

"Okay, keep me ten years old if you want to."

"Wait, you don't like my beard? I keep it trimmed."

"I don't care that you keep it trimmed. I like the goatee much better. Stop hiding behind that hair and those hideous hats. You should learn to love the public eye like me and Luke. I'm going to be rich like you one day and I'm going to love the camera being all in my business."

"That's a generational thing and I'm over it. You can have it all you want and you're already rich. You sure live the lifestyle of the rich and famous."

"That's because you're rich and mom and dad are rich. You're making me wait for my money until I turn thirty to be rich. I don't know why though."

"You know why and listening to you, I can see it's a good idea. Just like I told our brother, no money at thirty either if I don't see a college degree in your hand and I'm talking about a degree beyond undergraduate. You have nothing but time to get it done and that's the agreement."

"I know, I know. Whatever, so back to Ms. Phoenix. She is beautiful. She reminds me of Beyoncé's sister, Solange. They could be twins, except Phoenix is a little curvier. She's hot though and I know you've noticed."

"Didn't you hear me say she's engaged?" Gavin asked.

"So does that mean you can't find her attractive?"

"Of course not. She's beautiful. She's probably the most beautiful woman I've ever met and that's saying something."

"It is considering the number of women I know you know. When is her wedding?"

"In a few months. She's engaged to Carson Stone."

"What!" Layne screamed almost causing him to lose control of the car.

"Are you out of your mind? Why did you scream like that?" he said straightening the car.

"You're joking right? She is really engaged to Carson Stone, the star of so many of my dreams I can't count high enough. Now, that man is fine, but he's a bit of a player. I heard he was engaged, but I didn't believe it. I don't think anyone believes he'll go through with it. She must be some kind of woman to marry him knowing he has a penchant for sleeping with everything in Hollywood."

Gavin looked over at her.

"How do you know that's a fact?" he asked curiously.

"Seriously big brother, you have got to get out more. That man beds a different woman every night. Thanks to you and the fact that I'm twenty-one, I get invited to some of the best parties in Los Angeles and I've run into him a time or two before his father banned him from living there because he couldn't stay out of the headlines. I guess banishing him to Chicago was his punishment. I heard he was going to run the hotels on the east coast, but I don't think that's happened yet. He's still wild as ever."

"No one has to be banned to Chicago. It's a great place to live."

"Gav, living in Chicago for a few months does not mean you have lived in Chicago."

"Whatever," he said, throwing her favorite word back at her.

"Anyway, I hope Phoenix knows what she's getting into. I know that she likes you, so I'd say she knows a better man when she sees one. Too bad she's engaged. I know if you like her as much as I think you do, she's an incredible person and not just a sexy body. I know you like both, so she must really be something. Come on, it's me, you can admit anything to me. How much do you like her?"

Gavin looked quickly at her before putting his eyes back on the road. His brother and sister were everything to him and they always talked about everything. He had no problem being honest with her.

"I like her a lot. I like her a whole lot."

"Engaged and all huh?"

"Yeah, engaged and all. I keep my distance though. I know what it's like to have someone come in and throw a wrench in a relationship and I wouldn't do that to her. She may have no interest in me at all, so it would probably be a waste of time anyway."

"I doubt it Gav. That look of pleasure on her face finding out I was your sister was not your run of the way response. She was elated to know that I was not a weekend guest. She may be engaged, but she is as into you as you are into her. The question is, what happens next."

Gavin dismissed any notion that there was something between him and Phoenix. If she wasn't happy with Carson, she would leave him rather than be a doormat. It was obvious she wanted Carson and he would mind his own business.

"What happens next is we go for pizza and we leave Phoenix's life alone. How about that?" he joked. When he heard her stomach growl, he laughed and the car swerved.

"I guess that means I'm hungry," she said.

Gavin sped off with thoughts of Phoenix on his mind. Layne was right. He saw the jubilant look on Phoenix's face when he explained that Layne was his sister and not his date. He thought he heard a sigh of relief escape her lips. What did that mean, he thought.

Chapter 11

Gavin dressed and questioned his decision to attend tonight's celebrity party. It wasn't exactly his scene, but he agreed to go at Ellis' request to meet a music producer named Bingo. He didn't make it a habit of going outside of the company for talent, but Ellis was right about this latest guy and his music. He'd played a few tracks for him which had him dressing to attend a party Bingo was hosting while he was in Chicago for a few days.

Before he moved from California to Chicago, he'd heard that Chicago was becoming the new mecca for record producing and a lot of entertainment companies were setting up shop to tap into new talent.

The new video game he was developing was slated to be his biggest idea since he put out his first game and gaming system. The sound track was just as important as the game itself.

"Are you sure you're going to be fine if I still go out?" he asked Layne who had settled in front of the television with her laptop and a salad.

"You do know I can entertain myself, right?" Layne said.

"I'm just saying, if you wanted to go someplace, I'll leave the keys to the truck here."

Layne turned to him, excited.

"Wait, can I have the keys to the Jag?"

"Absolutely not. You are not ready to drive that yet. You're lucky I'm offering the truck. I'm driving the Jag tonight."

"I'm probably not going anywhere. This is the most rest I've gotten in a long time and I'm planning to chill, but yeah, leave the keys to the truck in case I change my mind."

"Alright. I'm heading out to meet Ellis at this party."

"Tell that sexy man I said, what's up!"

"Not happening on no day. I better not catch you flirting with him. You know how you can do."

"I only joke about it with you because it gets under your skin. Ellis is a cool guy and I know he's married. He's also rich, so that's two balls in the pocket!"

"Stop playing Laynie."

"Yeah, yeah. Have fun and if you bring a woman back, text me, so that I can go in my room and put on my noise cancelling headphones," she joked.

"That's not your room, so don't get any ideas and I'm not bringing a woman back here, especially while you're here."

"Right, that's because you got it bad for the hottie across the hall."

"I see I need to leave now since you're in your usual comedic form. I'll see you later tonight."

"Have fun Gav," Layne said turning back to the television.

**

Phoenix exited her bathroom after taking a much needed hour long soak in her tub. A perfect day for her ended with a bath in her favorite lavender scented oils. After her discussion with Carson about plans to go away, she decided to get herself ready for the trip, mind, body and spirit.

She spent the better part of the day getting pampered and shopping for a few new things for the trip. She was excited and hesitant at the same time. In the back of her mind, she felt like Carson was going to end up cancelling their trip, so she didn't want to get her hopes up too high.

Grabbing her favorite lotion, she sat on the side of her bed to apply it and heard her cell phone make a pinging noise that signaled a text message. She got up and reached for it on her dresser and her sister's name popped up. She opened the text and clicked on the image she sent her with the message, 'where is Carson?'

Phoenix looked at the picture and saw Carson in his element with a blond woman who looked to be more than just an idle friend. The look on the woman's face in the photo looked as if they were familiar with each other. She texted back.

'He's out of town with his father at some meeting.'

'Does that look like a meeting to you?' Reese typed back.

'Where did you get this picture?'

'From Adrienne. She was afraid to send it to you because she didn't want to upset you.'

She kept looking at the picture and the placement of the woman's hand which rested on Carson's chest, an intimate placement.

'You don't know that this picture was taken recently.'

'Phoenix, this photo was taken at some party right in Chicago tonight. Look at the date and time stamp on it.'

She wouldn't believe Carson had lied to her. No way was he in Chicago after telling her he was out of town.

'I'm telling you he's out of town. He is a lot of things, but he wouldn't lie and tell me he is out of town and be right here in Chicago. Too many people know us for him to try that lie.'

'I'm not trying to bring you down. I didn't want you to see this on some social media site or television entertainment news show. You see the caption?'

Phoenix looked closer and saw the caption that said, "Is this the same Carson who's getting married to Phoenix Graham soon? Who is the blond bombshell he's been snuggled up with all night?"

She was mortified to see her name in print. She hated the media. Who was that woman, she wondered and when was the picture taken? She refused to believe anything found in the media. That's the stance she knew she needed to take when it came to marrying a man like Carson Stone. Someone was always trying to tear him down and wreck their relationship. She loved her sister and appreciated the warning about the photo, but it had to be older than the date of the photo which was dated today.

She didn't respond anymore and the next text from her sister said, 'Sorry' with a sad face emoji. Phoenix closed her phone and threw it on the bed. There had to be an explanation. She would ask Carson about it and she was sure it wasn't anything other than the media making it out to be something bigger than it was. She'd seen other photos more compromising than that of him. He wasn't trying to hide and if it was from tonight, then she felt that he would know to hide from the cameras. Is this the life she'll have to endure once they're married?

**

Gavin walked into the party already in full swing. There were people occupying every corner of the place. There were waiters walking around with trays of food and drinks and music poured from the speakers placed throughout. He looked around and spotted Ellis talking to some people. Coming to the party was Ellis' idea and though he was hesitant at first, he was glad he'd gotten out for the evening. He grabbed a glass from a passing tray and headed in Ellis' direction.

"You made it. I just knew I'd get a phone call or a text telling me you'd changed your mind about coming," Ellis said when he walked up.

"I listened to Bingo's music again and yeah, I like it. Bingo has talent, I'll give you that. I think some of his stuff would be a good match for the game. Looks like a big crowd is here tonight, a who's who in the entertainment industry."

"Gavin, good to see you!" a voice said behind him as he was about to say something else to Ellis.

He turned around and came face to face with another gaming designer.

"Joey. It's good to see you."

"Yeah, it's been a long time. I've seen your team at a lot of the conventions lately, but you've been ghost. How's the telecom business going now that you've pretty much dropped out of the game?"

"Well, I haven't dropped out completely. I decided to take a little time and focus on something else."

"Ah, a new game I bet. Is it something you can share?"

He looked to Ellis, smiled and then turned back to Joey."

"Who said anything about a new game? I'm just taking some much needed time off."

"Right. I hear you're writing some book or something now. I know there's more to it than that, but I understand your desire to remain closed lip. I am the competition, so I get it."

Competition he is not, Gavin thought. His company was way ahead of anything Joey and his company could even dream of designing when it came to gaming. It was time to change the subject.

"What are you doing here in Chicago? I know you live and breathe the Los Angeles entertainment life. This doesn't quite seem like your set," he said.

"Hey, I go where the party is. This party has been the talk of the town for a while, so I flew in to check it out. In Los Angeles, this guy throws the best parties and not many people would miss it and it doesn't matter the location. I'm really surprised to see you here. You aren't one for big, lavish parties like this one."

"Yeah, I decided to hang out while Ellis was in town and he invited me to come along thinking I needed to get out."

"Well, it's always good to see you," Joey said walking away.

"The vultures are circling," Ellis said.

"Yeah, I see that."

"Everyone is wondering if you're secretly coming out with a new game soon and Joey smells blood," he added.

"They can circle all they want. No one is finding out about this one until it's completely in the bag and it's coming along great. Having a team in Chicago with me has been great. We're making great strides. I'm going to grab a bite to eat. I'll be back," Gavin said, walking off.

He walked around taking in the scene of the party when he thought he recognized someone walking into one of the rooms. He was hoping his eyes had been deceiving him as he followed, walking down the long hallway. He paused at the door with his hand on the doorknob not sure he wanted to enter. He was sure of one of the people on the other side of the door, although he wished he were wrong. He could hear laughing and giggling and hesitated before turning the knob and looking inside.

Neither the man nor the woman noticed his appearance at the door. The lights were on in the room and neither turned to look in his direction. The man was sliding the thin straps of the woman's dress down her arms until it pooled at her feet leaving her standing in front of him in only a tiny silver thong. Her large breasts were exposed and the man's attention was focused on them. As the man dipped his head down toward the woman's chest, his head turned slightly and Gavin had his confirmation. Carson Stone was about to get busy with a busty blond behind Phoenix's back a few feet away from him. Knowing what was about to occur, he backed up to pull the door closed just as the woman slid down to her knees and reached for Carson's zipper.

Gavin turned around and walked back out to join the crowd. He felt bad for Phoenix because he knew that Carson was a snake, but never thought he'd be an eye witness to it.

Rejoining the crowd and finding another friend from his telecommunication days, he struck up a conversation and tried to remove the image of Carson about to cheat on a woman who loved him, a woman that any man would be lucky to have and should be fully committed to. She deserved that and so much more as far as he was concerned. Carson didn't deserve her and as much as he'd like to pull out his phone and inform her of his infidelity, he didn't because his intentions would seem as if he were trying to find something to cause a wedge between them. He had no problem admitting to himself that he wanted Phoenix, but he didn't want her unless she came to him wanting him as much as he wanted her and she had to already be free of Carson.

"Hey, where did you disappear to?" Gavin heard as Ellis came up to join the conversation.

"I walked around a bit, checking out this place."

"Bingo wants to meet you. Are you up to it?" Ellis asked.

"Sure. Let's do it."

Gavin was ready to do anything to take his mind off of Phoenix sitting at home or out and about not having a clue of what her fiancé was doing.

Thirty minutes later after listening to several tracks, Gavin was more than impressed with what he was hearing. They had all gathered in the lower level recording studio with a group of others who were on Bingo's team. They were about to talk business when the door opened and a few more people joined them. Gavin's back was to the door, so he didn't see who had entered.

"Gavin Black, Ellis Mays, do you both know Carson Stone? He is the heir to the Stone Tower Hotel chain and our resident playboy."

As soon as Gavin heard his name, he turned around

and came face to face with a snake. Carson was obviously surprised to see him, knowing he was Phoenix's neighbor and now he knew Carson would finally find out where he knew him from. No words were exchanged as recognition covered Carson's face. Recognition turned to shock.

"I had to rescue this brother just now. Some woman was trying to break his back in one of the bedrooms. Somewhere I heard he was engaged, but you wouldn't be able to tell, especially after the noises I heard coming from the other room. Imagine my surprise when the bedroom door opened and out comes Carson pulling up his pants. I guess the headboard banging against the wall wasn't from a loud television in the room. I had to go and investigate because it sounded like a wounded wild animal and that wasn't her, it was him," one of the guys in the entourage said.

As Bingo laughed, Carson looked like he hoped a hole would open up in the floor and swallow him whole. He looked at Gavin and watched as the words that were just spoken registered. He knew that Gavin knew he'd just cheated on Phoenix.

Gavin decided to end the staring contest going on between him and Carson.

"Yes, we know each other," Gavin said, smiling.

"Yeah," Carson said nervously. He then turned to Bingo and spoke while turning his attention again on Gavin.

"Cool," Bingo said.

"You know nothing was really going on in that room.

I don't know what you think you heard. We were trying to find a quiet place to talk. She's a student going to college for hotel management and wanted to ask me some questions," Carson tried to explain. His words fell on deaf ears as he tried to explain to the group, but kept his eyes on Gavin, knowing he'd been caught.

"Carson, dude, don't worry about it. We're all bros here and no one is going to tell your secret. That fiancé of yours is fine, but I saw the headlights on that blond and I'd have tapped that too. She has been all over you since you got here. It was about time the two of you banged it out! We've all been there," Bingo said.

Not all of us, Gavin thought to himself. He looked at Ellis who he knew had the same sentiment. They had been friends for a very long time and he knew that Ellis loved his wife and would never step out on her, not even for a big, beautiful set of headlights, code word for breasts.

Gavin laughed at Carson's attempt to lie and he couldn't resist letting him know he was on to him and his extra curricula activities.

"I think I actually walked in on her as she was stepping up to the microphone," he said, making reference to the woman going down on her knees to go down on Carson.

The moment Carson realized what Gavin was talking about he faked choking.

"Got a hair caught in your throat?" one of the guys joked and the room fell into a fit of laughter as Carson recovered.

"Nah, I'm good," he said and looked again at Gavin. "So, I knew I recognized you. You're Gavin Black, huh? The only man in this place richer than me. Interesting seeing you here."

"I should be saying that to you. How's Phoenix?" he couldn't resist asking.

Carson faked coughing again and reached for the door to exit the room without answering him.

"I'm going to grab me a drink. Bingo, I'll catch you later."

Carson's sudden exit surprised everyone, but Gavin. He had no doubt Carson felt that his secret was out of the bag and soon enough, it would fall on the ears of Phoenix.

He would like nothing more than to expose Carson as the creep that he was, but he struggled with hurting Phoenix with the information while he also struggled with knowing about it and not letting her know she was being played.

"What did you think of the track?" Bingo asked interrupting his thoughts.

"I thought it was great and I think it'll be a perfect fit for the new game. Ellis has all of the information you'll need and he'll get the papers drawn up with the company lawyers. Look them over and let him know if you have any questions. Rumors have been out that I'm developing something new and big, but no one knows any details. There will be a lot of documents preventing you from divulging anything about it, but I think we're on the same page. Money for this game means riches for you, so you have just as much invested in this and on the line as I do. I look forward to working with you."

Bingo stuck his hand out to shake his and Gavin returned the shake, happy that they were able to make it work. Video games were nothing without the graphics and especially the sound and Bingo had the sound his game would need.

"That's good to hear. I'm looking forward to working with your company too. I've been trying to do so for a few years. If this becomes a success, I'd like to talk to you about partnering on a project to start a record label here in Chicago."

Ellis had mentioned that idea to him and he was considering it.

"I'm definitely up for talking about that. There is a lot of untapped talent and I'm thinking of expanding my portfolio. Let's talk soon."

"Sounds like a plan," Bingo said. "I hope you are enjoying the party."

"I am, but I think I'm going to make my exit. I had a long day and I'm drained. I appreciate the invite," Gavin said heading toward the door.

"Leaving already?" Ellis asked.

"Yeah I'm out. Are we still on for dinner tomorrow before you leave?"

"Is eight o'clock good for you?"

"That works for me. My sister has an afternoon flight out, so I'll text you with where sometime in the morning."

"Cool, I'm going to walk out with you for a minute. I

have a few questions for you," Ellis said, following him out.

As they walked toward the door, Gavin turned to him.

"You have questions for me?"

"No not really. What was that between you and Carson and what's the story about him and some chick in one of the rooms here? I know it couldn't have been Phoenix. From the woman you described, I don't picture her as the type to have sex in another room in a house full of people and she's not a busty blond. Phoenix is a beautiful sister."

"No, it wasn't Phoenix and I saw what Bingo's guy said he heard. I thought I spotted him going into a room with a woman and I followed him. I stupidly opened the door and I turned around and walked back out as the woman was dropping down to her knees, hence my comment to him about the woman stepping up to the microphone. We all know that's a metaphor for a blowjob. They hadn't gotten to the headboard banging part, but I had no doubt they would be getting to it."

"Damn! You mean he was cheating on her? That's messed up."

"Yeah it is, but it's none of my business."

"So, you're not going to tell her?"

Gavin looked at him surprised.

"Wait, you're the one constantly telling me to not cross the line with her and to stay out of her relationship with him because I'm too close. You know

I'm interested in her and if I told her what I saw, it would seem like I'm doing it to break them up. I've been on the other end and it's not a good place to be in. It would destroy her."

"True, but you're telling me you can look her in the face and listen to her talk about her relationship with him and not want to clue her in that her relationship is a fraud?"

"What do you expect me to do? Yeah, he's a creep and I'd like to pummel his ass to the ground, but it's not my place and I won't be that guy. I want her, but I don't want her like that."

"It's not just about that and you know it, Gavin. That guy just screwed another woman and the woman he's supposed to be screwing has no clue."

Ellis' choice of words angered him and he let his face show it.

"Wrong words Ellis," he said through gritted teeth.

"Whoa," he said throwing up the peace sign. "Sorry about that visual since I know, even though you won't admit it, that you've fallen in love with her, so I shouldn't have said that, but you know it's true."

"True or not, it's not my place. I would want her in a heartbeat, but not because I told her how much of a fraud her man and her relationship was. I don't know what to do, but being the bearer of that bad news is not the position I want to be in. I know she likes me too, but on the rebound from being hurt like that is not how I want to get her. I don't want the words that would crush her to come from my mouth."

"So my friend, you're telling me you have no problem letting her marry a man who you know will eventually hurt and destroy her and right now you have the power to prevent that. She may hurt a little now, but trust me when I tell you, she will hurt a lot more in the future when that truth and others I'm sure will come out. Think about that," Ellis said.

Gavin turned and walked away while his mind took in Ellis' last words. Talk about a dilemma.

Chapter 12

Gavin opened the door to his loft, still reeling from what he'd seen at the party. Phoenix was being played, used and as furious as he was, he had to remember it wasn't up to him to alert her. He wanted more than anything else to knock on her door and give her an earful of what he received an eyeful of, but he didn't do that.

After closing the door behind him, he could hear his sister Layne talking and laughing with someone. He followed the sound and found her and Phoenix in front of the television, sitting on the floor in front of pizza and half-eaten salad along with an empty bottle of wine.

"Hello?" he said with a questioning look on his face. The last scene he expected was to see Phoenix sitting comfortably and laughing in his place. It was a surprise and a pleasant one at that.

Layne looked his way first.

"Hey big brother. Did you have a good time at the party?"

"You went to a party?" Phoenix asked.

"Yes, I had a pretty good time. I didn't really go for the party aspect as much as I went to meet a producer who I'll be doing some work with. What are the two of you doing?" he said walking in and sitting in one of the chairs across from them.

"Well, we're enjoying watching Magic Mike XXL, two or three times. I think I lost count," Layne said, snickering.

"I think this is the third time," Phoenix added, snickering too.

Apparently they'd put that bottle of wine to good use.

"Is that right? Looks like that pizza, salad and an entire bottle of my best wine has seen better days."

"Gav, I need you to send me a case of this stuff. It's delicious."

"Layne, you're just old enough to drink. How do you know what good wine is and trust me you'll never need a case of it," he said, amused at how silly both of them were being.

"Well, my girl Phoenix here picked the best from the bunch and told me I would like it and you know what? I did."

"Did she now?" he asked, looking at Phoenix this time.

"I promise you, I asked her to let me see her

identification first to be sure she wasn't lying when she said she was over twenty-one.

"No harm done. I gave my brother and sister their first drink on their twenty-first birthday and I made them promise to drink with caution."

"How much more cautious can I be than to drink here in your place, under your watchful eye and Phoenix here monitoring my intake."

"Looks like I should have been here to monitor you both. I see I missed a good time."

"That you did brother, that you did. Phoenix knocked on the door looking for you and we started talking and before long, we were sitting around talking about men and all their crappiness and the bottle somehow ended up empty."

"I see that. No more wine for either one of you."

"You said you met with a producer? A music producer?" Layne asked.

"Yeah, Ellis and I are working on a new game and this producer is doing the music score for it."

"Did you know that my girl Phoenix here can sing? I mean really sing? She let me listen to a tape she made and I swear I thought I was listening to a professional singer."

"Yeah, I live across the hall from her remember? I have heard her singing through the walls and she is incredible. I've told her that many times and I've asked why she isn't singing professionally."

He and Layne looked to Phoenix to respond.

"I told you it wasn't in the cards for me. I took the

safe route I guess."

"Well, it's not too late, is it Gav?" Layne asked. "You could hook her up with your music producer guy and get her a record deal. She would blow the R&B charts up!" Layne said with slurred speech and all.

"I agree with you on that. I told her she should look into it," Gavin said.

Phoenix blushed. She knew she could sing, but she never thought to pursue it even though everyone who has ever heard her sing has told her she should. Well, everyone except Carson. He once told her it would be a waste of her time since he was rich. She didn't need the money, he said. That disappointed her for him to think she would do it for the money. She would do it out of her love to sing.

"It's just a dream," Phoenix said looking toward Gavin who turned his eyes away, avoiding hers.

"Dreams are meant to be lived out too. You should think about it and like Layne said, I can introduce you to someone if you ever want to consider it or at least look into it. Let me know," Gavin added before getting up.

"Where are you going?" Layne asked him.

"I'm going to bed and you should let Phoenix get to bed too. You have a flight out tomorrow, though it's not until the afternoon, but I'm sure the hangover you're going to experience will have you in bed for most of the day. Phoenix has to work in the morning. Did you both forget it's Sunday evening?"

Layne and Phoenix chuckled.

"We sure did," they said in unison and laughed at the coincidence of them saying the same thing at the same time.

"Gavin is right, I need to get across the hall, though it's not because I need to get to work in the morning. I'm going to take a few days off and Carson and I are going to take a mini vacation to the Bahamas after he gets back in town tomorrow evening."

Gavin heard that and his ears perked up. She thought Carson was out of town.

"Carson's out of town?" he asked.

"Yes, he's at some big meeting with his father showing him that he is capable of running things. He called me last night to tell me he would be back in town tomorrow and he wanted to take me away. I went on line earlier and booked us flights and a nice villa for the rest of the week."

"Sounds exciting," Gavin said walking her to the door.

"It is exciting. I think this is exactly what he and I need to reconnect."

Gavin saw Carson as lower than the lowest he thought he could be. He had Phoenix thinking he was out of town when he heard him talking to his female friend about spending the last couple of days with her including their little rendezvous at the party. Telling Phoenix the truth was on the tip of his tongue, but he didn't let it slip. He smiled though, he felt like he wanted to pound the air out of Carson's lungs.

"I hope my sister didn't talk your ear off."

"I had a fun time with Layne. She's an incredible young lady and she's going to make an incredible doctor."

Doctor? Layne was going to be a lawyer. It must be the liquor talking, he thought.

"I'm glad you had a good time. It's nice to see you smile and laugh. I miss seeing that and I've missed seeing you. I know you've been busy, but don't be a stranger."

"I won't and thanks."

"My sister said you originally knocked on the door looking for me. Was there something you wanted?" he asked.

Phoenix looked up at him.

"Yes, you."

"What? You wanted me?" he said, trying to understand exactly what she meant. He knew it was probably the liquor talking.

Phoenix sobered a little when she realized what she said.

"I'm sorry. That came out wrong. I wanted to talk to you, but I can't remember what it was about."

The words didn't come out wrong as far as he was concerned. He wanted them to be true.

"Well, if you think of it, stop over any time."

"I will. Good night Layne," she hollered around him.

When Layne didn't answer they both looked further into the room and in the time it took for him to walk her to the door, Layne had fallen asleep on the floor.

Gavin shook his head. He'd have to pick her up and

toss her in the bed.

"It looks like she had a good time too. I meant what I said about introducing you to a record producer. You have an amazing talent and the world needs to hear it. If I can help in any way, I'm just one door away," he added.

"You really are someone special Gavin Black."

"So are you, Phoenix Graham. I'll see you soon."

Phoenix walked across the hall and turned to look back at Gavin. Something in his face told her that he wanted to say something, but he didn't. She smiled before closing her door and listened for his door to close before she walked away after locking it. Once again, her mind turned to the woman who would one day win his heart and she knew that she would be the luckiest woman in the world.

Across the hall, Gavin shook his desire for Phoenix off and walked over to his sleeping sister. Before gathering her up to put her in bed, he cleaned up the leftover food and straightened the room.

"I like her Gav," Layne said.

Gavin turned when he heard her voice as she groggily tried to wake up.

"She's a nice person," he said.

"She's an awesome person and you know it and that's why you like her too. Why does she have to be engaged to that clown Carson?"

"She loves him Laynie."

"Yeah, but you love her don't you? I saw it in your eyes when you came in tonight and found her here. It's more than just like and you know what, it's more than just like that she feels for you too. The heat between the two of you almost sent this place up in flames."

"Go to bed Laynie or we could talk if you're up to it. You've been here two days now and I still haven't heard what brought you here to visit me, not that you ever need a reason."

He watched as she sobered up a little and sat up straight. He assumed she was ready to talk even though it was two in the morning. He gave her his undivided attention by sitting down across from her.

"Okay, here me out okay?" she said.

"I'm all ears sis. Lay it on me."

"I don't want to return to school in the fall. I want to take a year off and travel or do what people call a gap year, even though most students do that before they actually start college. I should have done it before my freshman year, but I don't think I could have handled the responsibility of traveling alone back then and I know mom and dad wouldn't have let me. You probably wouldn't have pleaded my case for me either. I think I'm ready now and I'm feeling a little burned out from school."

"That's what all the mystery was about? You taking a break from school?" he asked curiously.

"Not exactly all of it."

Gavin watched as she played around with her fingers and kept her eyes on her hands. There indeed must be more.

"As long as you don't tell me you're pregnant, I'll be

calm about anything else you have to say."

Layne looked at him with a quizzical look.

"Really Gav? I have no plans on having any children any time soon, so you can exhale right about right," she jested.

"Okay, I guess I'm ready for the rest."

"When I do go back to school, it's going to take me longer than one year to finish. I'm changing my major from pre-Law to medicine. Specifically Veterinarian medicine. I think dad is going to be pissed that I waited this long to change my major and that I don't want to be a lawyer, something he has always wanted me to be. Can you help me tell him?"

"Layne, you don't give them enough credit."

"You don't know how they are because you don't live at home. Luke can do whatever he wants, but Dad wants to plan my life out for me. I've done a lot of thinking and those are the decision I've made for myself."

Gavin leaned up and placed his arms on his knees.

"If you want to take a year off to travel, I think you should. Life is too short to live by rules of what people think you should do. Live your life the way you want. I think mom and dad will understand if you talk to them like you're talking to me. I know you and Luke look to me to be the go-between with mom and dad, but I don't think you need that filter anymore. I think it's great that you want to be a vet. You have loved animals since before you could walk. There was always some critter or another you'd be taking care of. At least you know what you'd like to do instead of law and they will respect that. It's not like you have no plan."

"You're so much better when it comes to dealing with them."

"That's only because I'm older and I don't need their permission to do anything. You're a grown woman, so you don't need it either, but you should still talk to them about the decision. As far as the travel part, where do you want to go?"

"Several places."

"You and Luke didn't plan this did you? First he calls to tell me he wants to spend the summer in Europe and now you want to travel."

"No, we didn't plan it, but I did tell him about it. I'm the only girl and everyone treats me like I'm fragile. I know dad is going to throw a fit when he hears I want to travel for a year. Can you help me with them? Please?" she begged

Gavin didn't need to wait to agree to help her. He could never deny his siblings anything.

"Yes, I'll help you explain everything to them, but make sure when the question comes up about where you want to travel, you can't say several places. That means you haven't thought it through. When you're ready, let me know and I'll come home to talk through this with them. I'm sure it will be fine."

Layne smiled, jumped up and gave him a hug.

"I like this new Gavin. Now that you're not running your company every day, you're less business like and more brother like. You're definitely a lot more relaxed.

You're finally living now and not just surviving and racing to the top."

"I've seen the top and I'm good down here in the cheap seats. Now go to bed, unless there's more."

"No there isn't. That's it and the biggest reason that I came was because I missed you and I wanted to spend some time with you in your world."

"I missed you too and I'm glad you're here. I'm going to tell Luke the same thing I'm about to tell you. Wherever you decide to travel, be prepared to look up and see me pop up. I'm not going to set you free for a year without seeing you and checking up on you in person."

"Big brother, believe me, I was already prepared for that, trust me."

Gavin smiled. That was easy, he thought.

"I wish I didn't have some appointments to get back to at home or I'd stay the rest of the week."

"Oh, no you don't. I don't think I could take you for a whole week. By the end of it, you'd have my place swarming with new friends hanging all over the place. You and Phoenix having your little drinking party was enough. She has a lot going on so I'm sure she loved the company."

"Yeah, the wedding is driving her nuts."

"I hope there will still be a wedding," he said out loud, thinking he'd said it to himself.

"What does that mean?"

He played it off.

"Nothing Laynie."

"What aren't you saying Gav?"

He exhaled and slumped back in his chair.

"I'm going to tell you something and you have to keep your cool. Deal?"

"Okay, deal."

"While she was leaving, Phoenix told me that Carson called her and told her he was out of town for a business trip and I know for a fact he lied. Not only is he not out of town, but he was at the party I went to tonight and I caught him in a compromising position with a woman that it seems he's been hanging with for a few days while Phoenix thinks he's handling business. He was having his business handled tonight, a vision I can never erase from my mind."

Gavin shook his head trying to rattle the memory free from his mind.

"What? He was getting busy at this party with some woman?"

"Yeah he was."

"What did Phoenix say when you told her?"

"I didn't tell her."

"Why not?"

"It's none of my business."

"Of course it is."

"No Laynie, it's not. Phoenix is a big girl and she can handle her own relationship."

"Not if she doesn't know."

"I think she knows. She has to."

"No, she doesn't. Tell her and then maybe there is something in the cards for the two of you."

"That's not how I want to get Phoenix."

"You always have to be the good guy, the better guy. I know you don't want to see her get hurt by this creep."

"No, I don't, but I can't get in the middle of that. If I do, it will be for selfish reasons."

"Why, because you want her? Well, that's quite obvious and I've only been here two days. By now, I'm sure she knows. Tell her Gav."

"I'm not going to do that and you better not either."

Layne stood and walked toward the bedroom and then turned back to face him.

"If it were me instead of Phoenix in that position would you tell me?"

"Of course I would. Right after someone paid my bail after I beat the daylights out of the guy for hurting you. A woman should be treated with respect at all times and cheating is never the answer to being unhappy. I've been through it and I know."

"Yeah, you've been through it and you know how it feels and if Ellis had known about Natasha, you would have expected him to tell you, right?"

"It's not the same," he said.

"Phoenix is your friend and now she's my friend and he messed around with another woman behind her back. That's nasty and tacky and you have to tell her. You would do it if it were me or any other woman in your life. Phoenix may not be your woman, but she is a woman and she deserves to know the truth about the man she's going to marry. I'm going to bed. I love you Gav."

"I love you too Laynie. I'll see you in the morning."

After Layne went into the bedroom and shut the door, Gavin stayed sitting in the chair as he struggled with what to do. He would like nothing more than to walk across the hall and tell Phoenix what he saw earlier in the night. She would know that Carson lied to her and that he'd committed the ultimate betrayal by cheating on her. He agreed with Layne that Phoenix needed to know and he needed to think of what he would say if he was going to be the bearer of bad news.

Chapter 13

Phoenix opened the door to her loft and was surprised to see Carson lounging in front of the television. They hadn't talked much all week after their planned getaway ended up going nowhere. At the last minute,

Carson came up with an excuse for having to back out leaving her to cancel their plans. She had been unable to cancel the reservation without paying a heavy fee because he didn't alert her that they wouldn't be going until the morning of the trip and she had spent the night before packing. Instead of taking an unnecessary week off, she went to work and had been busy and no longer focusing on Carson and his drama.

The last thing she expected to see a week later was him sitting in her living room lounging. She wasn't as angry as she had been a week ago, but she wasn't planning to let him off the hook easily by greeting him with a hug and a kiss like the dutiful girlfriend he expected her to be.

"You're here," she said glumly with no hint of excitement.

Carson turned at the sound of her voice.

"Yes, I've been pretty busy all week and I didn't like how our conversation ended last week. Though we've talked a few times I could tell you were still angry at me and I wanted to apologize and not just on the phone. I also wanted to know how everything was going with the wedding plans. I bought you some flowers. I already put them in a vase so that they didn't dry out. I wasn't sure how long you'd be."

Phoenix followed where he was pointing to a vase filled with red roses he'd sat on her kitchen counter. Nice gesture, she thought and it may have had the expected response if she weren't through with his phony attempts to placate her. She looked from the flowers back to him, expressionless.

Carson had been hesitant to bring up wedding plans when they spoke because he wasn't sure about the state of their relationship. By now, he had expected that her neighbor, Gavin, would have told her about his little secret rendezvous the weekend he'd told her he was out of town on business. That was the reason he cancelled their plans to go away. He figured if she knew, they could end up having a blowup while away and the best way to avoid that was to not go at all. So far, she'd said nothing about it, leading him to believe her neighbor opted to mind his business.

He couldn't believe her neighbor was Gavin Black, one of the youngest millionaires in the country. The money Gavin had, made his money look like pennies on the dollar. He was still wondering what a man like Gavin was doing living in a loft in Chicago when he knew he had houses all over the world and enough money to buy a mansion if he wanted to, but he opted for a loft in Chicago.

Phoenix walked on by him straight to the kitchen ignoring the flower arrangement. She knew Carson was expecting a different reception, but she wasn't going to give him one.

"Aren't you happy to see me," he said.

"Should I be? I mean, normally when you arrive you're already planning to leave, so I figured I would save myself the disappointment that you would have more than an hour to spend here."

"That's cold Phoenix. You're usually ecstatic when I'm here. I've missed you."

"I'm exhausted Carson and not in the mood for mind games."

"Mind games?" he asked.

"Yeah, mind games. You know how you screw up, apologize profusely, send flowers or promise to do better and then offer a consolation trip or an expensive gift. What do you have this time that you think will have me forgetting about the fact that you stood me up for another planned trip with another lame excuse? What only flowers this time?"

Carson yielded.

"Okay, I deserve that, but I'm here now."

"So, that's the consolation? You finally showing up

after a week? Yippee!"

Phoenix faked excitement and then turned her back to him.

"You do know in a few short months we're going to be married and there's some compromising we're both going to have to do. This is our test to see that we can overcome anything."

"I guess we're not doing a good job passing the test."

"Can we move on now to something happier?"

Her mind flowed back to the night her sister sent those photos. Something about it still didn't sit right with her and she wanted to clear the air.

"I've been meaning to ask you, how did your meeting go last weekend?"

"Meeting?"

Phoenix nonchalantly walked around her kitchen, talking without looking at him. She wasn't sure she had any fight left in her to save what was left of their relationship. It took her a week to realize it had been over for some time and only she had been fighting to keep the thin thread that held it together intact.

She turned and looked at him without saying another word.

"Oh, that weekend. It went well and I'm thinking my father is pretty close to turning more control over to me."

"How many times are you going to tell me that or how many times are you going to let him keep telling you that, if he actually is?" she said snidely.

"What's that supposed to mean?"

Phoenix had finally had enough and no longer wanted to play games.

"What were you really doing that weekend? Were you really at a meeting with your father?"

"Why would you ask me that?"

"Just answer the question and preferably without tossing out another question."

This is it, Carson thought. Gavin snitched and it took her this long to bring it up.

"He told you didn't he? You can stop playing this game with me as if I don't know what this is about."

Confused, Phoenix walked closer to him.

"What did someone tell me and who is he?" she asked.

Carson paced, clearly frustrated. Phoenix knew he was hiding something and whatever it was, he assumed she knew.

"So we're going to play this game? You know and that's why you've been different this week. You didn't ask me to come by or ask when we were going out. You didn't even mention the wedding this week and usually it's all you want to talk about."

Now they were getting somewhere she thought. They were about to be open and honest with each other for a change.

"That's interesting because you never bring it up and you've done so twice in the past five minutes. I guess you're acting just as odd as I am, according to you."

"Stop playing games and just say what you want to say or ask me what you want to ask me. I'm already tired of playing this game."

"We're playing a game? What game is that?"

"Okay, let me ask you something. Is there something going on between you and your neighbor? I get the feeling that there is more to him just living across the hall from you.

"What?" she said shocked.

"You heard me. Gavin Black, your neighbor across the hall? The two of you are too chummy for me and you're an engaged woman; engaged to me. Having him over here fixing a book case and I know you know who he is. He's richer than me."

"Well that's easy because you're not rich at all, your father is," she shot back.

"Ah, now the claws come out," he said with anger he'd never directed at her before.

"Hey, don't try to point me out as some money chaser. I know who my neighbor is and I know he's rich. What does that have to do with you accusing me of something?"

"Aren't you accusing me of something?"

"I'm not accusing you of anything. I asked you a question and I'm still waiting for an answer. Who was supposed to tell me something? Gavin?"

"Don't act like you can't tell this guy wants you. A man knows when another man is interested in his woman. Is the feeling mutual? Did something already happen and you're feeling guilty so you're trying to accuse me of something to clear your own conscious?"

Phoenix walked closer to him, leaving the kitchen.

She paused for a moment to check where the conversation was going.

"What are you trying to deflect?"

She watched as Carson nervously paced back and forth. He was hiding something and it wasn't jealousy.

"I'm not deflecting anything. I asked you a simple question and you should have easily answered it, but I guess no answer is really my answer."

"You're talking crazy," she said dismissing whatever he was trying to accuse her of.

"Right," he replied.

"Okay, so if Gavin is supposed to tell me something, I'll just go across the hall and ask him. Apparently he knows something that you're not telling me."

Phoenix walked toward the door.

"I bet whatever he had to tell you, you would believe it. The big and mighty Gavin Black. I had no idea that's who your neighbor was, though I recognized him, but couldn't figure out from where until the party."

Phoenix caught that and Carson realized he'd said it without meaning to.

"What party?"

It took her a minute, but she was putting the pieces together.

"Party? You were at a party with Gavin? When? That weekend you were supposed to be away? You weren't away? The text my sister sent me with that picture of you and some blond woman with gigantic breasts was a real picture? Gavin went to a party that same night. Was it the same party you were at? What the hell is going on? You better tell me or I will ask him and I'm sure he'll tell me the truth, something you're not accustomed to doing apparently."

Now she was angrier than she knew she could ever be. Carson was hiding a secret and Gavin knew what it was and she had a feeling Gavin knew that night when he came home to her and Layne having a girl's night in. She could tell he wanted to say something, but held back. She wanted to know. She needed to know.

"Last chance Carson," she warned.

"Okay. Yeah, I was at a party that night here in Chicago and not out of town on business."

"Had you been out of town at all?" she asked, though she already knew the answer.

"No. I was in Chicago the whole time."

"Doing what or do I even want to know?"

"It was a harmless party that Sunday night and yeah, Gavin and I ran into each other. I didn't know until that night that he was Gavin Black."

"So, what is it that Gavin knows that you thought he told me? Clearly whatever it is, it's something that would anger me because it's making you more defensive than you have ever been along with being accusatory of me."

For the few moments that Carson appeared angry, it was now replaced by a look that said he was trying to garner sympathy.

"Look, I had a few too many drinks and it was all innocent, no matter what you may hear happened. Nothing happened."

Phoenix was now frustrated it was taking him so long to get the story out.

"What didn't happen? Just say it."

Carson hesitated and came over to her to take her two hands into his.

"Phoenix, I love you baby. I swear I love you more than anything and I would never do anything to hurt you or cause you to not trust me, but you know how life can be sometimes and what it's like for me when I'm out partying. Women come up to me and sometimes I have a hard time resisting temptation."

Images invaded her mind of Carson with other women and she knew that's what he was trying to tell her. The picture her sister sent her wasn't the whole story. To her, the picture was the beginning. She pulled her hands from his and with unshed tears in her eyes, she stepped back. She knew what he was eluding to and she couldn't believe it.

"Say it Carson. Stop stalling. Just say it!" she demanded, holding on to the little composure she had left.

She watched as Carson stood to his full height as if he was about to face a firing squad. She assumed he felt that way by what he was about to tell her.

"So your neighbor showed up at this party and he may have seen me in a small situation and I thought maybe he came back and told you what he saw, which really wasn't anything."

Her heart raced and though she wanted to cry, she willed those tears to not fall. She wouldn't give him the satisfaction of crying over his deplorable behavior.

"How small of a situation did Gavin see?"

Carson looked at her with eyes pleading with her for forgiveness before he even said anything. She wouldn't let him off that easy.

"Okay, here it is," he started to say as if he was going to ease into a story and thinking up a lie at the same time.

Enough was enough, she thought. Was this the man she had planned to marry?

"Stop it Carson! Man up! Isn't that what guys say to each other? Spill it. What happened that night? You're already in hot water because you lied about being out of town and I still don't know why. I've never tracked your comings and goings and then you try to throw shade at me about something going on between Gavin and me, something I would never do. I already know you weren't out of town, but I wasn't sure until now. My sister sent me a picture of you at some party with some big-boobed woman all over you. The picture looked as if the two of you knew each other, intimately. I'm assuming it was a picture someone took from that night. What else happened? You may as well finish telling me now."

Carson knew there was no getting out of this one and if he didn't tell her, he knew she would ask Gavin and he didn't want his version to be the one she heard. Ripping the Band-Aid off, as the metaphor goes, he said it pointedly.

"I slept with her."

That's when the staring match began. Phoenix had no words after the sting of the ones that just came out of the mouth of the man she loved and she thought loved her. Where would she begin in responding to that? She'd heard rumors for a long time that he'd been stepping out on her, but she never wanted to believe it. To hear him say it she felt like she needed a hot shower to wash off his filth.

"You slept with her at the party?"

"Yes, but it was nothing, baby. I promise it was nothing. I barely remember it because I was drunk."

"So you were drunk and your body slipped into hers by accident? Lately I've barely been able to get you in mine on purpose."

"That's cold," he said.

Phoenix saw fire.

"Cold? I'm being cold. You just admitted to sleeping with another woman two months before your wedding to me and I'm being cold?" she screamed. "What the hell kind of party was this?"

"Just a regular party and like I said, I got a little drunk and one thing led to another and then it happened."

"It? That's what we're calling this? 'It' happened?" she exclaimed.

"Baby, I'm sorry and I swear it will never happen again."

Phoenix needed to take it all in and she wanted it all so that she was clear with the decision she already knew she was going to make.

"What does Gavin have to do with this?"

"He saw me."

"He saw what exactly?" she asked.

"I don't know, but according to him, he saw an eyeful. I didn't know he was there and I assumed he told you what he saw since I know he wants you. That would have been his in to get you."

"What am I some consolation prize? Nobody gets me. I decide who my life is spent with and this is all childish play. You are a grown ass man who apparently can't control his hormones except around the one woman he should be letting them free with. How many times have you cheated on me since we've been together?"

Carson turned pale, if that were possible with his brown skin.

"Seriously Phoenix?"

"Answer the damn question. How many times? Thankfully we've always used condoms."

She watched as Carson formed his mouth to respond, but didn't. When he remained silent, she had her answer.

"That many times? Wow. Here I was thinking we had something special when all along you were giving that something special away with a coupon. Get out," she said softly. She was trying to not lose control and reach for the closest thing to throw at him.

"Phoenix, now wait a minute. We're standing here talking about this like two adults and I think we can get beyond this."

Hearing that fueled the fire boiling over in her. What did he take her for? What kind of woman did he think she was? She wasn't the type to let a man walk all over her, disrespect her, cheat on her while still saying he loved her and his expectation was that she would accept it and move on. Home-girl didn't play that. She inhaled and exhaled to calm down before she spoke. There was no need for shouting or hitting below the belt. They were over and nothing was ever going to change that.

"Carson," she said then paused.

"Baby," he responded.

She ignored his term of affection. He should have tried using that months ago and perhaps tried a different approach besides sliding up into another woman. That word held no weight. She continued on.

"I don't know who you thought you were involved with or engaged to, but the kind of woman who would forgive and forget your indiscretions is not who is standing in front of you. I'm not a doormat and I deserve a hell of a lot more than to have a man who would treat me this way. I've never given you reason to doubt me and this mess with you thinking something is happening with Gavin was just a cover for your mess, so I'll let that go. I'm not a cheater. It doesn't deserve me telling you it's a lie. There is no way in hell I would ever forget what you did, but I will forgive because there is no need to hate. You are a grown man and you made a grown man decision, though it was a boyish thing to do. Men don't need to cheat. If I wasn't satisfying you, all you had to do was tell me I wasn't the woman for you, but you didn't have to cheat on me, disrespect me and embarrass me. I can't be involved with a man like that, nor could I marry one."

Carson stiffened at her words. Was she backing out of marrying him? He was Carson Stone and no woman walked away from him, ever.

"Whoa, wait a minute. This has nothing to do with us getting married. We are still getting married. I probably need some counseling or we could go to couple's counseling to work out our problems, but this isn't an end to our plans to get married. I love you and I told you I was sorry."

"What are you sorry for? Are you sorry for what you did or are you sorry for getting caught? If you were sorry for what you did, you would have come to me that night and told me everything. I can't say I would have reacted any differently than I am now, but you waited over a week and that was because you thought someone else had told me. You avoided me all this time for that reason and that's pathetic. I'm done and like I said a minute ago, get out."

"Phoenix, I'm not leaving like this. You can't call off this wedding. There is too much at stake and it's two months away. My family has spent a lot of money pulling off this wedding of a lifetime that you wanted and you're going to let something like this ruin the great life you can have with me? Who does that? Why don't you take a few days and think about it and we can talk then," he said going toward the door.

Clearly he wasn't paying attention if he thought he was in control of the situation.

"Carson, do not misunderstand what is happening here. You are not in control of this. I said I'm done and that means the wedding is off. Now you can tell your family and figure out how to cancel everything that's in play or you can have your mother showing up in her beautiful dress with all of her guests and no bride. The choice is yours."

Phoenix watched as something in Carson changed. Gone was the apologetic pleader who wanted everything to go back to normal. What she was looking at was a Carson who now knows that he is defeated, but he wasn't planning to leave giving her the last word. She was looking into the face of a harsh, cold man, not the one she had been in love with and had been ready to marry. From his body language, he had gone from Jekyll to Hyde.

"You know what? Fine! If that's the way you want it, that's fine with me. Do you know how many woman would love to be in your shoes about to marry me? Carson Stone? Huh? You are lucky I chose you over every other chick out here. I had my pick and I chose you. I should have known you wouldn't be able to handle a man like me anyway. You weren't ready for all this. You want to cancel the wedding? Fine, consider it cancelled. When I leave here I'll make one phone call and shut it all down since that's what you want? Is that what you want? You want to walk away from all I have to offer you?"

Phoenix didn't know if he was expecting an answer or if the question was rhetorical. She was tired of talking. She'd already answered that and he didn't need to ask.

"Oh, now you have nothing to say. Well, I'll say what I need to say then since you had a lot to say. I'm over this and I think I have been for a while. Gavin across the hall wants you and he can have you as long as he's ready for the ice princess in bed. You want to know why I cheat? That's why because you're not enough for me, so I had to get it someplace else."

Phoenix thought she was going to let him say his peace and she tried to stay above the belt, but clearly he didn't get the memo that they were adults. He was resorting to nastiness and she didn't have to take that standing in her own living room.

"Get out Carson and if I ever see you again, it will be too soon. Get out!" she screamed louder than she intended. She was hurt with the vile words that spilled from his mouth. How dare he try to hurt her by blaming her for his cheating? She'd heard enough.

"I'm leaving," he said, finally opening the door. "I'm Carson Stone and I don't have to beg a woman to stay with me. It's your loss."

He looked like he was about to say something else and she cut him off from doing so.

"Get out!"

With that, she watched Carson open the door and slammed it behind him. She ran over to lock it and put the chain on before he came back in. She needed to get her locks changed immediately and let the guards know Carson was never allowed in the building again.

Overwhelmed by what just happened, she held her tears which now threatened to fall, until she reached her bedroom. Throwing herself on the bed, she grabbed a pillow and cried into it. She knew she wasn't going to walk away unscathed and so she would cry as long as she needed, but when she got up, she would get up knowing it wasn't her fault that the relationship ended or that he cheated on her. Her self-esteem would stay up in the heavens because nothing would bring her down to a level that would make her forget the powerful woman she was raised to be. Carson Stone didn't deserve her and once she cried over the failed relationship, she would never shed another tear for it or him again.

Chapter 14

No woman was worth all this, Carson thought as he walked from the elevator to his car and before reaching it, he found himself standing toe to toe with Gavin Black. Gavin was about to walk by him and he stopped him.

"She's all yours," he said.

Gavin turned around at Carson's words. His plan was to ignore him and keep walking. Apparently Carson had another idea.

"What?"

"I said she's all yours. It's what you wanted right? You think I don't recognize when a man wants my woman? Well you can have her. I hope you have some thick blankets once you get the ice princess between the sheets."

Usually Gavin could walk away from chumps talking mess, but he'd reached his limit quickly with Carson.

Before he knew what he was doing, he grabbed Carson by the collar and shoved him against the wall and put his face right up to his so that the meaning of his words were clear and concise.

"You never deserved a woman as wonderful as her and if I had a chance with her, I wouldn't throw it away with a pair of fake books and over bleached hair. You aren't even worth the hassle of trying to explain what a real man would do and a real man is exactly what Phoenix needs. Whether I want her or not is none of your business because unlike you, I don't like my private business on public ears."

"Let go of me," Carson tried to get out while being hemmed up. He was no match for Gavin's strength.

It took everything he had to not lay a punch on Carson which would open him up to a lawsuit, but he would gladly pay it for just one lick.

"Do you know how hard it is for any woman to trust a man these days with the internet and dating sites that make it easy for a man to cheat? You had a good one and you didn't know what to do with it. Go on back to your wild party chicks and leave the good women to men who will treat them right," he said finally letting Carson down.

He prepared himself for any physical comeback Carson would have, but he knew it wouldn't happen and it didn't. Carson wasn't the type to really be a man when he needed to be. He was too busy hurting good women.

"I knew you wanted her and the truth is, she

probably wants you to, so the two of you deserve each other. I bet she probably cheated on me with you."

"Trust me, if I wanted her, I wouldn't have to have her cheat behind your back to get her. She's much more than that and I wouldn't treat her like a plaything. Believe me when I tell you, I'm better than that."

"What you think you're a better man than I am?" Carson asked.

"I don't have to think what I already know. I am a better man than you."

Before Carson could get another word in, Gavin straightened his shirt and walked to the elevator. He got in and turned toward Carson who was still standing in the same spot. When the doors closed, he muttered one single word to himself.

"Punk."

He smiled right before frowning at what Phoenix must be going through. He would stop in to see her, but he figured she needed space. He would give her that and remembered he'd told her if she ever needed to talk, he was available. He was taking a trip to visit his family in a few days, but he'd reach out to check on her if he didn't hear from her before he left. She had to be hurting and he hoped in the end, she would realize she was better than she was with a man who didn't show her an ounce of respect.

**

"Do you need me to come over?" Reese asked Phoenix after listening to what happened between her and Carson.

"No, I'm fine. I just needed someone to talk to."

"So, it's over? You're calling the wedding off?"

"Of course. He cheated on me and this latest incident wasn't the only time. There is no way I'd marry a man who openly admitted to me that he cheated on me and then wanted to blame it on me. I wouldn't marry a cheater period. Once a cheater, always a cheater."

"How could it have been your fault? You didn't tell me that?" Reese said.

Phoenix knew she hadn't told her. No woman would repeat the horrible things he said to her about her being cold in bed. For a second she questioned herself, but she knew she gave as good as she got, so if there were problems in bed, he never said anything. Though she would have liked to have experienced more sensuality and passion, she never told him she wanted more, so it seems neither of them were getting what they wanted sexually. He called her an ice princess and no matter how hard she tried to shake those words, they stuck with her like a piece of gum on the bottom of her shoe; the thing that wouldn't go away.

"Let's just say he and I had some parting words that I don't want to repeat."

"What do you need me to do for you? Make any calls to cancel everything?"

Phoenix had actually braced herself for her sister saying she told her so, but that never came. Reese was being supportive, which is what she needed at the moment.

"No, I told him he needed to cancel it or his family and friends would show up to a wedding with no bride because I wouldn't be there. The invitations were going out next week so I can stop that. I just need to tell our family and friends."

"I'll take care of that," Reese offered.

"Are you sure?" she asked.

"Of course. Anything for you. Why don't you take some time off from work? Do you think you can get a couple of weeks off?"

Her job, she thought. She wondered what would happen to her job since she worked for Carson's family hotel chain. Surely he would see to it that she was fired. She had a feeling he was just that bitter.

"I may not have a job to worry about. Carson will probably have me fired. It's his father's company and one he will one day inherit. All he'd have to do was make a phone call."

"Yeah? Well, let them try it and we'll sue them. You haven't done anything wrong as far as your job is concerned, so they have no grounds to fire you."

Phoenix smiled at the harsh tone of her sister's voice. Reese was ready for a brawl!

"You are serious about this. More so than me."

"Girl, some fool hurt my baby sister and he's lucky I wasn't anywhere near there. I'd be in jail right now."

"That's why it's a good thing you're not."

"You know what I think you should do? I think you should take some time off and visit Andre in Paris. I know he'd be happy to see you and you can tell him all about the wedding being called off. Get away from Chicago for a minute and regroup."

That was a good idea, she thought. She needed some space between her and Carson and the news that will spread in the next several days about their split. She didn't want to be around to hear or see anything about it."

"That's not a bad idea. I can't think straight right now. I'll work this week, as long as I still have a job, and put in for a few weeks. I was taking some time off after the wedding anyway to prepare for our move to California. I'll just move the time off up to now."

"It'll do you some good. Let me know what I need to do for you while you're gone and I want you to go and enjoy some down time."

"Thanks for always being in my corner. I love you Reese. I need to call and talk to mom to let her know what happened. I think she knew this was coming."

"I think we all did and I'm glad you finally saw it to. I love you too kiddo and if no one else is in your corner, you know I am. Let me know if you need help packing or just want some company and I'll be there."

"Thanks. I feel a lot better now. I'm going to try and make something to eat and relax. I have a lot to think through and work out in my mind."

"I know you do and remember, I'm here for you."

"Thanks. I'll call you later."

Phoenix hung up and her conversation with Carson flooded her mind. She should have known he was cheating on her. The signs were there, not to mention the many stories in the media she tried to avoid.

Her thoughts also turned to Gavin. He had a chance to tell her about Carson and he didn't. She wasn't upset with him because babysitting and reporting on Carson wasn't his job. She was more concerned about what he thought about her. What kind of woman would put up with a man like Carson? Gavin must think of her as a weakling if she put up with his shenanigans. She bet Gavin would never treat a woman the way Carson did.

Picking herself up from a slump she'd been in since Carson left, she headed to her bathroom to run a hot bath. That always relaxed her and it was what she needed the most. She would deal with the aftermath of her breakup with Carson when her head was clearer.

**

Gavin shook off his encounter with Carson and exited the elevator, walking to his door. He turned toward Phoenix's door, prepared to knock to check on her and he decided against it. He knew she had to be hurting and he felt hurt for her. Breaking up isn't easy and he didn't know the circumstances, but whatever it was, it couldn't be good. He wondered if their break-up had anything to do with what he witnessed Carson doing at the party. He never told Phoenix what he saw, but wondered if she somehow found out and confronted him about it. Maybe she was tired of him treating her like she didn't matter and she finally walked away. Either way, he knew she was hurting and as much as he wanted to comfort her, it wasn't the time; it wasn't his time.

Turning toward his place, he went inside and hoped that Phoenix was okay on the other side of her door.

**

Gavin was startled awake by the ringing of his doorbell. He'd fallen asleep in front of the television after a conference call with his team. He jumped up knowing it could only be Phoenix since no one else would have access to their level. He opened the door and looked into her somber face.

"Hi, Gavin. I know it's late, after eleven, but you said anytime I needed to talk?" she said, hoping she wasn't disturbing him.

"Sure, it's okay. Do you want to come in or do you want to talk in the hallway?"

"Do you mind if I come in? I don't think I feel like sliding to the floor here to sit and talk."

He moved to the side to let her in.

"Of course. Come on in."

"Did I catch you sleeping?" she said walking in on a scene that looked like he may have been working and then fallen asleep.

"Sort of, but I'm awake now. I had a late conference call and I was looking over some work and must have fallen asleep. Have a seat," he said moving the papers to a table so that she'd have someplace to sit and he took the seat across from her.

Phoenix looked like she'd had a rough day, though her beauty wasn't touched. Happy or sad, to him she was incredibly lovely. Even now, she was dressed down in jeans and a tank top and looked sexier than any woman sporting an evening gown in full make-up, walking the red carpet. He looked into her face and knew that it wasn't the time to weigh in on her beauty. Phoenix needed a friend. She looked nervous and he wanted her to feel comfortable.

"Can I get you something to drink? A bottle of water?"

Phoenix perked up a little. He thought that maybe she needed a moment to get herself together.

"Water would be great," she said and he got up to get it.

When he returned, he watched as she held on to the bottle, not drinking it, but thinking hard. He would be quiet until she found the words.

"Carson and I broke up and let me just say he told me about the night of the party. He didn't tell me everything and I'm sure I don't want the details. Prior to that, I pretty much knew that things weren't going to work out. I've talked with my mother recently about reservations and my sister is never one short on words, so I've gotten an earful from her recently too. I think deep down, I knew that Carson wasn't being faithful to me, but I chose to ignore the signs and I don't know why. Perhaps because I loved him and I could see into the future and see a great life together with him, but that wasn't going to be enough. It should never be enough for anyone."

"I'm sorry to hear you're going through this. I can't say I'm sorry to hear that the relationship is over and I promise I'm not saying it for any selfish reasons."

Phoenix smiled at him.

"Carson told me you saw him that night. You didn't tell me," she said and looked him square in the eyes.

Gavin leaned forward in his chair.

"I'm sorry Phoenix. I struggled with doing the right thing to either tell you or mind my own business. I went back and forth between my reason for telling or not telling you. I saw him and the woman, but I didn't see him and the woman, if you know what I mean. I walked away when I saw what was about to occur. It made me sick to know what he was going to do and how much I knew it would hurt you. I didn't want to see the hurt in your eyes and I didn't know the kind of relationship the two of you had. I'm sorry."

Phoenix lifted her hand to stop him.

"I'm not upset with you at all and you don't owe me an apology. I know there are women out here who accept that type of thing, that open kind of relationship from their men, but I'm not one of them. I want and expect honesty and commitment and most of all fidelity. I don't understand how I could have been so stupidly blind for so long."

"Hey, don't put any of this on you. This is all Carson and you know it. You weren't necessarily blind as much as you were in love and he knew it."

"I knew the kind of philanderer Carson was when I met him and when I fell in love with him. He's always been the same, though I wanted to see him change and be as in love with me as I was with him. Now I find that he never really was and he said some terrible things to me."

Gavin didn't want to pry, but he wanted to know how far Carson tried to take her spirit down.

"Do you want to tell me what he said? Remember he spoke out of anger."

Phoenix spoke softly and told him everything Carson said including the fact that he called her an ice princess in bed which was why he cheated on her. She didn't give him what he needed.

It took everything within him to not leave her sitting and leave to go find Carson and not hold back from knocking him out. He had no doubt Phoenix was everything a man could want including intimately. He watched as Phoenix, out of embarrassment, lowered her head and began to cry.

"Phoenix, look at me," Gavin spoke softly. He hesitated when the desire to reach out and comfort her came over him. He pulled his hands back knowing that if he touched her, he would want to pull her into his arms and do more than just comfort her with words.

He watched as a play of emotions crossed her face and she began doubting the kind of passionate, loving and incredibly sexy woman he knew she was. He wanted to curse Carson for the emotional turmoil he placed in her head, making her think that she was anything less than desirable or that she didn't have what it took to satisfy a man. What kind of man does that to any woman? Not a real man, he thought. He shook off those negative thoughts and turned his attention full on to Phoenix who was hurting.

Phoenix tried to look away after raising her head to look at him.

"Don't turn away," he said lovingly. Gavin wanted to reassure her that the hateful words that spewed from Carson's mouth were not how a man was supposed to talk to or treat a woman. He watched as her chin lowered and he reached out to raise it so that they were looking into each other's eyes.

"I'm embarrassed. I can't believe I just told you all of those awful things Carson said to me."

"Don't make excuses for him. He didn't just say them out of anger; he said them out of a lack of who he is, not a reflection of who you are. A man like that doesn't deserve a woman like you and he never did. Intimacy between a man and a woman is not the sole responsibility of a woman. It's a mutually shared experience and if he felt that you were anything but hot and sexy, then I say it's because he wasn't giving you what you needed in order for him to get what he needed. Don't ever let anyone have you lowering your head and thinking less of yourself. You're more than that and I've known it since the moment we met."

Gavin wanted to curse himself. He didn't want to turn their conversation into how he felt about her, though he's been aching for months to tell her. Even though she was no longer with Carson, it still wasn't the right time.

"I really thought he loved me, but now I know he didn't. I think I was the means to an end. I believe his family wanted so much more for him and the lifestyle he was living wasn't going to cut it for them. His circle consisted of wild, partying women and none that his family would approve of. I think he saw me as a means to an end. I don't doubt that he cared for me, but not the way I needed or wanted to be cared for. I didn't realize that before, but it's crystal clear to me now."

"Are you going to be okay? What can I do for you to put a smile back on your face?"

Phoenix smiled just hearing his words of comfort knowing that he meant what he said. She knew he was that type of man.

"Thanks for being my friend. That makes me smile and the fact that you don't judge me for the horrible choice I made getting involved with him."

"Phoenix, people are who they are, including Carson and he let you see who he wanted you to see and you took that at face value. That's nothing to be ashamed of and I'm always going to be your friend."

Phoenix saw so much love and affection in his gaze and she felt ashamed that hours ago she ended her relationship with Carson and now she was sitting across from Gavin wishing she could have found a man like him. She knew she wouldn't be where she was now if she had.

Her thoughts went temporarily back to her conversation with Carson when he accused her of having something going on with Gavin. Could he see that her feelings for Gavin had grown over the past few months even though she was engaged? She never did and never would have acted on the attraction she had for him then, but what does that mean going forward? Is she acting on the rebound if she told Gavin that she considered him more than a friend?

"There was one more thing Carson said to me that I haven't told you."

"What's that?" he asked.

"He accused me of cheating on him with you. I didn't even dignify that with a response. He should try to be half the man I feel like you are and maybe we would have had a better relationship. It ended up being exactly what it was supposed to be."

Gavin wasn't surprised to hear her say that Carson thought they had something going on. He was never one to hide his feelings and Carson had told him that he could see that Gavin had more than just neighborly feelings for Phoenix. Should he tell her? He didn't want to keep anything from her, but he didn't want to make a play for her when she was vulnerable.

"There is no secret I find you attractive or that I've had thoughts about you as more than just a friend, but I never, ever would have acted on that then nor would I now. I believe in respecting relationships and even though Carson is a creep, you were involved with him. There isn't a man who wouldn't have an interest in you and I'm not just talking about a physical attraction. We've gotten to know each other as friends since I've lived here and to me you are the epitome of the perfect woman. Carson knew that and he was jealous that I recognized it as well, though he didn't appreciate it. You and I never had anything going on and don't let him make you feel bad by accusing you of something that wasn't there."

Phoenix tried to read his face to see if there was anything but truth on it and there wasn't. Her truth matched his, but she felt ashamed that even for a minute, she had thoughts of more than friendship with him while she was still with Carson. To her, that made her no better than him. She looked at him and hoped she wasn't speaking out of hurt over her relationship with Carson and looking for comfort so soon.

"What if he saw something in me that made him think that I was interested in you? What if it showed on my face when I spoke about you or he heard something in my words? Gavin, you are an incredible man and I've said that many times. Carson could learn a thing or two from you. It wasn't until I met you that I realized there was something in my relationship with Carson that was missing."

"Thank you. I'm not perfect and believe me I have my own flaws, but I've never disrespected a woman or talked down to one in order to build myself up. That was his flaw. Whatever you felt about me, there is nothing wrong with that. Attraction between a man and a woman has been there since the beginning of time. You didn't cross a line like he did and thoughts never hurt anything until you do. You will need some time to heal from the end of your engagement and all that will happen as a result. The media will have a field day raking you both over the coals and I'm sorry for what you will have to endure because of who you were engaged to. I'm hoping Carson will take the high road and not try to slam you to make himself look good. I'm sure he'll feel like he has an image to uphold."

Phoenix was afraid of that and knew that it was coming. That's why she was going to leave for Paris in a few days to visit with her brother. She hoped a few weeks away would give her the time she needed and the media would forget about her by the time she returned.

"I'm leaving in a few days to spend some time in Paris with my brother. The media attention to this will be crazy and I want to be far away. I wanted to stop over to let you know what happened and to say thanks for always letting me vent to you."

"I told you, anytime you need to talk, I'm here. I'll miss you while you're gone. I hope we can stay in touch while you're there. I want to know how you're doing."

"I'll miss you too and I'll keep in touch."

Phoenix stood to leave and felt much better than she did when she showed up.

"Have a safe trip and let me know if you need me to keep an eye on anything with your place while you're gone."

"Thanks Gavin."

She walked to the door with him following close behind her. She reached for the door handle and stopped. She turned to face him and without thinking, she moved close, hoping it wasn't a bad move. She reached her arms out and hugged him, laying her head on his chest.

Gavin reached around and pulled her snug up

against him and hugged her back. This was the first time he'd been this close to her and it felt good. She felt like she belonged in his arms. Before he could say anything, Phoenix pulled away, smiled up at him and left. He waited until she opened her door, went in, waved back at him and then shut and locked her door.

Alone with his thoughts, he knew that he would give Phoenix the time she needed to deal with her breakup, but when she returned and was ready, he wanted to show her that he wanted to be more than just her friend. He hoped she'd give him an opportunity to show her how a better man would treat her.

Chapter 15

"How are you holding up sis?" Reese asked Phoenix the moment she answered.

Phoenix was better than she thought she'd be. After calling off her wedding she took some time off from her job and visited her brother to get a break from the backlash in the media about her being the only woman in the world who would turn down an opportunity to marry Carson Stone. She had been gone for a month and had been home only a few minutes when her sister called to check on her.

"I'm holding up fine. I'm tired from the long flight home. How have things been here?"

"Well, the media seems to have moved on to a new story finally and playboy Carson is back to his philandering ways. He's been worrying mommy and daddy because he couldn't find you to talk to you. Apparently he felt like you were going through pre-wedding jitters and if he gave you some time, you would get over it. He found out you were taking some time off from work and wanted to know where you were after going by the loft and not being allowed in by security. Of course you know how that went when he started throwing his name around and how childish he got when it didn't work. I guess he's the only person you didn't give your new cell phone number to."

"Yeah, he started calling it nonstop so I changed it and didn't give it to him. I'm glad no one else did either. I got several emails from him, but I haven't read any of them. I was tempted when I first got to Paris to call him, but Andre threatened my life and promised me he would hurt Carson and no one would find the body if I didn't keep my distance from him. I admit I missed him until I remembered what he did and then I remembered why I was done."

"Well, it's over, you're back and Carson is history. Let's not waste a conversation on him. As you can see I kept your place nice and clean."

"I see that and thank you. I also see the huge stack of mail you left for me."

"I put them in order of when they came in. When do you go back to work?"

"Next week. I thought after what happened with Carson, I would be out of a job, but his father called me directly to tell me he still expects me in position and he understood why I did what I did. He was the one who told me to take a month off to regroup and when I returned, he expected the same level of work out of me that he'd received before."

"Yeah, I hear his father appointed a new CEO and it wasn't Carson and in response to that, lover boy has been seen at a different party almost every night."

"It's what he wanted all along which is why I knew marrying him wasn't a good idea."

"I'm glad to have you back home and maybe things can get back to some semblance of normalcy for you. So, have you seen Gavin yet? I ran into him several times while checking on your place and he told me the two of you had been in contact often."

Phoenix had thought about Gavin on the flight home. They had stayed in contact mostly via text and email. The time difference didn't work when it came to phone conversations, but they managed to get in a few. He was concerned about the impact the negative media coverage of the breakup would have on her life, but thanks to him and her family, she stayed unscathed.

Gavin turned out to be the friend she needed and he never failed to send her an encouraging text or email letting her know that she would get through all the press and that he was sorry for what she was going through. Besides hearing from her family, she anxiously awaited contact with him while she was away.

"No, not yet. I literally walked in the door five minutes ago."

"Oh, I thought your flight got in a few hours ago?"

"It did. I made a few stops. I thought about knocking on his door, but I didn't see his car in the garage, so I assume he's out."

"What now, sis?"

"As far as what?"

"As far as you and Gavin? I know you like him and I know he likes you. I talked to him a few times and he's really smitten with you, but he wanted to give you space and not crowd you right after your breakup. I know you think it would be too soon after you ended things over a month ago with Carson, but time waits for no one. Gavin is a great guy and he deserves you as much as you deserve him."

"It's too soon for me to even think about anything other than being Gavin's friend."

"The best relationships start with the greatest friendships."

"I'll keep that in mind. Can I call you a little later? I'm exhausted from the flight and I think I'm going to grab a long nap."

"Alright. Call me if you need anything."

"I will. Love you sis."

"Love you too."

Thoughts of Gavin being across the hall from her again had her wondering if she was on his mind. Their conversations in the month that she was away had taken a turn from a basic friendship to something much more. She looked forward to hearing from him and she couldn't wait to send him her latest batch of photos from Paris. For the first few days after she arrived, she moped around wondering how her life had taken such a bad turn after falling in love. Love wasn't supposed to hurt as much as she had been hurting. She had hurt more for the loss of the relationship than over the loss of Carson in her life. He'd caused her a hurt that she never thought she'd feel. Despite that, a few days later things started looking up. Her brother was in between jobs and took some time to show her around Paris. After being in a city known for romance, she felt better and Carson had become a distant memory even with his attempts at trying to reach her to apologize and make things right. Nothing he could ever do or say could make her go back to him.

Her brother was the rock she knew he would be. She laid the entire story out to him, including Gavin and he told her to follow her heart. She told him of her hesitation with jumping into anything with Gavin so soon, but her brother was right when he said you aren't supposed to time and plan out love. If what she wanted was to follow her heart and tell Gavin how much she liked him, she should do it and go with whatever happens. He told her he never liked her with Carson, but that he supported her decision to marry him because he wanted to see her happy. Once he told her that, each conversation with Gavin got better and better.

She was excited when he told her that he'd gotten a boost of inspiration and was able to complete over half of his book and he expected to be completely finish by the time she got back to Chicago. She told him that while she was in Paris, she put her fears aside about singing publicly and had participated in a few open microphone nights at a pub or two and she'd received a standing ovation. She never thought she would get the kind of reception she did and it was great. Gavin was excited for her and told her when she returned, nothing should prevent her from pursuing her love for music if that's what she wanted to do. She decided music is exactly what she wanted to do. Not knowing how far a career in singing would get her was the excitement that fueled her desire to do it. The unknown is what intrigued her the most.

Gavin had been a lifeline and much more than just a friend. Neither of them spoke of it, but it was in the air. Now that she was back home, she wondered if he was open to exploring more than just a friendship with her. She hoped he didn't think it was too soon because she didn't. It was time for her to move on and she'd be a fool to walk away from someone as great as him. She was ready and she wondered if he was home. She'd give him some time and she'd stop over. For now, she had a lot of unpacking to do and needed to clear the coat of dust that covered everything and then she'd decided what to do about Gavin.

She continued to struggle with one big truth which was, in the month that she'd been away, she'd fallen in love with him and she still wondered if it was a good thing. Was she falling in love too easily, especially after her breakup? Did she give herself enough time to be alone to work out her own life before falling so hard for Gavin? She knew her love for him didn't come overnight and had started prior to her leaving for Paris and most likely before her breakup with Carson. Gavin was as close to perfection as she ever came across. No woman in her right mind would pass up the chance to get closer to him and she was no exception. She wanted to be ready if what she felt in his words meant more than just friendship. She hoped so.

**

"So, big brother, are you going to make your move and let Phoenix know you're in love with her?" Layne asked as Gavin loaded the trunk of his rental car to head to the airport.

"No Laynie I'm not. She's just getting back in town and probably to get her life back on track after all that drama. I'm not planning to add to it by pouncing on her with my feelings. She needs time to heal."

"Aw, man! You guys are something else. What makes you think she hasn't healed already? It's been a month and women are extremely resilient especially after going through something like what Phoenix went through. She was in love with a jerk and after the things he said to her when they broke up, trust me when I tell you, she is over him. That relationship and the residuals of it are dead, buried and stinking."

Gavin laughed.

"Your way of saying things and the visuals are killing me," he said.

"I'm just saying what needs to be said."

He closed the trunk and turned to her.

"How do you know what Carson said to her?"

"You're not the only one who has been staying in

touch with her while she was in Paris. We're like sisters now and we could actually be if you got your game on and made that move. You know you love her and I'm guessing she loves you, too. She should be back home by now, so she'll be there when you get back home tonight. Thanks for coming home and convincing mom and dad to let me travel for a year."

"You're welcome and remember that means I'm dropping in on you at any time and watch out for those island men."

"Please, there is no man anywhere that can get over on me and have me falling all head over heels in love. I want to take the year and have fun, not get all serious about anyone."

"Remember you said that."

"I got that, now back to your love life."

"We're not back to my love life. I know how to handle women and what I plan to do about Phoenix is none of your business."

Layne huffed at him and folded her arms across her chest. Gavin relented, not knowing how she was easily able to get him under her spell. He pulled her in for a hug so that he could get going to not miss his flight from California back to Chicago.

"I promise you, I have no plans to let Phoenix walk out of my life or into the arms of another man. That's not going to happen. I'm not going to push her, but I will let her know how I feel about her and we'll let things naturally happen from that point on. How does that sound?"

Layne smiled brightly.

"That works perfect and I'll start researching places for the wedding," she quipped.

"Funny. I love you and remember, before you take off on this journey of yours, come to Chicago so we can hang out for a few days."

"I will and thanks for everything. You are the best big brother in the whole world."

"Yes I am," Gavin said before getting in his car and driving off.

He thought about Phoenix on his drive to the airport. He hadn't spoken to her since she left Paris for Chicago two days ago. By now she was settling in at home and preparing to go back to work. He couldn't wait to see her. Talking to her over the phone or texting and emailing wasn't enough. He needed to see her beautiful face. They had grown closer over the past month and he hoped she was ready for him because he was coming for her.

Gavin was able to gather that Phoenix was completely over her failed relationship and was ready to move on with her life and he hoped that meant she was ready to accept more from him than just friendship. He wondered if she was going through the same nervousness over seeing him that he was experiencing over seeing her.

The media had died down around her broken engagement to Carson and because of the kind of person Carson was, he'd done several stupid things since then that has taken the attention from him and

Phoenix to several other newsworthy screw-ups. He was happy about that and Phoenix would be able to get back to her life without the public scrutiny.

Layne's words rang in his head and though he wouldn't openly admit it to her, he was in love with Phoenix and he wanted nothing more than to tell and show her, but he needed to move forward with caution. The last thing he wanted to do was push her into something she wasn't ready for.

Pulling his car over to the side, he parked and pulled out his cell phone and called her.

"Gavin!" Phoenix said with excitement and that gave him hope.

"Hello to you. Are you home and settling in yet?"

"Yes, I've been home since yesterday and have been asleep for most of it. I was hoping to hear from you. I didn't want to disturb you if you were busy working on your book."

"You'll be happy to hear I've finished it. I sent the draft off to my editor and I'm looking forward to seeing his feedback on it. I'd love for you to read it."

"Really? You want me to read it?"

"Of course. I don't trust sharing it with anyone, but you."

"I'm honored and I would love to."

Phoenix felt giddy. Her feelings of them growing closer weren't a dream.

"Good, now that we've gotten that out of the way, I'm actually out of town, flying back today and I was calling to see if I could invite you out for dinner to welcome you back home."

"You're out of town?"

"Yes. I flew home to help my sister with an issue with my parents."

"That must be about her taking a year of."

"Yes, now that it's all worked out, I'm heading home and I was thinking about you."

He hoped that wasn't too much for her to take in.

"I've been thinking about you too and I'd love to do dinner. Do you want to meet someplace?"

"How about I stop my luggage off at home and knock on your door when I get there?"

"Sounds like a plan."

Silence invaded their conversation and Gavin knew what he needed to say next.

"I've missed you, Phoenix. I've missed you a lot," he admitted.

"I've missed you, too and I can't wait to see you," she added.

To Gavin, those few words meant everything.

"I'll see you in a few hours," he said, before hanging up and pulling back into traffic.

Chapter 16

As soon as Phoenix opened her door, Gavin's heart felt like it was going to beat out of his chest. He had never seen a more beautiful sight than her standing in her doorway with a big, bright smile on her face and that greeting was all for him. Before he could gather any words to say, Phoenix leaped into his arms, wrapping her arms around his neck. He held her so tight, he was concerned he was squeezing her too tight. She felt damned good and he never wanted to let her go. They stood like that for several minutes not saying a word, but held on to each other.

Gavin finally released her.

"Welcome back," he said.

"Thank you."

"I swear, I don't know if I can stand it if you get any more beautiful. You are glowing!" he exclaimed.

"I'm feeling the best that I've felt in a very long time

and seeing you standing on the other side of my door just made my day. Do you want to come inside while I grab my things? We're still doing dinner?"

"I wouldn't back out on dinner for any reason. Besides the fact that I'm starving, I'm looking forward to catching up with you and hearing all about your trip to Paris besides what I read in your emails and in the pictures you sent."

He followed her inside and shut the door.

"I have a lot more pictures to show you. Paris is so beautiful. I hope to go back one day."

"I'm sure you will. I also want to hear about this singing. Are you ready to let the world hear that incredible voice?"

Phoenix came back into the room.

"I think I am."

"Do you want my help connecting you to some reputable people? I want to be sure no one tries to take advantage of your talent."

"I trust you," she said looking up at him.

Gavin's heart leaped with the way she was looking at him. In front of him was no longer a woman he was simply friends with. Instead, she was replaced by the vibrant beauty that he was in love with. He felt and heard his breath as it poured from his mouth as his body tried to keep up with the rapid beat of his heart. He felt his smile disappear as he thought about his next move. Stupid or not, he was going for it or he'd never make it through dinner.

"Are you alright? What's wrong?" Phoenix asked.

She had seen the change in his demeanor.

"Phoenix, I want to do something, but I don't want to make you uncomfortable. I have not been able to stop thinking about you and seeing you after a month, I feel like I can live and breathe again because you're back. Besides that, I have dreamed about holding you in my arms and kissing you, but if I'm moving too fast or thinking in a way that you aren't ready for, stop me now because before we leave, I need a taste of those lips of yours."

Gavin moved closer to her and she moved in his direction without hesitation. He watched her move in what appeared to be slow motion to him and he was glad. He wanted to take in every step she made in his direction knowing she was coming to him because she was now ready for him.

Phoenix knew Gavin didn't need permission because she wanted to kiss him as much as he wanted to kiss her and there was no need for any pretense. She dropped her keys and her bag in the floor and never missed a stepped walking into his embrace.

When Phoenix's response was to meet him halfway, he had his answer. When she was a whisper away, he pulled her close to him and lifted her chin all the way up so that he could have access to her full lips which were covered in a clear gloss. He wasted no time leaning in to capture lips that were waiting for him to take charge. His first contact with her lips was explosive and he heard rockets going off in his head. Torrid waves of uncontrolled passion seared through him as his mouth covered hers. He increased the intensity of the kiss the moment his tongue touched hers and the feel of her joining him in the kiss by caressing his tongue with hers was sure to be his undoing. Touching her was what he wanted, kissing her was what he craved, but her reaction to him was more than he could have imagined. He never imagined the thrill of her mouth opening to take him in.

Phoenix didn't know what was happening to her. Was this how a woman was supposed to be kissed? Was she only being kissed because it felt like her mouth was being made love to? She felt lightheaded, she felt completely possessed by Gavin's mouth as his tongue staked a claim on hers letting her know that if she had any doubt about his intentions, it was pretty crystal clear now. She couldn't think of anything at the moment that she loved more than the feel of his lips, his tongue as they went at each other like two starving beings. She needed and wanted even more as she moved even further into his embrace. When she felt his hand reach up to hold the back of her head, making sure she didn't go anywhere, she felt herself leaping like she was trying to climb to the top of a mountain and that mountain was Gavin. Her heart raced as she desired more and more of him. With his height she couldn't get a grip on him like she wanted to and she whimpered her displeasure.

Gavin heard and felt Phoenix's plea for more, so he reached down, grasped her hips and pulled her up, lacing his hands beneath her ample behind to hold her to him. It's what she wanted, he knew, when her arms circled his neck and she didn't hesitate to devour his mouth when he thought he was taking the lead. Her kiss was demanding, blinding and penetrating and he coiled his tongue around hers while they fought to draw every bit of their fierce desire from each other. His hands roamed, her hands caressed and the only sounds in the room were of moaning, escalating his hunger for her to a whole new level.

The heat in the intimacy of the kiss made Phoenix feel weak as they claimed each other with a zest that said they had been holding back for a long time and the kiss was their relief.

Gavin knew it was time to pull back when his mind took him to a place where they were naked and sweating it out. For now the kiss would have to do. He willed his body to soften in all of the places that had grown hard at the sight of her.

Phoenix didn't know how long the kiss had lasted, but whatever it was, it wasn't long enough as Gavin slowly pulled his lips from hers and stared into her eyes. The burning acknowledgement of how much he wanted her stared back at her as he finally lowered her back to the floor, both of them breathing like they needed to find a chair before they passed out.

"Mmm," Gavin moaned.

Phoenix stepped back ran her finger across her lip still feeling him there. She hoped the way her heart was beating she wasn't about to have a heart attack. If so, she was ready to die a happy death. She'd never been kissed like that before and for the first time, she felt wanton as she kissed him with a fervor she never knew she had in her. Who was this wild woman who practically climbed his body hoping there was a way to get even closer?

Now that was how a man is supposed to kiss a woman. Yeah, she'd been missing out.

"Wow!" she exclaimed, when nothing else could come to mind.

"Wow is right," Gavin added. "I've waited a long time for that kiss and it was well worth the wait. One more taste," he said and leaned down and captured her lips again, this time not going as high-powered as he did the first time, but still enough to let them both know that the first kiss wasn't a fluke.

"Yes, one more," Phoenix said breathlessly as his mouth closed over hers.

It was quick, but packed a powerful punch.

Gavin lifted his head and smiled.

"I won't say how long I've wanted to do that because it wouldn't be right. I will say thoughts of kissing you consumed me for the entire flight here. It was the longest flight in the history of the world."

Phoenix knew exactly how he felt. No longer would she deny herself the chance to be close to him. Kissing him was more amazing than she could have imagined.

"I've never, ever been kissed liked that before. That was amazing!"

"Yes it was and I knew it would be. Okay, we need to leave for dinner and get a cold glass of water before I need to go across the hall for a cold shower. I needed that and now I need food. Shall we go, beautiful?"

"I'm ready," Phoenix said following him to the door after picking up her bag and keys that she'd thrown down when she needed to be in his arms. What she didn't say was she was ready for a lot more than just that kiss and dinner. She had a feeling more was on its way.

**

Gavin knew if he could pick three days out of his life to label as his happiest, today would be one of those days. He was sitting across the table from Phoenix and he no longer had to fight his attraction to her. The kiss they shared before leaving for dinner was a sign for him that they were both ready to move on and possibly do so together. He'd taken a chance and went for it hoping she'd missed him as much as he'd missed her, even though when she left to visit her brother, they were nothing more than friends. That friendship grew through text, email and phone calls. He looked forward to the many pictures she'd sent him sharing her day and the highlight of his day was when he received a simple text that said, 'hello'. That was all he needed.

He knew the moment things between them had changed. She had been gone about two weeks and throughout that time, he tried his best to be her friend and comfort her through the loss of her relationship with Carson. He knew it had to be hard for her even though deep inside, he was happy that she'd come to the conclusion that he wasn't the man for her. He knew it, but he wouldn't be the person to tell her so. It was something she had to have her own eyes opened to without any coercion from him.

After about two weeks in, conversations about Carson stopped and she started asking him more about what was going on in his life, how his book was coming along and congratulating him on the progress he was making with his latest game. He was able to talk to her more about her own hopes and dreams, especially about her singing. He had a feeling singing was therapeutic for her and he knew great talent when he heard it and Phoenix was an incredible talent.

She's shared with him that her job would be waiting for her when she returned home and that Carson's father had no ill feelings toward her about the breakup. To him Carson was a big boy and could handle his own issues and not have them impact the professional relationship she had with the hotel chain. He let her know that she was doing a great job and he wanted her to continue to run his human resources division and he was thinking of adding a few more of the hotels under her management because that's how much he appreciated the hard work she did for them.

Now, having her back, sitting across from him, he couldn't help, but think of the possibilities they could have. He didn't want to rush into anything too quickly for her. He would wait as long as she needed and when she was, he wanted to be the person she gave her next chance at love to.

Gavin looked at Phoenix as she checked out the

menu. He loved that she was no longer on edge or thinking about negative things, but could finally enjoy just doing her.

"You seem happier now that you're back home," he said.

Phoenix looked over at him and smiled.

"I am extremely happy and ready to get back to my life. I can't tell you how exposed and vulnerable I felt when I left for Paris. I felt like everything in my life was up in the air and would crash and burn any minute. It didn't and I survived and now I'm looking ahead to what life has to offer me now."

He hoped that included him.

"Well, I'm glad you're back and I hope there is room in your life for me."

Phoenix thought back to that heated kiss and knew that it did.

"I could tell and I have no doubt you could tell how happy I was to see you too and there is plenty of room for you. I have a space in my life that's yours alone."

"No doubt at all?" he asked never breaking the stare. The connection between them was off the charts.

"None," she said without hesitating.

Phoenix looked away first. She had to because any minute, she thought she would burst into flames his piercing eyes were so magnetic. It was like looking into an ocean of waves that drew her in to where she wanted to hop in and let the waves take her away. She needed a new subject before she suggested they skip dinner.

"What's the latest on your game? Are you expecting

a launch soon?"

"It's coming along good, but I don't expect a launch for almost a year. There is a lot of testing that'll start in a few months and if that goes well, we're on schedule to launch around this time next year."

"I didn't know it took that long to get a new game developed and out."

"It does for me because I only want to put out the best product and I have some of the best games around the world as part of my test market. They can make or break a game launch so I give them time to play it and give feedback on the experience."

"Are you thinking of returning to the company after your book is out?"

"Not on your life. I didn't realize I could be this happy walking away from that crazy life. It'll always be my company and I'll always sit on the board, but Ellis likes running things and I like him at the top. I still keep a close eye on everything, but he runs the day to day and does a great job. I'm thinking of getting in the music business and that was inspired entirely by you."

To say she was shocked was an understatement.

"Really?"

"Yes, really. I like new ventures and Bingo, that producer I was telling you about, and I are thinking of collaborating on something big and depending on what you decide to do as far as music, you may be our first artist."

"Oh, my that's exciting. You go for the things you want in life don't you?"

"Yes, I do."

Gavin said those words with so much zest, he wanted her to know that the thought extended to her because he wanted her.

"You're really serious about this aren't you? You think I could really be a singer?"

"You're already a singer. Now, you just have to take the next step. I see great things for you and after working with Bingo on the game, I think I want to dive into the business. I've been meeting with him regularly and I'm thinking of partnering with him and getting some fresh faces on the music circuit. I didn't think about that until I met you and heard you sing."

"You are a jack of all trades, huh? I like that. You're always open to new and exciting things."

"I am and now the question is, are you?"

She hadn't thought a lot about it, but now hearing that Gavin would be a part of paving the way and helping her with everything, maybe she was ready.

"I admit I haven't thought a whole lot about it, but I trust you and I know that I wouldn't have to worry about the unknown. Your success alone leaves me with no doubt that you'll hold my hand along the way."

"Yes, I will. If you're open to it, I want to set up a meeting with you and Bingo and let him hear you sing."

"I'm ready whenever you are."

"Sounds like a plan. Now, let's talk business another time because right now I want to talk about you and me."

Phoenix was nervous.

"Okay," she said giving him her full attention. The waiter walked up at that very moment to take their order. After placing it, they turned back to what was next for them.

"What would you say if I considered this an actual date between us?" he asked.

"I'd say I'm happy about that."

"Are you sure?"

"I haven't been surer of anything as I am about that. I think we both know something changed between us while I was away and I've thought about nothing, but getting back home to see if that connection was because I was away and not across the hall."

"The connection started for me before that, but respectfully I kept my distance. I don't plan to do that anymore and we can go at whatever pace works for you. I've been attracted to you for a long time now, pretty much since we met and unless you tell me you're not interested, I don't intend to let you get away from me."

"Trust me, I'm not going anywhere that doesn't include you and me," she admitted.

After the waiter brought their meals and they were halfway through eating, the band for the night took to the stage and several couples got up to dance. Gavin didn't want to miss an opportunity to hold her in his arms again.

"Would you like to dance?" he asked.

"Yes."

After getting up to come around to escort her to the dance floor, Phoenix was in heaven the moment Gavin pulled her into his embrace and they swayed to the slow jazz music. The lighting of the restaurant was low with just enough lighting for them to make out each other's faces.

"Have I told you today how incredibly beautiful you are?" he said, leaning down to whisper in her ear.

That small, innocent act made her quiver. His voice was deep and seductive and made her think of all kinds of wild, crazy things that involved them being naked.

"Yes and I appreciate it every time you do."

Phoenix leaned into his chest and closed her eyes as they swayed to the music. She didn't know if he realized it or not, but she felt his fingers as they made small circles across her back as he held her. As they moved in rhythmic perfection together, Gavin began humming to the music and the only thing that existed in the world for her right now was him and her.

"You feel incredible in my arms and I'm hoping this song plays all night, so that I can continue to hold you like this."

Phoenix lifted her head and looked into his dark eyes filled with so much promise for them. The sexual energy between them was unhurried, but real and enveloped them in a heated lust. She didn't move away when his head leaned down toward hers, knowing he wanted another taste of her lips. She bit her lower lip in anticipation and when he lowered his head all the way down to her mouth, she leaned up and took the assault full on. The kiss started out slow and sexy and then turned heated, blazing a hot trail that traveled her bloodstream, firing embers of explosive sensations. When he pulled up, she saw a raw hunger in his eyes that told of the depth of his longing for her.

"I think I'm already addicted to kissing you," he whispered while placing smaller, sexy kisses to her thoroughly kiss lips.

"It's the one kind of addiction I'm in full support of," she said as she laid her head back on his chest. She needed a moment to get her body back in check. This was the kind of feeling she'd longed for feeling when she was in the arms of a man and Gavin was all that.

"I want to be sure around me you know what I'm thinking and how I'm feeling about you. This isn't a beginning as much as it is a continuation of what I've been thinking and feeling about you for a while. I hope that's okay."

"It's more than okay," she said, moving in a little closer so that their bodies looked like they were one person. She loved being this close to him, hearing his heart beat and feeling his body sway with her to the soft music.

Phoenix laid her head on his chest, closed her eyes and relished in the feeling that if she had any doubt about being with Gavin, it was completely washed away the minute he kissed her. She couldn't wait to see where things between them would go.

Chapter 17

"I had a great time at dinner," Phoenix said on the ride back home.

They ate, danced and talked until they looked around and most of the guests had already gone. Once the band finished, the restaurant had put on slow jazz music and they continued dancing, neither wanting to let go of the other. They decided to call it a night when they noticed the staff looking at them strange because they wanted to go home. Even though they stayed late, the staff welcomed them back anytime, especially after seeing the extremely large tip Gavin had left for all of them. There were grins from all of them as they left. Gavin was some man, she thought.

She'd never felt so raw and animalistic as she has been feeling since Gavin kissed her crazy. That kiss at her place had been on her mind while they ate and combined with the one he planted on her while they danced, she knew every kiss would be as powerful. Several times while dancing, his lips searched out for hers and she was ready each and every time to take what he offered. She wondered if he was the type of man who liked for women to be open about her wants and desires. That had never been her, but with Gavin, she was ready to spill her deepest secrets and desires.

"I'm glad. To me, it was a perfect evening and topped off my busy trip home and back. The highlight was seeing you when you opened the door. I dropped my luggage off and took the quickest shower in the history of the world because I wanted to get to you."

"You must be exhausted after the long flight and no sleep."

"I am, but I wanted to see you and we both had to eat."

Phoenix smiled over at him and leaned back in the soft leather seating of his car and closed her eyes. This day couldn't get more perfect, she thought. What could have been an uncomfortable coming together had been made easy when he took the first step and kissed her to let her know just how much he'd missed her. She left for Paris with them being friends and had returned ready for more.

"You could probably use extra rest after that time difference of being back from Paris."

"I do, but like you, I was anxious to see you and I can sleep anytime. I have a week before I'm due back at work."

Her eyes opened the moment she felt his hand reach

down and cover hers. Without thinking, she linked her fingers with his and they rode like that all the way home.

The elevator ride up was intense. Gavin stood on one side never taking his eyes off of her and Phoenix stood on the other trying to use her mind to tell him how much she wanted him to pull her to him and kiss her like he did earlier. How did women do it, she thought. She wanted to scream and beg for him to please kiss her again. The words were on the tip of her tongue, but nothing came out. When the door opened, he waited until she exited first and then he followed her out, still no conversation happened.

They reached her door and she turned to him.

"Thanks again for dinner."

"It was my pleasure."

To Phoenix the words rolled off of his tongue with so much erotic undertone that her body shivered. There was something about that voice that sounded familiar and made her think of hearing it in her ear while they made passionate love.

"I'll talk to you tomorrow?" she said trying to prolong their time together.

"Of course. I'll be right across the hall. All you have to do is knock," he said, still staring at her like he wanted to devour her.

Before she could think of what was next, she felt herself being pulled into his embrace and saw his lips search out hers. She instinctively opened for him as if she'd been kissing him all of her life. The kiss was sweet and when he deepened it, she returned the mating ritual with as much fervor as he poured on her. When he pulled up, she could see the willpower he possessed knowing how much they wanted each other, but he said he wanted to go at her pace and so she knew it would be her that would need to make the first move to something more than a kiss.

"Those lips are going to consistently be my undoing," Gavin said.

"I enjoy you," she said.

"And I you. Until tomorrow?" he said.

Phoenix didn't speak, but nodded her head as she reached for her keys and unlocked her door.

Gavin went to his door and looked at her one last time with a heated gaze that turned her into a puddle of mush before they each went inside their respective apartments and shut the door.

Gavin had walked two steps when he heard a quiet knock on his door. He turned back thinking something was wrong because it could only be Phoenix and when he opened the door and she was fine, he exhaled.

"Are you okay?" he asked since the last he'd seen her she had gone into her place and locked the door.

"I'm doing fine, but I could be doing better."

Phoenix was breathless. She'd never been bold and brazen, but with Gavin, it felt second nature to be this way. She had been in her apartment for a few minutes when she realized she didn't want the night to end and she wanted him. If it was going to take her making the first move to let him know that she was ready, then she was more than ready to do that. She threw caution to the wind, exited her apartment and went across the hall to his.

Gavin looked at her with a confused look.

"How could you be doing better?" he asked.

No hesitation, Phoenix said to herself.

"I could be doing better if you invite me in and make love to me."

Who said that, she thought. She was surprising herself.

There she said it. For the first time in her life, she opened her mouth and told a man exactly what she wanted.

Gavin didn't give her a chance to say another word. He pulled her to him, pushed the door closed behind her and locked it while moving her back a few steps until her back was against the door.

"Are you sure?" he asked. "Are you ready for that step with me?"

"Yes," Phoenix said on a whisper.

"This is big for us and there's no turning back. When I say that I mean this isn't something casual or something to scratch an itch. I want more than something casual with you. Making love with me tonight means commitment and no regrets in the morning. Are you read for that?"

"I'm ready for it all. I've been thinking of nothing but you and me and I want this between you and me more than anything. I've been fighting this feeling and I know you have, too. There is no need for either of us to continue denying what I know we both feel. I've never told a man I wanted him to make love to me before. I've never said much about my wants, but with you I want to give my all and that begins with being open and honest."

Gavin didn't speak, at least not with words. He pressed forward against her so that she could feel how ready he was for her. He'd discovered that he was always in some state of arousal whenever she was around and now, tonight, he was about to burst through his zipper with want for her.

He kept his eyes open as he kissed her sweetly, nipping at her lips, first the top and then the bottom. Phoenix reached for him and he felt her move her hands across his chest trying to get in. He made it easy for her by reaching down and pulling his shirt up and over his head leaving his chest bare for her to touch. The emptiness he felt when he had to pull away from her lips to remove his shirt had him quickly capturing her lips again.

Phoenix new she had to have died and gone to heaven the moment Gavin removed his shirt and gave her access to his muscled pecks. The feel of him hard and powerful under her hands was magical. Taking the step to go for what she wanted, she didn't stop her hands as they moved further down his chest to his flat stomach until her hand rested on the buckle of the belt in his jeans. She moved quickly to remove it and then unsnapped the button before reaching for his zipper. When Gavin breathed hard into her opened mouth, she knew he enjoyed her aggressiveness, a new action for her. What she saw standing in front of her was the sexiest specimen of a man she'd ever seen and for the moment, he was all about her, wanting her, loving her since his gaze spoke volumes.

"Baby, we need a bed," he whispered against her now very kissed, puffy lips.

Phoenix didn't speak, but nodded her agreement and when Gavin reached down to pick her up, she went into his arms and wrapped her legs around his taut waist.

Gavin walked with her in his arms straight to his bedroom and when he encountered the mattress at his knees, he slowly lowered her to it and followed her down.

She closed her eyes as he lavished her face, neck and exposed chest area with light kisses sending her desire for him higher and higher. She felt him painstakingly slow opening the buttons to her blouse. When he reached the last and the sides fell open, the stir crazy look on his face told her everything she needed to know about his desire for her. She helped him remove the shirt and with nervous fingers, she helped her remove her pants. As he slid them down her legs, removing them along with her heels, he licked a path all the way down to her feet and back up her bare legs, stopping at the apex of her thighs.

Gavin couldn't believe he had Phoenix in his bed. Thankfully he'd always left a light on and they weren't in total darkness. He wouldn't miss a chance to see her in all of her glory. As he moved up her body, he inhaled her essence deeply, soaking up and taking in her scent making sure it would be forever imprinted on him. He stood briefly and removed his pants and stood before her in nothing but black boxer briefs which showed the impression of his massive erection.

Phoenix looked at Gavin standing in front of her with his hardness at attention and ready to please her.

"I know this is a very bad timing to bring this up, but are you sure?" he asked, giving her an out even though they were nearly naked. He didn't mind a cold shower if it meant not moving faster than she wanted.

Phoenix knew the time for talking had passed as she reached up and unclasped the front closure of her bra and let it fall away, leaving her open to his gaze. The heated passion she saw looking back at her was almost more than she could bare. Her body felt like it was about to explode before they'd gotten to the good part.

He needed no other words as he leaned down and sucked one nipple into his mouth and using his hands to test the weight of the heavy mounds. Phoenix moaned as he moved between the two large globes kissing and licking his way across her chest, giving each equal attention. He moved them higher on his bed and joined her as he reached over into his nightstand to withdraw the protection they would eventually need. He had other things in mind and his first dealt with moving back down her body, never taking his eyes from hers.

Phoenix knew what was next and she held her

CHERYL BARTON

breath as he spread her legs and moved his head between them. She closed her eyes the minute she felt his hairy chin caress her thighs.

"No, don't close your eyes. Look at me. I want you to know it's me that's giving you want you want and need. Watch me love you and never forget this feeling," Gavin said.

Phoenix opened her eyes and as soon as she did, she thought back to the dreams of her faceless lover. Night after night he brought her to the brink, yet she never knew who the man of her dreams was. When Gavin slid her lace panties down her legs and to the floor, he moved down and lowered his head, passing his tongue over her hooded nub, her hips rose to meet him as moan after moan escaped her lips. Her hips moved of their own accord as she reached her hands down and gripped his shoulders. He felt familiar though she knew he should not have.

Her body felt like it was climbing a mountain that had no top. She rose and rose and her mind went wild as he gave her everything she needed. He had a masterful tongue and the feeling was a new experience for her.

Gavin opened her wider for him draping her legs over his shoulders. His tongued teased her, claimed her, possessed her and with an ardent plea, she spoke her desire.

"Please, please," she begged.

"Please what baby? Tell me what you need? Does this feel good," Gavin said as he took another swipe with his tongue.

"Yes," Phoenix uttered.

"What about this?" he said adding a little sucking motion to the swipe.

"Oh, yes!" she moaned a little louder. "What are you doing to me? More, more!" she screamed as her body rose again and this time a wave overtook her and she crashed as her orgasm slammed through her. She felt her head tossing from side to side as she held on to Gavin's massive shoulders while his mouth locked on to her, not letting up. His mouth rode her until the motion of her hips slowed. Her sex exploded with such magnitude that she thought she'd smother him with her thighs.

She kept her eyes on him as he watched her come apart in his arms.

"Better baby?" he asked and Phoenix felt her body rising again. He said the word better and she knew, he was the man from her dreams. He was her faceless lover though she didn't know it back then and the thought sent her quickly over the edge again as Gavin continued to feast on her until her body finally did calm and she fell back onto the plush mattress.

"You are so beautiful. I don't think I will ever tire of declaring that. My thoughts of being with you are no comparison to having you here with me in my bed. Are you ready for me?" he asked with a husky voice.

"Yes," she said softly.

Gavin reached for the protection and once he'd removed his shorts, he slid the protection in place before rejoining her on the bed and climbing between her welcoming thighs.

"I love watching you come apart in my arms. I can tell your release flows through your entire body and I want to be sure each and every time, you get any and everything you need from me. Your pleasure is my pleasure," he said before kissing her. He used his hands to spread her thighs wide and after bracing them with his elbows, he placed his hard as steel shaft at her entrance and used the wetness he found there to ease into her body, slowly at first. With his size and her small frame, he went slow, giving her body a chance to get accustomed to how thick and long he was.

He kissed her moan right into his mouth as he withdrew and then went in slowly again. He watched her face for any sign of pain and when he saw only the glow of a woman in the throes of passion, he went in to the hilt giving her all of him. He loved her slow at first until the pressure built up and he felt his body calling for him to increase the pace. Phoenix matched him stroke for stroke as she rose her hips from the mattress to meet every one of his downward thrusts.

"You feel incredible," he whispered with a controlled strain to his voice.

"I love how you feel. I love how you make me feel," she said with a wild abandonment she didn't know she possessed. She wanted him and as she opened her eyes and took him into her heart while receiving him into her body, she knew this was where she was meant to be.

They rode higher and higher together as the pace of their lovemaking increased faster and faster. Gavin was giving her everything he had and he had the sweat that was gathering on his brow to prove it. Phoenix wiped the moisture away that had beaded up across his forehead while he put in work to make sure she was satisfied and satisfied she was. Without warning, her body spun out of control as she surged higher and higher bringing Gavin with her. Pressure was building in the area between her legs where his body was intimately connected to hers. She felt him all over her. There wasn't a part of her body that wasn't reacting to him.

They were together. Gavin felt her body's reaction to him and they were reaching the precipice of a powerful release together. He rode her as she swirled her hips to match his strokes. The minute her body climaxed, he gave her everything to make it more pleasurable. Her screams elicited something in him as he joined her in an orgasm that stole his ability to breathe. In what sounded like a guttural growl, he poured out his release as his body shuddered over and over with the raw mating of their bodies. He held on to her luscious hips until his body calmed and he collapsed over her making sure to not place the weight of his body on her. He hoped he'd be able to breathe and move soon because never had he experienced an orgasm that powerful. He knew it would be with Phoenix and only with her. He soothed her body with caresses as he noticed her body trying to return to normal after a powerful experience.

Bodies spent and drained, Gavin placed soft kisses across her sweat covered body before rolling to the side and pulling her along with him. He reached for the blanket to cover them, pulled her into his embrace and knew no words were needed. What they had just experienced, neither one of them could have predicted it would be as powerful as it was. She was his now and he knew it would always be like that between them. They were meant to be and this was the beginning of the love he looked forward to sharing with her. He hoped she was ready for everything that came with being involved with him. He planned on showing her the way she should be treated and loved. He pulled her as close as he could get and together, they fell into a slumber.

Chapter 18

Gavin woke and knew he was the first to do so. He could hear Phoenix as she slept, snoring lightly and the sound was music to his ears. He was delighted to know that he had not dreamt their night together because if he had, he'd be full of disappointment.

Their night of making love had not been planned and though he knew they should have waited before taking such a step, the passion between them had been building for some time and they spent the entire night fueling that passion over and over again.

After the first time, they fallen asleep and when he work an hour later, he wanted her again and she was ready, coming into his arms as the feelings stirred in their bodies. Sometime before the sun had come up, he rolled toward her again and once again, she opened her body to him, loving him and letting him love her.

He should be as tired and exhausted as Phoenix was,

but the moment he sensed it was morning, he woke to make sure she was with him in his bed.

He let her sleep while he got up and went into the bathroom that wasn't in his room and showered so that he wouldn't wake her. After slipping on a pair of jeans, he headed for the kitchen to brew some coffee and find the makings for breakfast whenever she did wake up.

As he cooked, his thoughts drifted to what Phoenix's reaction would be when she woke up to the light of day and realized that they'd slept together. Even though their coming together throughout the night had been hot and passion-filled, he wondered if she would second guess the decision in the light of day. As far as he was concerned, nothing had changed except for the fact that they'd shared an intimacy that had been building up.

He wiped his hands on his jeans and walked back to his bedroom to see if Phoenix had woken up. When he entered the bedroom, she turned and smiled at him and any reservations he thought she might wake up with disappeared.

Phoenix heard Gavin the moment he'd entered the bedroom. She had been woke for a few minutes trying to gather her thoughts. Images of the two of them, lips locked, bodies locked pleasuring each other throughout the night flooded her mind. She'd never had such an amorous night of lovemaking in her life. Gavin was an incredible lover and because she had already been falling for him, she knew he was a wonderful man. She wondered if he found regret now that it was the next day. Was he waiting for her to leave? She didn't know what to do, but she wouldn't shy away from the fact that what happened between them was one of the best nights of her life. He made her feel things she'd never felt in bed before.

Gavin had brought the tigress in her out and now that she knew she could be so free sexually, she never wanted to hold back ever again and hoped that their first night wasn't going to be their last. He'd told her that he'd wanted her for a while, but he wanted more than just getting her naked. It was now or never, she thought as she looked up at him standing in the doorway. She pulled the covers up around her naked breasts remembering she was naked under the covers.

"Good morning beautiful," Gavin said taking in her early morning beauty.

"Good morning."

"How did you sleep?"

Phoenix hadn't slept that good in a minute.

"Your bed is incredible. I slept very well."

"Was it just as incredible when I was in it with you?" he asked, digging to see where her head was. He wanted no regrets.

Phoenix felt her body heat up thinking of him being in bed with her. She looked at him standing in the doorway, leaning against the frame with his legs crossed at the ankles. He looked delicious in jeans that rode low on his hips, shirtless and shoeless. The man should be labeled as detrimental to any woman's health. His sex appeal was lethal!

"It would be if you came back in and joined me."

Gavin walked over to her, leaned down and took her mouth in a kiss that showed how badly he wanted to crawl back in bed with her. He pulled the blanket from her hand, removed his jeans and joined her between the sheets. He would never miss an opportunity to love her.

**

After showering, Phoenix slipped on the t-shirt Gavin had set out for her to put on. She could run across the hall and gather up some clothes to put on, but she liked the feeling of walking around in his t-shirt. Once she had the shirt on, she laughed when it went past her knees. He was a giant compared to her small stature since she stood at five foot seven to his height which she knew was well over six feet.

She walked out of the bedroom to join him in the kitchen to see if she could help, only to find that he was done and had set a place for them to eat. She saw omelets, her favorite, fresh fruit and muffins and she was starving.

"This looks delicious. Don't tell me you cook too?"

"I love to cook. For years I didn't have to cook my own meals, but I've always enjoyed cooking. It just so happens, you're catching me at a time of cooking where breakfast meals are my specialty. Breakfast is also my favorite meal of the day."

"Mine too," Phoenix admitted.

"Well, have a seat and let a brother feed you," he said excited.

"Smells wonderful," she said admiring his handy work.

"You look wonderful, especially in my shirt. I'm trying to focus on getting this all set up, but I can't stop thinking about what you may or may not have on under it.

Phoenix felt the heat rise in her cheeks at the thought that she was wearing nothing under the shirt and hoped he wanted to explore to find out for himself. The magnitude of the thought of making love with him again had her mind crazy with want. She'd never had sex as many times in a short period of time as she had with Gavin and she surprised herself that every time, she wanted him more and more. She saw the look in his eyes and knew what he wanted. Eventually, she guessed they would actually get to a meal.

"Well, I'll never tell. I guess you'll have to keep wondering or come find out for yourself."

Before she could say another word, knowing Gavin was a man to act on whatever he was thinking especially if challenged, she laughed lightly when he came around to her side of the counter, turned her chair around and ran his hands up her legs, causing a hitch to catch in her throat at the intimacy in his touch and the intensity in his look.

While he used his hands to explore her body, Gavin leaned down and kissed first one corner of her mouth letting his hot, minty breath cascade across her cheek. After kissing the corner, he used his tongue to travel across the seam of her closed lips to the other side where he placed another soft kiss before covering her lips with his, using his tongue to beg for entrance into her mouth. The moment she felt his tongue touch and mate with hers, she felt his hand slide up her inner thigh until a finger slipped between her sweet folds. Phoenix opened her legs so that he could have easy access to that spot he wanted the most. The moment his finger enter her, first one and then two, she felt her essence coat his fingers as her breath quickened and her hips began a twirl around his probing fingers.

"Mmm, I thought we were eating breakfast," she was able to get out between kisses.

"Breakfast is good any time of the day. Right now, I want to feast on you."

When his fingers began moving around, in and out of her taking her mind completely off of breakfast and placing it on how his fingers were making her feel, she moaned lightly as her head dropped back giving him access to her neck. She reached up and held on to the back of his head as he place open mouth kisses across her neck. She felt lightheaded as she gave herself over to him with a reckless wanton feeling that left her feeling dizzy in a sexy, hazy way.

Gavin gave into the need to have her without waiting a minute longer. He picked Phoenix up from the stool and carried her over to the large brown leather sectional and was about to sit down when he remembered he left protection in the bedroom.

"I'm going to lay you here on the chair while I go get protection, but don't you dare move."

"Let me," she said softly. "Where is it?"

"My nightstand."

Phoenix was like a flash of light leaving him. She wanted him inside of her as much as he wanted to be there. While she was gone, he divested himself of his jeans which were cutting off his circulation he was so hard. He carefully pulled the zipper down and removed them before grabbing a towel from the basket of clothes that sat on the floor that his assistant had left there the day before. Placing it under him, he sat down just as she returned.

When Phoenix had protection in hand and entered the room, she found Gavin casually sitting on the leather sofa with one arm across the back of the chair and the other in his lap stroking his long, thick, powerful erection. He was clearly waiting and ready for her. She walked over, ripped the package open and when he reached for it, she pulled her hand back. Covering his massive hardness was a task she couldn't wait to do.

"Let me," she said straddling his lap and placing the condom over his hard as steel flesh. She kept her eyes on him as she slowly rolled it in place watching the show of emotion on his face as he fought to remain patient.

"You're trying to kill me," he said through gritted teeth.

"Oh, I'm dying right along with you," she said.

Rolling the condom on, she stroked him up and down loving the feeling of his hot flesh in her hands.

Gavin reached forward and pulled the shirt up and over Phoenix's head as her breast stared back at him. Without pretense, he leaned forward and took one nipple into his mouth as he gave attention to the pebbled tip. Not leaving out the other, he moved his head to the other side and sucked in the other nipple, nipping on it slightly causing Phoenix to squirm on his lap. He kissed his way up her chest to her lips.

"Are you ready for me?" he asked as he tweaked both of her nipples between his fingers while his shaft stood strong and hard between them, fully covered and ready to take them higher. He reached between her legs and feeling how wet and ready she was for him, he didn't want to wait another second and apparently Phoenix was thinking the same thing.

She answered him by raising up on her knees, positioning him at her entrance and sliding down over his heated flesh. The rush of heat that overtook them both stole any thought in her head away that didn't focus on him and his hot flesh sliding deep in her, stretching her walls to take him in. She could feel the swell of his manhood growing even longer, thicker and harder as he moved his hands to her hips to raise and lower her while he used his hips to slowly pump up into her. His movements, so methodically slow were driving her mad. Though Gavin guided her hips, she added her own level of grind to the action as she quickened her movements to increase the pace.

"Yes," she uttered.

"It's all you baby. Take what you need," he groaned

out.

Gavin rolled his hips as Phoenix moved faster and faster chasing her release and taking him along with her.

Phoenix tried to stifle her moan, but the intensity of his thrusts up into her was more than she could hold on to.

Between his thrusts up and her forceful strokes down, Phoenix felt her orgasm building and the moment she crashed, she bounced up and down on his lap knowing that if he hadn't been holding onto her hips, she would have bounced off of his lap to the floor.

Gavin held onto Phoenix while she was in the throes of her release at the pinnacle of ecstasy. Her orgasm triggered his as he threw back his head and growled out his release so powerful that he was temporarily blinded. He closed his eyes and focused only the feel of her heated warmth surrounding him in her body. Together they rode the wave of frenzy until they collapsed into each other, sitting in that position until their breathing returned to normal.

"Now that was better than any breakfast we could ever partake in," Gavin said the minute his mind cleared up enough for him to focus on getting words out of his mouth.

"I don't think I can move even one muscle," Phoenix declared.

"Baby, you don't have to go anywhere. I love the feeling of you just like this."

All thoughts of eating a real breakfast dissipated as

Phoenix slumped onto his shoulder while he cradled her body close to his.

"You're mine Phoenix and I never want to be anyplace other than with you and inside of you. I love you," he declared before he realized what he was saying.

"I love you too, Gavin."

Phoenix pulled back so that they were looking at each other. She wanted him to see the love she had for him and not just hear it.

"Are you sure this isn't too much for you right now? I don't want to scare you with my feelings for you so soon after," he said.

He didn't want to elaborate on what that meant, not inviting the idea of anyone else into their moment. He wanted their time to be about them only.

"Falling in love with you could never happen too soon and I'm walking into that love with a clear head and of course a satisfied body."

"I couldn't ask for more than that."

His stomach growled at that exact moment and they both fell into a fit of laughter.

"Well, I guess you could ask for something more, like some sustenance?" she asked, still laughing.

"Okay, maybe I could ask for one more thing," he said and then kissed her again.

Chapter 19

"Phoenix, you are a star girl! I don't know where you've been hiding this talent, but I'm glad you brought it here. That was a test first take and I thought we'd do a couple of those, but I think you're ready to record this. Let's do this!" Bingo said.

"With a super producer like you, a girl can't go wrong. Thanks for helping me bring my music to life," Phoenix said to Bingo.

They were in the recording studio finishing up the final song for her new CD release. No one would have ever been able to convince her to do this except for Gavin and her sister. Reese had been behind her the entire time, pushing her to stick with her decision to quit her job at the hotel and focus on her music career only after Gavin had put together a showcase for her to let a large crowd of people hear her sing for the first time. She was a hit from the first word of the first song.

Her night had almost been ruined by the sudden appearance of Carson in the audience. He tried to get close to talk to her, but his attempt was blocked by Gavin and the security he'd hired which was led by Wallace, an ex-football linebacker. No one messed with him or got by him. She'd told Gavin that Carson had tried to reach her a few times at the hotel and it wasn't until she finally told him that she was seeing someone that he stopped trying to connect to get her back. She had no plans of going back to an unhappy place in her life especially when she was at her happiest.

His showing up at her showcase was a surprise. She had no doubt that seeing her with Gavin, he knew any thoughts he had of them getting back together were over. Ever since that first night that they'd made love five months ago, that had sealed their fate and they were happily in love.

Now that he was helping her chase her dream of being a singer, they had released a single and it immediately went platinum. From there, Bingo and Gavin had her back in the studio to record a full CD.

Reese sat on the other side of the glass enclosure cheering her on and making eyes at Bingo who seemed to be eating up the extra attention Reese was giving him. She wasn't surprised, but shook her head at Reese anyway. There was never a dull moment when she was around.

Phoenix put her headset back on and gave the thumbs up that she was ready. She turned around to get one quick sip of her water and when she turned back to the microphone, Gavin was walking through the door. She didn't think he would make it because he had a big meeting about the release of his book, though he said he would try.

Gavin was a busy man and she knew he had a deadline he had to meet for getting the final draft of his book to his manager. She didn't want to disturb him by reminding him of her recording session which is why she scheduled it right after leaving the hotel on her last day of work. Reese and Wallace had accompanied her just in case Carson decided to show up, which he didn't. His father had pretty much told him to stay away from the hotels since there were no plans in the immediate future for him to be involved in the business.

Their love had grown more and more each day and now she couldn't think back to a time when they weren't in love. She now knew what real love was like and what she'd been missing out on not being with the better man for her.

After several discussions about a musical career, she decided to take the leap and jump in not knowing if people would accept her or not. After that first listening session Gavin had put together, inquiries came in from every direction with the question of when she would release a full CD and Bingo had wasted no time writing and producing songs she knew were going to be a hit since he was a writing genius.

He and Gavin and collaborated to launch a music label right in Chicago, a mecca for new talent which now included her. She was happy he'd made it in time for the recording since this was a song that he hadn't heard. She decided to surprise him by co-writing the love ballad with Bingo and she did so with the love she felt for Gavin on her mind as she wrote and sang the words.

When he smiled at her, she waved at him frantically and blew a few kisses his way. She giggled like a little girl when he mouthed, 'hi baby' to her. Bingo played the track and she began to sing.

Gavin lit up the moment he realized he didn't recognize the song, but knew without a doubt that she was singing to him and about him. His love for her grew with each passing day. They had been on a rollercoaster of love since she returned from Paris. They spent their days staying focused on their business lives, but at night, that time was reserved for them to spend together either relaxing watching a movie or going out and getting involved in the Chicago night life.

A few months back, he was no longer able to hide his identity and he didn't mind one bit. He had to hire extra security for them so that they could be out and about and not be disturbed. For a hot minute, the media had a field day trying to figure out how he ended up connecting and falling in love with the woman who had walked away from Carson Stone. One story after another crept up and he and Phoenix agreed to not pay attention to any of it. They were in love and couldn't care what anyone thought about it.

He watched her sing and was mesmerized at how

natural singing came to her. He couldn't believe she waited so long to let her talent take her to the next level. He was more than happy to lend the love of his life a helping hand.

Going into business with Bingo had been a great business decision and they were waiting for the new office park he'd contracted to have built to be ready. They had signed on several new artists and couldn't wait to rival some of the largest record companies in the business and Phoenix was going to send them into the stratosphere with her talent. Her CD was going to be an instant hit, especially after the success of her single which they were able to get recorded and on the streets in two months. Money gets people moving, especially when you have as much of it as he did.

As the song ended, he and Reese clapped like they were at an actual concert. Phoenix removed her headphones after Bingo gave her the thumbs up and joined them.

"That was incredible. You were meant to sing," Gavin said lifting her up, kissing her and spinning her around.

"Oh, get a room," Reese said.

"Oh, stop being jealous of our happiness," Phoenix responded.

"You wish!" Reese shot back at her sister.

"I still can't get over the fact that you've been keeping all of this talent in and bottled up, not sharing it with the world," Gavin said.

"Thanks to you baby, I'm following a dream I never

thought I'd get the chance to do."

Gavin blocked out the fact that Bingo, his team and Reese were in the room as he planted what started out as a soft kiss on Phoenix's lips that then turned into an assault on her mouth. He loved the feel of her, the taste of her and her response every time he reached for her. Even now he wanted her, but had to remember where they were.

"Seriously dude, follow Reese's advice and get a room," Bingo said.

Gavin released her lips and they laughed at how easily they could block out everyone around them and focus only on their love and desire to get a taste of each other anytime, anyplace.

"I'm taking my love out of here if you're done?" Gavin asked linking his fingers with Phoenix's.

"Yeah, I'm done. She knocked that out the park with one take. Your woman is a natural."

Gavin knew that already.

"Tell me something I don't know," he said before heading out.

"Sis, I'll catch you later," Phoenix said to Reese.

"I'll be right here keeping Bingo company."

Phoenix shook her head as she followed Gavin out.

"I hope Bingo knows what he's getting into," she said to Gavin after they got on the elevator in the building which housed the temporary offices and studio of their record company until their office park was ready.

"Oh, believe me he knows and he's still running

toward it," he joked. "I think she actually likes him and not just for a quick roll in the hay. You told me that's her usual M.O."

"Yeah, I think you're right. She talks differently about him than I've heard her talk about other guys. It'll be interesting to see what happens with them next," she said as the elevator door opened to the top level where his office was.

"I'm more interested in seeing what's going to happen with us next."

Gavin opened his office door and after Phoenix entered and sat down, he locked the door behind them.

She knew that look. The one gazing back at her said that he didn't care that they were in his office, he wanted her naked. The moment she looked at him, her mind and body began preparing for the love she knew she was about to receive. She loved that he made sure they didn't confine their lovemaking to the bedroom. He was an adventurous lover and he'd brought out the adventurer in her. They made love in the car, in the elevator, on his plane and just about anywhere else their desire led them to not wait another minute before joining their bodies and living out their passion.

"I'm assuming dinner is about to wait?" she asked as she began unbuttoning her shirt, more than ready for him.

"Dinner and possibly breakfast tomorrow may have to wait. I've been thinking about you all day, hoping your last day at work was a good one and wondering how long I'd have to wait for you to finish at the studio before I took you back home to have you in my arms all night. We've been so busy lately, I feel like I'm neglecting you, something I never want to do," he admitted.

Phoenix needed to reassure him that they were in this together.

"Baby, I never, ever feel neglected, even when you're busy. I know who you are and what your day is like and the moment we do come together, it's always special, fun and most definitely hot. I miss you like crazy when we're apart, but I also know that at the end of the day, I get to feel you and love you and that's all that matters."

"I'm happy to hear that, but right now, I need you. I need to hear you moan out my name."

Gavin walked over and helped her remove her blouse and skirt and when she stood before him in high heels, a thong and bra that barely covered her full breasts, his desire for her skyrocketed. He reached for her, no longer wanting to talk. As soon as his lips touched hers, the fire that never seemed to burn out when they came together, burned hot. He drank from her lips like a man thirsty after walking through a desert. He lifted her up so that she could feel his need for her through his pants. He turned and walked with her in his arms.

"You know I bought this chaise lounge chair for my office because I love making love to you on the one in your place. I say we christen this one the right way," he said while lowering her to it.

As he removed his clothes, his mouth watered the

moment he watched Phoenix reach up to undo the snap that held her beautiful breasts in place, finally releasing them for his attentive eyes to behold and a beautiful sight they were.

"I love you, baby," he said, removing his own clothes in order to join her on the chair.

"I love you too and I hope no one comes looking for us, trying to get in this office."

"I wouldn't recommend it if they don't want an eyeful because I'm about to make love to the woman who makes every day worth getting up for."

After removing his own clothes, the only piece of clothing he had left to remove were his boxer briefs which were now barely containing his hardened shaft. The tip of his flesh peaked out over the top of the band around his waist and before he could slide them down, Phoenix reached out and ran her finger across the slippery slit in the top of the full mushroomed head of him. Gavin sucked in a breath as she took the essence of him that had already seeped out and spread it around the head. The touch of her hand on him was about to end things before they were able to get started.

Phoenix began to stroke him through the thin layer of his briefs watching as his veiny member throbbed under her touch. She leaned forward and placed soft kisses around his navel following a thin trail of hair that led to his member. When her chin graced him lightly, she felt Gavin shiver and knew that he was already close. She snaked her tongue out and with her eyes locked on his, she licked around the wide head loving the soft, but rugged feel of him on her tongue. They loved tasting each other and it had become one of her favorite things to do to bring him pleasure.

She was about to pull her briefs down and take him fully in, as she loved to do often when he stopped her.

"You know I love having your mouth on me, but if you do that, this will be over before I can get in you and you know that's where I want and need to be right now. I say we save that for later and let me in."

Phoenix had no plans to fight what they both needed. She sunk her fingers into the waistband of his briefs and slid them down his powerful legs, tossing them to the side. She then leaned back as he joined her on the chair and lifted her hips so that he could pull her thong down her legs. After he tossed them on the floor, she spread her legs wide welcoming him into her warmth.

Gavin laced their fingers together as he took her mouth at the exact moment that he entered her body, thrusting all the way in on his first push causing them both to cry out with pleasure.

"Hold on tight baby because this is going to be a very bumpy ride," he said.

Phoenix dueled with his tongue while she gripped his shoulders to heed his advice. With each forceful, tantalizing push into her body, she lifted her hips to meet him thrust for thrust, grind for grind. He gave her what she always wanted and needed from him, never missing an opportunity to provide her with copious amounts of love and attention, always taking her to heights she'd never known before. Her body screamed at the perfection of his lovemaking which left her mind dazed with lust

Gavin was in pure animalistic mode as his heart pounded matching the pace of his surges into her body. He grunted uncontrollably loving the feel of her walls pulling him in and holding him with a grip that left his body trembling. They rocked into each other, until the pressure built as they loved with enthusiasm that only two lovers who were familiar with each other's wants could experience.

Before too long, Phoenix felt her body quake as she went over the edge, experiencing an orgasm that had her softly screaming his name. She wanted to shout, but had to remember where they were. She let go as the intensity of her orgasm shattered her very being. Her orgasm triggered one in Gavin as he poured himself into her body and his love flowed from his heart to hers.

Gavin's body tried to calm from the powerful orgasm, but it took longer than he expected. Ripples of it continued to flow through him and he continued moving in and out of Phoenix's body, never wanting to extricate himself. He tried to move to take his weight off of her, but she held him close. He knew that after lovemaking, she loved staying connected to him intimately and holding him close. In her arms is where he had yearned to be and never missed a chance to stay there.

They were both encased in a post-coital haze as their

breathing returned to normal and the sweat that covered their bodies was cooling off and causing a chill.

"This good loving is going to kill a brother, you know that right?" he said laughing and turning over so that he was on the bottom and Phoenix lay sprawled across him. He ran his hands up and down her body loving the feel of her rounded curves.

"We are in that kill-zone together then because my body isn't ready to even entertain moving a muscle.

Gavin held her until he felt her go limp in his arms surpassing being exhausted.

"We can't stay like this forever. Eventually we have to get up and get out of here. I know I couldn't wait to have you, but now I wish we were back at the loft where we wouldn't have to get up."

"I know me too, but the sooner we get up, the sooner we can get to the loft and find this exact same position."

"Okay, that's a deal only if we get to this position the same way we got to it this time," he chuckled, planting kisses across her face making sure to get a taste of her lips.

"Deal," she said, finally moving to first sit up and then stand up. "I'm going to go into the bathroom to clean up. Would you care to join me?" she said sheepishly as she stood and wiggled her behind at him.

"Now I know why I was happy when this office came with a bathroom in it. I have the best luck," he said.

"Well, you could get even luckier if you follow me."

Gavin jumped up so fast, he stumbled and they laughed.

"I guess that means I'm anxious."

"Anxious, I like."

Chapter 20

Phoenix combed her hair, fluffed it, lifted it, let it down and still couldn't get it to look the way she wanted. Tonight was perhaps the best night of her life, second only to the day she met the love of her life, Gavin. Tonight was going to be a magical night, not just for her, but for them and she wanted to look perfect.

Gavin walked up behind her and nuzzled her neck pulling her back, flush against his body. Phoenix went willingly into his embrace knowing that as long as she lived, she would never tire of being this close to him. For a few seconds, she didn't care what her hair looked like because she could only focus on him, the man who'd shown her what it meant to be loved unconditionally.

"Seriously Phoenix? I don't know why you didn't call in a stylist to get you ready for tonight. That would have been an easy phone call and we could have had the top person in the industry in here within hours."

She turned in his arms so that they were facing each other. She leaned up as close to his lips as she could get before she smiled, seeing that he was leaning down to meet her. Excitement shot through every limb in anticipation of the feeling she knew she'd get the moment their lips met. Before she could think about it or prepare for it, his lips captured hers and she exhaled knowing this is where she belonged, in the arms of a man who never failed to make her feel sexy, desirable and loved. No longer did she feel second to a man who only thought of himself first, second and third. She wished Carson no ill-will, but being in love with a man who really loved her and showed her every day was unmatched to anything else when it came to love.

Gavin reached down and wiped the smeared lipstick from Phoenix's lips and smiled at his handy work of smearing the bright red lipstick all over her lips knowing his lips probably looked exactly like hers.

"Now you'll have to reapply your lipstick and if you don't stop looking at me in that sexy way you always do, I may end up smearing the next application as well."

He leaned down and kissed her one last time before turning to head to the bathroom for something to wipe his lips.

"Oh, so that's what you do huh? You mess up my makeup and then exit to clean yourself up."

She smiled when seconds later he returned with a

towel to clean her face also. She had no doubt he would because he always thought about her and made sure she knew it.

"I never think of me without thinking of you," he said wiping her lips for her.

The action made her shiver knowing that if she could see her face as he wiped it, the small action of his wiping her lips would appear to be the most erotic scene she'd ever been in, second only to the many nights of lovemaking that never failed to satisfy her beyond her belief.

"I know that look in your eyes baby and if I had time, I'd remove that sexy ass dress you have on and get inside of you before you took your next breath, but tonight is about celebrating you and I wouldn't miss it for the world. This is what you've been planning for and dreaming about and I'm the happiest man in the world knowing that I get to share this night with the most beautiful woman in the world."

"Are you sure you're okay with this? I know how private you like to be. "

"Baby, nothing would be able to keep me away from being with you tonight and I don't care how any paparazzi are out and throwing questions at me from all corners of this earth. Tonight is your night and I want to show the world how proud I am of the woman I love."

"Can I admit that I'm a little nervous? Actually a lot nervous. I've never been the center of everyone's attention like I will be tonight."

"Baby, you be as nervous as you like here with me, but once we get out there, you make sure you own this night. This is the biggest night of the year for the music industry and never have they invited an artist who just released a CD to open up the show. Do you know how big this is? This is your first CD release and it has topped just about every chart from the highest grossing release from a new artist to topping the charts as the second female artist to ever release that many CDs in the first week of the release. It's only been out for three months and is setting record after record. You received nine nominations tonight including the best collaboration of the year with the hottest country singer in the world. Who would have thought a female R&B singer would make a hit record with the biggest country star? You know who thought that? I did because I know the talent you have. You've been hiding that for years."

Phoenix blushed.

"I've always been told I could sing and I've always loved singing, but who knew I could make it a career. If it wasn't for you, I never would have taken that leap and given it a try. I love you for having so much faith in me and for supporting me from the start."

"I love you Phoenix and I knew it the moment I met you and we said hello, but I couldn't claim it at that time."

"I knew it too, but that was some situation, huh?"

"It was."

"What would you have done if I'd gone through with marrying Carson?"

"Do you want the truth or do you want me to say the politically correct response?" he asked smiling.

She looked over at him as he leaned against the dresser in his finest navy blue tuxedo. No other man would ever look as good as he did in that tux with gray shirt and accessories. The man could wear a suit and she loved looking at him fully clothed or in nothing at all. It's the thought of him in nothing at all that had her heart racing. She wished they did have time for at least a quickie, but they had an awards show to get to. Tonight the world would be watching her.

"I want the truth," she said and waited.

"I've never told you this before, but I was going to be selfish for once in my life and I wasn't going to let you marry him without telling you I was in love with you. I know it would have been wrong because I've been hurt before by someone coming between me and my ex, but deep down, I knew I was the better man for you. It's not that I didn't think that you could make your own decision about who you wanted to be with, but I have never felt for any woman what I felt for you and I needed you like I needed my next breath. It wouldn't have been that way if Carson had been a better guy, but it practically killed me knowing how terrible he was treating you. I knew that if given the chance, I would always be the better man for you and you would never, ever regret giving me your love and your heart."

Phoenix walked over to him and looked him in the eyes.

"I have never regretted knowing and loving you. I

have never been as happy as I have been since we met. Even before we fell in love, I was happy every time I saw you or talked to you. At one time I knew I wanted you too, but I felt obligated to see things through with Carson because I believe in being faithful and giving it my all, but when I found out he didn't share the same values, it was over. It was actually over before that and I knew it, but I was going to give it all I had because I believe in commitment and honesty and I tried my best with him. It didn't work, not because I tried to sabotage it after meeting you. It didn't work because his heart wasn't in it either. I know he cared about me, but he wanted to marry me to prove to his family he could settle down and that he could do it with a woman who wasn't after his money or interested in running around from one club to the next and spending life together blowing through money. I understand that and I don't hate him because of it. I'm glad that we parted ways, though it wasn't under the best of terms."

"Well his loss is my gain and I haven't looked back since. So, now that you are rich, what's the one thing you want to do that you've never been able to do?"

Phoenix thought about it and knew what she wanted to do."

"After spending a few more months promoting the album, I want to take a month and go away to someplace with a beach, blue water and fruity drinks with cute little straws in them. I want to swim, dance and enjoy time away from the spotlight."

Phoenix turned away and walked back over to the

mirror to apply her lipstick.

Gavin moved away from the dresser and pulled a small red box from his pocket and walked up behind her, leaning down close to her ear.

"What do you say to doing all of that for our honeymoon?" he said, pulling the box around so that he held it in his palm in front of her.

He smiled seeing the look of shock and wonder on her face as she stopped moving. Since they were standing in front of the mirror, he looked into her face through the reflection and waited for her to look down. When she did, he heard her intake of breath when she realized what was happening. He watched as tears formed in her eyes before she even opened the box.

Gavin stepped back and turned her around to face him. Still taking in the look of amazement and confusion on her face, he did what he had been waiting to do for weeks. He went down on one knee while holding out the box and looked up at her as tears flowed down her face.

"Phoenix Allure Graham, I have loved you from the moment I met you. I shared my love for you with your parents, your sister and your brother and they told me if you'd have me, they wholeheartedly gave their approval. Will you do me the honor of being my wife? I love you baby and on this night, one of the biggest in your life and mine too, I want to seal our love with this," he said opening the box, showing her the fifteen carat, platinum princess cut, floating diamond engagement ring. The ring was so large and beautiful, it lit up the entire room.

Phoenix tried to speak, but only whimpers came from her mouth as her lips trembled and tears streamed down her face. She had no doubt she wanted to marry him and there was no reason to delay her response.

"Yes!" she shouted before watching as Gavin stood to his full height and slid the diamond from the ring box to her finger. She looked at it in every direction and marveled at its beauty. She'd never seen anything so big and beautiful before in her life. She wanted to leap into his arms and Gavin must have known what she wanted to do because he stopped her before she could do so.

"Now, any other time, I would welcome it with open arms, but you're already in your dress for the red carpet and I don't want to be the blame for some fashion expert comments on some blog tomorrow about how wrinkled your dress looked. We'll save our celebration for later tonight. For now, I'll take one of those kisses I love sharing with you."

"You know you don't have to ask for that. I love you Gavin, more than anything. Thank you for making my life complete."

"I'm the complete one, baby," he replied.

**

Gavin exited the limousine and went around to help Phoenix out as her stylist exited first. She didn't want any help getting dressed for the red carpet, but he insisted on making sure someone kept her in pristine shape as she walked the carpet, checking her hair, make-up and dress.

As soon as Phoenix exited the limousine, camera flashes went crazy and the crowd standing in the raised bleachers along the red carpet path went crazy screaming her name. His heart swelled the moment she went into full superstar mode and owned the night like he wanted her too. He knew that this was all new to her and he wanted her first walk on the red carpet to be the most memorable of her life. He followed a few steps behind her giving her the spotlight and only getting closer when she wanted him to join her for a photo opportunity. Reporters screamed her name, flying one question after another at her as they walked then stopped for her next group of photos.

The biggest names in entertainment were also turning to look at the rising star, wanting pictures with her as well.

"Hey Phoenix, is that an engagement ring or the hope diamond on your finger? Did you and Gavin Black get engaged?" one reporter screamed.

"It looks like Phoenix Graham is permanently off the market," another reporter screamed.

Crowds of reporters turned away from other artists and turned all of their attention on Phoenix and the huge rock on her finger. The secret was now officially out and she couldn't be happier. Thankfully, they called their parents before leaving the hotel for the awards show to tell them the great news. Her family already knew and so did his parents. They made a conference call that also included Luke and Layne who were equally as happy for them. She had her ring on her finger and she was planning to never take it off. She knew people would spot it on her finger and she wanted to be sure her family knew that she'd said yes, first. She'd taken the time to call her sister during the limousine ride over. Her sister was joining her at the event, coming in her own limousine tonight and Phoenix couldn't be happier that she could share the night with her. Her parents were already in the audience and thanks to Gavin, they were sitting on the front row, front and center. This was a night for them all.

"Hey Phoenix, you sure are having some year! An album with three songs already at the top of the charts and now a huge diamond engagement ring on your finger. Gavin is a lucky man!" yet another reporter shouted at her. She turned to look at her handsome fiancé and knew that she too was lucky. The man of her life liked it, loved it and put a ring on it and she was living on top of the world.

"You look gorgeous baby," Gavin leaned down and whispered in her ear.

Phoenix smiled and did what he'd told her to do; she was owning the red carpet.

Epilogue

Gavin escorted Phoenix up the stairs to the plane that would take them back to Chicago. They'd had a night that topped all nights. After winning six awards, including best new artist, they mingled with some of the top artists in the industry and answered a million questions that were thrown at them before leaving to head back to the hotel. He assumed they would be staying a few days in California to continue the celebration, but surprising him, Phoenix wanted to go back to their home in Chicago. Even though they could go anywhere they wanted, she wanted to go back to the quietness of their loft.

Three months ago when they'd decided to move in together and not being able to decide which loft to make their home, Gavin had the entire top floor where they lived remodeled after her brother decided he wasn't coming back to his and told her to do whatever she wanted with it. Gavin bought him out and what had been two lofts was now one big loft and it was their place of peace. That place is what she wanted right now and he would do anything to make her happy.

"Are you sure you're okay with going home right away?" she asked.

"Baby, you're the star, not me. You know I'm most comfortable out of the limelight and as long as you're smiling and happy, we can go wherever you want."

Phoenix settled into her seat on the plane as Gavin gave the instruction for the pilot to take off as soon as the airport gave them clearance.

"I love this plane," Phoenix said sitting back to relax.

"You can use it anytime you want."

"I still can't believe you own a plane. I'm still learning so much about you."

"Truthfully we own a plane because the minute we're married, what's mine is yours," he said leaning over to plant a soft kiss on her lips.

"Last night was amazing."

Phoenix was living a dream and it was all because of the man who sat across from her and loved her unconditionally. That's the kind of love every girl dreams of from the man she loves.

"You were amazing. You opened that show and at the end of your performance, I thought the applause would never end. The crowd loved you! You were born to be in the spotlight and definitely born to sing."

"I love singing and I never thought it would get me

to where I am, but you know what I want more than being a star?"

Gavin looked at her questionably.

"What is that?" he said. He knew if he could give it to her, it was hers.

"Being married to you and having tons of babies!"

"Tons?"

"Yes, tons. I've always wanted to be a mother and though I love where my career could go, that's not a priority for me. I owe you so much for helping me get here and I hope you don't think I don't appreciate it if I take some time away from it."

Reassuring her, Gavin took her hands in his while they waited for the plane to take off.

"I wanted to help you fulfill what I knew was a dream for you and that was what I did. Whatever is next for you, I'm in it with you all the way. We can have as many babies as you want to have and I will love you and them more than anything in this world."

"I'm going to do the press junket for the CD and spend a little more time touring and promoting, but then after we're married, I want to focus on us and our lives and our family."

"Whatever your heart's desire is, is what we're going to do. We have our entire lives together and we'll do whatever we want to do and if that means a house full of babies, our parents will love us even more and I'm looking forward to it."

Phoenix felt like she wanted to cry, but instead wrapped her arms around his neck and pulled him in for more than just a quick kiss.

"If we don't stop, we're about to join the mile-high club," Gavin said, shifting in his seat to ease the strain on his zipper. Phoenix never failed to have that effect on him.

"I can't help myself once I'm in your arms."

"I know the feeling. Let's table this until I know we're someplace where the staff on the flight won't walk in and interrupt us. Now, let's talk about the wedding so that I can focus on something other than getting you naked," he said.

"Okay, let's talk about the wedding. You're not the only one who needs a reprieve," she said fanning herself.

Gavin pulled back and shifted in his seat to calm the growing hardness in his pants.

"Okay, let's talk wedding so that my body has a chance to calm down."

Phoenix laughed at his antics to will his penis to soften.

"I don't want a big wedding," she said.

"Are you sure?"

"I'm positive. I just want you. I don't need a big fancy gown or hundreds of people celebrating with us. I could slip on a pair of tennis because you know that's how I like to roll, put on a wedding dress off the rack and say I do in a little chapel and I'd still be just as happy."

Gavin laughed so hard, he started coughing and choking through his laughter.

"Now that is some picture you just painted. You in a wedding dress and me in a tuxedo with sneakers on. Our mothers would kill us," he said gathering himself.

Phoenix had to laugh too, though she meant every single word of what she'd just said. All she needed was the man she loved and someone to marry them. What was important was that she was loved by Gavin Black, the better man for her.

**

"I need to call my sister," Luke said as he and his friends enjoyed the final moments of the party he hosted in Gavin's villa in Hawaii. He had been expecting Layne, but instead, he received a cryptic message from her that said she decided not to come because of some guy. He wasn't sure what she was trying to say, so he tried again to reach her and this time, she answered on the second ring.

"Layne what were you trying to say about not coming to Hawaii? Your year of taking a break from school is just about over and this was supposed to be your last hoorah before going back to school."

"I know, but I've changed my mind."

"You've changed your mind about what?"

"I changed my mind about going back to the states to go to school. I'm going to stay here in the Bahamas permanently."

"What? Are you crazy? Mom, dad and Gavin are going to lose their minds. Why would you want to stay there?"

"I've fallen in love with a great guy and we're going

to get married. I haven't told Gav or anyone else yet, so don't say anything."

"Married? You're getting married? When?"

"I'm going to do it before I tell the family, so that they can't stop it and we both know they'll try to."

"You can't get married Layne."

"Why not? Gavin is getting married and no one is squawking about that."

"He's not running off to secretly get married. He and Phoenix have been together over a year now. You've been in the Bahamas for three months after leaving Turks and Caicos and several months before that you were in Mexico and now you're talking about getting married already. Who is this guy?"

"Just be happy for me Luke and promise me you won't tell anyone about this. I'm going to fly home after the wedding and introduce him to everyone. By then, it will be too late for anyone to try and stop the wedding. Promise me!" Layne shouted into the phone.

Luke didn't want to, but Layne was his twin and they were close and always kept each other's secrets.

"Okay, I promise I won't tell, but wait until I get there. I'm going to fly out this weekend. I want to talk to you in person. Promise me you won't do anything until I get there."

Luke waited for a response, but got none.

"Layne, say it," he pushed.

"Okay, well I wasn't planning on getting married until next week anyway so I'll wait until after you get here, but don't come to try and talk me out of it because it won't work."

"Just don't do anything until I get there."

"Okay, and you promise to not tell anyone?"

Luke relented.

"I promise."

"Okay, I'll see you in a few days. You're going to love him."

"Really. What's his name?"

"His name is Marco and of all the men I've dated, trust me when I tell you he's the best man for me."

Luke hung up the phone and immediately dialed Gavin. Best man my ass, he thought. If anyone could talk some sense into Layne and stop her rush to the altar, it would be Gavin.

"Gav, we have a problem," he said the minute Gavin answered the phone. He knew that Gavin and Phoenix were heading back to Chicago after the awards in California. Gavin had called all of his family on a conference call earlier to tell them that he had proposed to Phoenix and she said yes. They were planning to spend some time in Chicago before flying out to California to visit the family.

"What kind of problem?" Gavin asked.

"What's wrong?" Phoenix asked him the moment she saw the change in his facial expression go from happy to one of concern.

"I don't know yet. All Luke said so far was there was a problem."

"Luke, what's going on?" he said turning back to the call.

"It's Laynie. I just spoke with her. She's in the Bahamas talking about not coming back home and marrying some guy named Marco."

Gavin stood and with his tall frame, he almost hit his head on the ceiling of the plane.

"What are you talking about? I just spoke with her when we announced the wedding and she didn't say anything about meeting a guy and getting married. When did you speak to her?"

"Just now. She was supposed to join me in Hawaii before flying home to get ready for school and she left me a message saying she wasn't coming. When I called her back, that's what she said."

"Who is this guy and when is she planning on getting married?"

"I don't know who this guy is, but she said she was going to marry him next week and then tell everyone after it was too late to do anything about it."

Gavin was livid as he paced back and forth inside the cabin of his private plane. Layne had done some crazy things before, but nothing this outlandish. Married to some guy none of them had ever heard of? He knew that wasn't going to happen. For one thing, she would eventually be a very rich young woman and because he knew how much she liked spreading information about who she was and who her brother was, that left her open as a target. He needed to know who this guy was and do it before Layne got in too deep that he wouldn't be able to get her out of it.

"I'll take care of it."

"What are you going to do? She's going to be angry I told you after I promised her I wouldn't. I've never broken a promise to her before."

"Luke, there are some promises you shouldn't keep and this is one. I'm glad you called me. I'll take care of it, so don't worry."

"Okay, I was going to fly to the Bahamas to talk to her.

Should I still go?"

"You can come if you want, but don't tell mom and dad. I need to handle this before they have a heart attack over this. When are you flying to the Bahamas?"

"I was going this weekend because she is planning on marrying this guy next week."

"What!" Gavin shouted, causing Phoenix to stand and join him in his pacing.

"Sorry Gav. I'm supposed to be looking out for her."

"Don't blame yourself. Layne is a grown woman, though immature most times, she's still a grown woman and we're not babysitters. Don't get too worried and worked up about this. I'll see you when you get to the Bahamas."

"Thanks Gav. Thanks for always being there for us. Will you be at your house?"

"Yeah I will and looking after the two of you as just as much my job as it is mom and dad's."

Gavin hung up and told Phoenix everything Luke said.

"You're close with Layne and you talk to her all the time, more than me I think. Did she say anything to you about meeting a guy or thinking about marrying him?"

Phoenix shook her head no.

"No. I love Layne and you know that, but if she had, I wouldn't have kept that from you. What is she thinking?"

"I don't know, but I'm about to put a stop to her thinking and any plans she has to marry this guy."

"You're going to the Bahamas?"

"We're going to the Bahamas unless you want me to drop you at home first."

"Not on your life. Where you go, I go and I want to be able to help with Layne in any way I can."

Gavin nodded and went forward to tell his captain that they need to report a new flight plan. They were bypassing going home to Chicago to fly to the Bahamas. Whoever this guy Layne thought was the best man for her wouldn't be as soon as he got his hands on him. The best man for his sister this guy is not and would not be and he would see to that.

Read more of Layne Black's story in, "The Best Man" a Valentine's Day release on February 14, 2017.

Enjoy chapter 1 of "Bossy" a new release from Cheryl Barton – available now

Cassidy Bostic walked across the pristine kept green grass that covered the grounds of the cemetery that had become just as familiar to her as a place she loved going to everyday. This was a familiar walk for her since she'd done it consistently on the same day, every year for the past fifteen years.

As with previous years, the moment she spotted the headstone, apprehension invaded each step. Her legs began to wobble and it wasn't due to the five-inch stilettos she was wearing. She shivered at the sight of the dark gray concrete headstone that boldly proclaimed in embedded calligraphy, the name of who was buried there.

A chill shot through her body and it wasn't due to a chill that wasn't in the air since it was a nice spring day, unlike the day of the events which had unfolded years ago that set into motion her trek to this cemetery every year. Her anxiety had her pulling her suit jacket a little tighter around her shoulders as she held tightly to the large bouquet of flowers she'd brought along with her.

Without thinking, Cassidy looked back at her driver and the moment he began to move toward her, she knew it was because he saw the solemn look on her face. He'd seen it many times before when he'd driven her here. She raised her hand to stop him and tried hard to plaster a slight smile on her face to let him know she was alright. This, she went through every year when she arrived back in Las Vegas, Nevada, to the place where her life had changed forever.

As she finally reached the grave, the name inscribed brought unshed tears to her eyes as she tried to hold on to her composure to not allow herself to get as emotional as she did during every visit. She'd hoped that the many years that had passed would lessen the pain, but today, she knew it hadn't. Cassidy's heart ached, her chest tightened and her body felt numb as the feeling of a love she once shared being snatched away from her overwhelmed her. She held out hope that this would be the year that the loss of Leon Wright, the first man she ever loved and the first to ever love her unconditionally, would not hurt as much as it did in previous years. No such luck, she thought.

Cassidy reached down and turned the iron flower holder over to secure it in the plate in front of the headstone. She unwrapped the flowers and placed the large bouquet in it and fussed with it to get it just right while she got her emotions in check. Reaching inside of her purse, she withdrew the small container of wipes and cleaned off the top of the headstone so that it shined once again. Stepping back, she began the conversation that had now become second nature for her whenever she traveled to visit the resting place of the love of her life.

"Hi Lee, the name she called him. I'm here and I'm doing very well. I know that lying here beneath my feet isn't you, but just the remains that were once the vessel for your spirit. I know you wouldn't want me coming here every year like this to visit, but as the day gets closer and I say that the prior year would be my last year for taking this trip, I find myself booking the flight to get here anyway. I use the excuse that I can visit my Los Angeles office while I'm on this coast, so I may as well stick to the routine of visiting you. Enough of the small talk though. Let me tell you about your son who is his father all over again."

Cassidy began feeling better once she mentioned her son who meant everything to her.

"Landon is tall and handsome like you and at fifteen years old, he is the only sophomore on the varsity basketball team. With his height, he's a star center and there has already been talk about him heading to the national league after high school. Now, don't turn over in your grave just yet. You know that's not going to happen because I know you wouldn't want that and I've told your stubborn son that fact. He understands that I want more for him than a basketball career, but to have something to fall back on in his later years. No one knows if basketball will take him far even though he has the talent now. He's a good boy and he does pretty well with his grades. Like his father, he hates math, but I stay on him about that and I make sure there is always a math tutor on speed dial."

Cassidy laughed because she and Leon often talked about school and his first comment was about how much he hated math and even though their son had never met his father, as soon as she brought up the subject of math with Landon, his first words were how much he hated math. That made her think of Leon and the fact that he wasn't with them to share in their life.

"Too many girls and even some women are on the prowl for him, but I've been schooling him about these chicks out here the exact same way I know you would. I don't hold any punches and I give it to him straight, no chaser because that's how they are coming at him. These fast tail girls are ready to spread their legs wide open without being asked and I don't want Landon caught up."

Cassidy hoped that everything she poured into her son was sinking in because she knew all it took was one slipup and he would be caught up. It wasn't just his stardom on the basketball court that drew girls to him, but also because of who his mother was and she feared the limelight would have him making the wrong decisions. So far, he'd been able to stay focused on school and sports and though she knew he liked the attention he got from girls, she could see that he understood the dangers of letting down his guard.

"Landon asks me questions about you often and I tell him what I know when he asks. We didn't have a lot of time together and wished we had so that I would have more to share with him about your life and your family, but I kept my promise to you and I never told your family he existed. I know you were terrified at the thought that even after all of these years, someone would come after him or me if they knew of my connection to you and your past. He's safe and thanks to you and how you took care of us even from the grave,

I've been able to always provide for him. He's still at that private school and I know you wouldn't be happy that he lives on campus throughout the school year and not at home, but I felt it was best so that he would be able to focus and not get too caught up in being hounded by the media and paparazzi wherever he went. He comes home on weekends when he doesn't have games or other events. This school is strict when it comes to anyone being on the grounds who is not a parent or who didn't get special permission. He's safe there and he likes it. My company is still continuing to grow exponentially and I know how much of a workaholic I am so I wanted to be sure he was in a great environment for getting the best education. I still haven't told him where you're buried and I won't until I know I'm ready for him to visit. He seems okay not knowing as long as he knows that even though you left us before he was born, you loved him and talked about him daily. He knows he was loved and I made sure he knew that you loved me more than anything in this world and as a result of that love, you and I had him."

A car horn honked close by disturbing Cassidy's concentration, rattling her. Though no one should know or remember her from her time in Vegas, she was nervous every time she came back even though she knew the threat to her and Landon was no longer an issue. She saw her security detail jump out of the truck that followed her limousine as they made sure that whoever else may be at the cemetery wouldn't have a chance to get to her if they tried. She smiled when she noticed it was only a bunch of kids playing around and when they continued on, her detail got back into their car and she turned back to finish giving Leon an update on her life.

"The business is doing great and I've followed my dreams as you asked. All of what I have I owe to you and I love you for your sacrifice. I would still give it all up if I could get you back because that's how much I still love and miss you. No one has taken your place in my heart, though several have tried. I can't seem to find anyone that has the qualities that I'd like in a man for anything long term and my friends all say I'm too bossy and too stuck-up to even be open to love again, reminding me that love as a young girl in my teens is nothing compared to love I could have now in my thirty's. Right now, I don't care because I'm all about the business and making it bigger and better than anything. There are days I long for the simpler times when I lived in that apartment in Las Vegas and my only care in the world was what I was going to wear when I saw you. I miss you Lee and every dream for me we talked about, I'm making it happen. This fashion world is not joke, but like you once told me, I am Cassidy Renee Bostic and I am 'Bossy' so yeah, I got this! I love you baby," she declared, wiping away one tear that streamed down her face. As much as she loved the feeling of relief saying his name and visiting his grave every year, it was time to go.

Cassidy turned and walked back toward the long, black SUV limousine and she thought back to the time when she believed she and Leon were about to live the kind of life that some people only dreamed of until the night their lives changed forever. That was the night the love of her life made the fatal mistake of trusting someone who literally shot him in the back.

As she settled into the plush gray leather seats of the limo, she looked out of the window and thought about where it all started and how it went so tragically wrong in one night.

Bossy is now available in paperback and for your e-pub device at www.cherylbarton.net

Some think they are ready for Hollywood playboy, Cade Weston in, "Heartthrob," but few are! Enjoy this short excerpt.

"Mr. Weston, can I get a moment of your time?" a voice shouted.

"Cade! Over here please," another voice bellowed in the crowd.

"Cade, what was the most challenging aspect of your most recent film?" a male shouted over all the other voices.

"What do you like most about being Cade Weston, being an actor, running your own record label, having a successful apparel line or is it the countless number of women who throw themselves at you daily?" a female voice shrieked.

"Cade, can I have your baby?" That question made him laugh, something else he heard daily.

"Mr. Weston, what's next for you, is it a new movie or a brand new business venture?" another voice hollered.

"Mr. Weston, are you single? I have a daughter and I think she'd be perfect for you!"

Cade smiled as questions were being thrown at him from the crowd that gathered outside of the Los Angeles television station. It was daytime, but he had just wrapped up the taping of his appearance on a late night talk show. He was told to expect the crowd once word got out that he would be there. He expected a crowd, but nothing like what he encountered as he exited the building while his team of security made a path so that he could get into the waiting limousine.

"Cade, what do you think of the nickname everyone has given you, calling you 'Heartthrob'? I hear it's because of the number of broken hearts you leave behind and the throbbing bodies women and some men experience just by getting a glimpse of you?" yet another voice shouted.

Cade stopped in his tracks at hearing himself being called heartthrob.

Recently, that pseudonym had been plastered on the cover of every magazine and news story written about him. He liked it, especially when people tried to define the title with their own characterization. He found it hilarious each time he read a new story about him and his sexual prowess, something that kept his name in the headlines.

"You don't have time to stop and answer questions Cade," Abby, his personal assistant said, urging him to keep walking.

Cade knew she was right and though he was tempted to answer some of the questions, he continued on to the limousine and got in followed by Abby and Aaron, his chief of security.

"That is some crowd, especially this early in the morning," Aaron said.

Aaron was not only Cade's chief of security, but also one of his best friends since their college days.

"It is and I am who I am because of crowds like that."

"I see this heartthrob thing isn't going away. I'm beginning to think you're enjoying the title, brother."

Cade didn't answer, but gave his friend a slick smile. Being labeled a heartthrob and plastered on the cover of magazines certainly had its benefits.

"What's on the agenda for today?" Aaron asked.

"I'm going home to work out and then I believe I have several meetings at the record label. My artists are climbing the charts and because of that, we've been getting in demos from aspiring artists from around the world. There are a few my team who is responsible for new talent want me to hear. Then, later tonight, I'm going to be eye candy on the arm of Ms. Diamond at a fundraising event. Does that about cover it Abby?" he asked turning toward her and making sure he hadn't left anything out. He noticed she had yet to lift her head from her cell phone no doubt booking him for another public appearance somewhere. He didn't question her; he just followed along.

"That's pretty much it. You asked me to clear your calendar after the event with Ms. Diamond tonight."

Aaron knew what that meant. Cade was often called on to accompany some of the most beautiful women in the world to events to keep the buzz about them in the media. He knew that Cade believed that all press was good press in Hollywood. He had, after all, recently been named the sexiest man on the planet. Everyone wanted to be seen with him and all women wanted to get under him, literally. Aaron had a feeling Diamond would be engaging in both before the evening was over.

"Abby, can you get my usual suite ready for tonight and since I'll be entertaining, roll out the usual including my staple gift. Check to be sure it's not one that I've given Diamond in the past."

"Do you want me to add flowers this time as well?" she inquired.

Cade thought about it and knew it wouldn't be necessary with Diamond.

"No flowers tonight, but make sure my driver sticks around since she won't be staying all night."

Abby didn't respond or even react since they were all accustomed to Cade's penchant for entertaining and then moving on. This was going to be one of those nights. He would be doing his part to keep Diamond in the spotlight by being seen with her and in turn, she would spend the evening in whatever way he chose. He was Cade Weston, media mogul, box office smash, actor and of course, according to the entertainment world, 'heartthrob' and he planned on living up to that name tonight.

Get "Heartthrob" now at www.cherylbarton.net in paperback and for your favorite e-pub device.

More from Cheryl Barton – The Bachelor Series

Book 1: "Bachelor Not For Sale"

The "Bachelor Series" continues with "Love at Last", Brian's story of love that almost wasn't.

The series started with Bachelor Not For Sale with the love story of Duron Knight and Taija Charles. Duron had been hurt by a previously relationship and thought that the playboy life was for him until he met and fell for bombshell, Taija Charles one night at a bachelor auction. She had been a beautiful vision in red and he knew from the moment he'd met her that she was his. Taija wasn't expecting to find love at a bachelor auction, but no woman in her right mind would ever turn down dinner with Duron Knight, every woman's dream man. In the midst of falling in love, someone from her past showed up and threatened everything she and Duron had. Their love is threatened by his inability to trust her and by her poor decision to open her door to an old flame.

Book 2: "A Designed Affair"

In the second installment of the "Bachelor Series", "A Designed Affair", Duron's sister Loren Knight an interior designer knew that the perfect man had already been designed for her, but the problem was, he was her brother's best friend, Michael Bailey, who was also a well-known playboy. If anyone knew of his playboy ways, it's her brother. She knew there was no way her brother would approve of anything happening with Michael, but with fate and temptation came an opportunity that neither of them could resist. The biggest hurdle was keeping their love affair from her brother, but what happens in the dark always comes to light and when it does, she hopes their love can survive the turmoil that could cause Duron to lose his best friend or Loren could lose the man she's loved since high school.

Book 3: "A Perfect Combination"

In the third install of the Bachelor Series, "A Perfect Combination", Tyrone Davis, Duron's other best friend and partner in his architecture firm never thought he would meet a woman that could hold his interest for more than a romp in the sheets. On a business trip, he runs into Victoria (last name), the best friend of Duron's wife Taija and sparks began to fly as they flirted over drinks. That flirting turned into the best sex of his life and when he woke the next morning to find Victoria gone, he knew he wanted more than one night of incredible sex with her. What he didn't know was that Victoria had a fiancé back in Boston and though he knew he should let it go, he couldn't. To him, they were the perfect combination and fiancé or not, he knew what they shared was nothing casual and he set out to prove that to her.

Book 4: "Love At Last"

The next installment finds Duron's brother Brian struggling with the news that he may have fathered a child with a woman he thought had loved him as much as he'd loved her. As a college professor, he'd met Shelly Braxton, a college junior at a football game. By the end of the game, he thought he'd met the perfect woman for him and the nights of passion they'd shared, he knew he'd never have that with another woman. Not knowing what happened, Shelly left school and left word that she never wanted to see him again. He tried to contact with her only to be met with silence. Letting her go, he went on with his life until a friend told him he saw Shelly with a little girl that looked exactly like Brian's sister and would have been the right age for a daughter he could have conceived with Shelly. Brian took a leave of absence from work and went to Baltimore to finally confront Shelly on her disappearance and why she wouldn't tell him that she'd had his child. Ready for a fight, Brian is surprised to find that love they once shared still burned as hot as fire.

Get your copy of, "Love at Last" in August 2016 at www.cherylbarton.net

From Cheryl Barton – "Un-Break My Heart"

Dr. Mackenzie Ellis suffered a loss so great, she never thought she'd fall in love again, especially with someone close to her.

Travis Blackwell, III never dreamed of crossing the line with Mackenzie until his heart would no longer allow him to deny the love he has for her and the passion he wants to share with her knowing that he is the key to mending her broken heart.

Get your copy at www.cherylbarton.net

From Cheryl Barton – "Amorous Occupations: The Electrician"

The party invitation said everyone had to wear a masquerade mask the entire night, a New Orleans tradition. Dara Marshall couldn't resist the opportunity to spend an uninhibited night of passion with National Football Association coach Nelson Riley, the guest of honor, knowing that her identity was hidden by her mask.

Dara's world turns upside down when she discovers the gorgeous coach is the newest client of her father's business and after she's sent on a job at his condo, she does everything in her power to not give away the secret of who she is.

Nelson could never forget the sexy temptress he'd spent an unforgettable night with, even when she tries to hide behind a mask and baggy overalls.

Get your copy at www.cherylbarton.net

Coming soon from Cheryl Barton – "Advantage, Love"

Professional Tennis player Leah Duncan thought that all she needed was life in the spotlight until she discovered there was more to life and its name is love.

Derek Kennedy fell for Leah Duncan in what he called love at first sight until he experienced déjà vu with a woman who may not be happy when all he has to offer her is his love.

Love shouldn't have a price and Leah and Derek will need to find a middle ground if the love they want and need is to survive their different lifestyles.

Come share in Leah and Derek's story to see if love conquers all. For release in August 2016 at www.cherylbarton.net .

ABOUT THE AUTHOR

Cheryl Barton lives in Maryland and in her spare time she loves to read espionage novels, cook, watch Sci-fi movies, spend time with family and friends and enjoy Maryland steamed crabs.

Find more romance and inspirational novels by Cheryl Barton on her website at www.cherylbarton.net.

I am because you read and I thank you! - Cheryl

Connect with me

Visit my website at www.CherylBarton.net
Twitter – @Author Cheryl Barton
Instagram – AuthorCherylBarton
Facebook at Author Cheryl Barton
Email – Cheryl@CherylBarton.net
Blog - https://mswriterinmd.wordpress.com/

www.ingramcontent.com/pod-product-compliance
Lightning Source LLC
Chambersburg PA
CBHW020553260626

47157CB00003B/677